FOR THOSE WHO DARE

JOHN ANTHONY MILLER

For my family – and all that's most important

ACKNOWLEDGMENTS

Special thanks to Donna Eastman at Parkeast Literary and the entire team at Next Chapter.

1

EAST BERLIN

August 13, 1961 at 5:08 a.m.

Kirstin Beck lay awake, tossing and turning, her blond hair spilling across the pillow. It was a difficult decision, months in the making, a path that once taken, would alter more lives than her own. Some would thrive, reaching uncharted destinations, while others faced destruction, caught in a spinning spiral that could never again be straightened. As the clock ticked, marring the eerie serenity that lives in the hours before dawn, the time to act arrived.

She eased her slender frame from the mattress, ensuring the springs didn't squeak. She paused, sitting on the edge of the bed, and listened to the rhythmic breathing of her husband lying beside her. When satisfied she hadn't disturbed him, she stood, remained still for a moment, and then tiptoed from the bedroom into the hall.

She glanced at him again, ensuring he still slept, before going into the bathroom, removing her nightgown, and quickly dressing in black slacks and a grey top. She opened the door to the linen closet and reached to the back of the bottom shelf, behind a stack of towels, to retrieve a small satchel. It contained her personal papers: birth certificate, identity cards, important phone numbers, addresses, and money – West German Marks and American dollars – that she had painstakingly saved and hid from her husband. Careful not to make any noise, she quietly closed the door, cringing as the hinges faintly creaked. She stepped back into the hall, moving carefully in the darkness, and stopped at the bedroom door.

Her husband still slept, facing away from her. He snored faintly, his breathing rhythmic, before muttering something in his sleep. She watched as he moved his arm, his hand feeling the empty space she created when she climbed from bed. He stirred, lifted his head from the pillow, and sat up.

She stepped away from the door, barely breathing, as seconds quietly passed. The bed springs squeaked as his weight shifted and then it was quiet, the silence punctuated by the moving hands of the clock. She waited a moment more and peeked around the jamb.

He lay on his side, facing the doorway, but she couldn't see if his eyes were open or closed. She glanced at her watch, knowing she shouldn't wait much longer, and walked quickly past the door, hoping the aged floor boards made no noise.

It was quiet. He didn't speak, so she assumed he was sleeping. She hesitated, just to be sure, and then crept down the hall to the stairs. As she descended the steps, she stayed near the wall where the treads had more support, carefully descending one step after another. When she was halfway down she paused and listened but heard no noise from the bedroom. She went down the remaining stairs to the first floor, crossed the foyer and looked into the parlor. She could see the radio in the darkness, the record player beside it. A stack of records sat in a holder, all American – Patsy Cline, the Shirelles, Roy Orbison, the Platters – her most prized possessions. For a brief moment she thought of taking them, but realized they were only belongings, easily replaced, and there was so much more at stake. She entered the dining room and then the kitchen, where she grabbed her pocketbook from the table.

She took a note from the satchel and laid it on the table. Written days before, it explained why she was leaving, why she had no other choice, and how each would be better for it. She knew it was a cowardly way to end their relationship, but she couldn't risk telling him – he was too strong, too determined, and he would argue and plead and gradually whittle away at her resistance until it no longer existed. It had to be done this way, in the darkness of night. She eased the door open and paused, taking one last, lingering look at the house that had been her home before stepping outside.

It was chilly for an August evening, barely fifty degrees, and she crossed the small yard behind her end-unit rowhouse. It was more garden than grass; she had crammed every flower she could into the limited space, creating a kaleidoscope of color in an otherwise drab landscape. Now she would miss it. But she knew she could plant more flowers, just as she could start a new life.

Her narrow yard ended at a wrought iron fence, old and rusty, that marked the edge of a cemetery. The fence was bordered by overgrown shrubs and a lane that led to tombstones, graves and mausoleums. She walked along the fence and crossed a strip of grass between her residence and the neighboring Church of Reconciliation. Staying in the shadows, close to the overwhelming brick building that was dominated by spires and arched windows, she edged toward the rear. There was little light, only a quarter moon, and she realized the nearby street was dark. She hesitated, wondering why the streetlights weren't lit, especially when her clocks ticked and her refrigerator hummed as she exited the kitchen door.

3

She sensed something wasn't right but didn't know what it was. She left the shadows cast by the church and crept quietly into the cemetery that stretched behind it. The graves were surrounded by neglected shrubs and trees, reminders of a once beautiful location that had since fallen into disrepair, just like the rest of East Berlin. Many of the graves were old, the tombstones worn, separated by dirt walking paths spaced evenly between them. Kirstin stepped cautiously, moving from one tombstone to the next, and was halfway across the cemetery before she saw them, silhouettes at first, and then more distinct as she got closer.

Several East German soldiers, spaced four or five yards apart, stood at the edge of the cemetery. Others were huddled in pairs, whispering, and she saw the faint flicker of a cigarette held in a soldier's hand before he moved it to his mouth. Their grey uniforms were barely visible, blending with the darkness. She studied the string of soldiers, stretching like a ribbon in both directions, and knew something was drastically wrong.

In the distance, thirty feet from where the soldiers stood, was a simple stone wall, barely three feet high, that marked the edge of the graveyard. The old wall, and twenty or thirty feet of graves adjacent to it, was located in West Berlin. She only had to get to it, scale it and she was free, fading into the West like thousands of others had done before her. But tonight, it was different. Tonight, a line of soldiers stood on the border, waiting in the darkness. But waiting for what?

Germany had been divided since the end of the Second World War – communist East Germany and free West Germany. The city of Berlin was also divided, the communist East, administered by the Russians, and the free West, governed by the French, British and Americans. Kirstin lived in East Berlin, in the Russian half, but her grandmother lived in West Berlin, in the French section. Residents had always moved freely between the sectors, even though many went to the West and never returned. It never seemed to matter before, but she realized with a sinking feeling, that maybe it mattered now.

She heard the hum of machinery, distant at first but growing louder. She peeked from behind a mausoleum, wondering what was happening. The noise came closer, an engine, a truck or some sort of vehicle. She paused, eyeing the short stone wall only sixty feet away, but guarded by soldiers standing before it. Should she risk escaping, running through the cemetery, past the soldiers, and leaping over the wall, hoping they couldn't catch her?

Before she could act, the noise came closer and the border was bathed in light. A searchlight sat in the rear of a truck parked along the edge of the graveyard. It cast a bright light along the wall, directly in Kirstin's path. She crouched, hidden, as men in worker's clothes and more soldiers exited the vehicle. Disillusioned and frightened, she retreated, hiding behind shrubs and tombstones, slipping through the shadows on her way back home.

2

Steiner Beck woke when he heard vehicles in front of his townhouse. He rolled over, thinking a neighbor arrived home late and that the noise would stop. When it didn't, he sat up in bed, rubbed the sleep from his eyes, and reached to his nightstand to turn on a lamp. He felt the empty space in the bed beside him, finding the sheets cold.

"Kirstin," he said softly, thinking she might be in the bathroom.

He could see his reflection in the mirror above the bureau, his hair mussed, his gray eyes dull. His face was marked with creases from the pillow, just above his neatly trimmed beard. Barely fifty, he was twenty years older than his wife, an age difference he was acutely aware of as he got older. A handsome man who women found attractive, he noticed his hair was starting to thin, more gray than black, and his face showed wrinkles dug deeper than the marks made by his pillow.

He yawned and listened for his wife downstairs. "Kirstin," he called again, just a bit louder, wondering if she had fallen asleep on the couch.

There was no reply. He waited a moment more and went

to look at the street from his bedroom window. He saw military vehicles parked near the church, two trucks and a jeep, with another truck farther down the road. He crossed the hall and went into the second bedroom, a shared office for him and his wife, and glanced out the window at the cemetery. There was a troop truck by the back lane of the graveyard, near the wall. A searchlight in the back streamed a path of pale light along the border, growing dimmer the farther it travelled, showing a string of soldiers fanned across the border.

"Kirstin!" he yelled, now worried.

He hurried to his bedroom and grabbed a pair of trousers from a straight-backed chair beside the bureau and put them on. He went to the closet, took a shirt off a hanger, and found his shoes and a pair of socks. Once dressed, he went out in the hall and down the steps.

"Kirstin," he called again.

He opened the front door and looked out. The trucks were still parked along the curb, their engines running, a driver seated in each. A row of nineteenth-century townhouses lined the opposite side of the street, some still showing damage from the war, even though it had ended sixteen years before. Neighbors parted drapes and peeked from windows, while others stepped out of half-closed doorways in pajamas and robes, curious but careful, as if knowing they witnessed something tragic, but didn't know what it was. With the West Berlin border so close, some may have suspected what little freedom they had could be slipping away, vanishing like a morning mist melted by the rising sun.

He closed the front door and went into the kitchen. "Kirstin," he said loudly, but still got no response. He opened the kitchen door but paused, noticing a note on the table.

Kirstin then walked through the opened door. "Steiner, I think they're closing the border," she hissed.

She seemed winded, but he didn't know why. "Darling, what are you doing?" he asked. "I've been calling you."

"I woke with all the noise," she explained. "I went outside to see what was happening."

He studied her closely, wondering what she was doing, but then his eyes strayed to the paper laying on the table. He started to reach for it.

"Steiner, come look," she said, tugging his arm. "There are troops in the cemetery."

He hesitated. "I saw them from the window," he told her. "What are they doing?"

"I'm not sure," she said, edging closer. "There are workman there, too."

He studied her for a moment, pensive, but didn't reply. The edge of the cemetery marked the border with West Berlin. Perhaps she was right. Maybe they were closing the border. For a moment he wondered why he hadn't been notified. But then he realized he couldn't be; few probably were. It had to be kept secret. Or all of East Berlin would have crossed to the West.

"What am I going to do with my grandmother?" Kirstin asked anxiously.

"I'm not sure," he replied. "We'll have to see what happens." He wondered what prompted the border closure. Was there an international incident? Or some sort of friction between East and West? He again looked at the paper and reached across the table for it.

She moved in front of him and snatched the note away. "My list of shortages," she said hastily. "Coffee, potatoes, cosmetics, toothpaste, bananas... can you think of anything else?"

A loud noise attracted his attention, like a truck tailgate dropped in the down position. "What is going on out there?" he asked, losing interest in her shopping list.

"It's probably the soldiers," she said. "They extend as far as I could see, past the clothing company next to the church and all the way to *Strelitzer Strasse.*"

He was confused. "But why close the border now?" he asked. "Could we be at war?"

She hesitated, as if the thought hadn't occurred to her. "I don't know," she said. "Wouldn't we know if we were?"

"I'm not sure," he replied. "But they wouldn't close the border in the middle of the night unless they had a valid reason."

"Maybe they don't want us to leave," she said simply.

"They've closed the border before," he said, deciding it was nothing serious or he would have known about it. "And it was only temporary. Just as this is."

"But what if it isn't?" she asked.

He wrapped his arm around her. "Then we'll accept it," he told her. "With everyone else in East Berlin."

3

Tony Marino had spent almost two months in Germany gathering information for his next book. Commissioned by Green Mansion Publishing for their *History of Nations* series, he had already written *The History of France* and *The History of Belgium*. Now he was writing *The History of Germany*. He had planned to leave Berlin a week earlier to visit his home in the States but decided not to because he was behind schedule.

Almost thirty-five, he bore a striking resemblance to Elvis Presley, although his eyes and complexion were a bit darker. He was raised in Philadelphia, home to many Italian immigrants during the first half of the twentieth century, by a single mother who still spoke broken English. Fluent in Italian, French and German, he did a stint in the U.S. Army as a translator and then went to college on the G.I Bill. A natural talent for writing and an interest in history led to the publication of several magazine articles before he landed his current assignment with Green Mansion.

He stood in front of his coffee pot, yawning as he waited for it to brew. Having just crawled out of bed, he turned on the radio to catch the baseball scores from the American military news network. From the time he first played stick ball in the streets of South Philly, he had been addicted to baseball, almost obsessed. And the Philadelphia Phillies were his team. But it was tough to be a loyal fan; the Phillies were horrible, the worst team in baseball. The evening before they had lost to the Pittsburgh Pirates, 4-0, managing only five hits, and they had lost the day before that and the day before that. Actually, they had lost fourteen games in a row. But the announcer barely mentioned the Phillies. The entire country was focused on the Yankees. Roger Maris hit his 43rd home run, still on track to beat the Babe's record for most home runs in a season. Fans were mixed, some pulling for Maris, hoping a modern star could take the record, others were loyal to the Babe.

Marino was distracted by noises outside his third-floor apartment, located in the French section of West Berlin, and he looked outside to find an army of workman and soldiers destroying the tranquility of a Sunday morning. His apartment building bordered a cemetery defined by a three-foot stone wall, and soldiers were strung across the edge of the graveyard, standing a few feet apart. Workers were pounding wooden poles into the ground, while others strung barbed wire between the posts. He could see their faces as they built the barrier, the soldiers directing them, some smoking cigarettes. It seemed surreal.

It was a large cemetery, the section along the border shaped like the bottom of the letter L, the Church of Reconciliation and a row of old townhouses at the edge of the street beyond. The rest of the cemetery, the side of the letter L, extended several blocks back into East Berlin. *Strelitzer Strasse* was the closest street intersecting East and West, and Marino saw concrete barriers blocking the road, soldiers spaced evenly around them. The border had been open the day before, easy to travel in either direction. But now, for some reason, that luxury no longer existed. He wondered if the entire border with East Berlin was being walled in.

Even though the barrier was hastily constructed, by early morning it ran in both directions for much of the urban landscape. The barbed wire was almost four feet high, crossing the western edge of the cemetery and leaving a few rows of crooked tombstones, eroded by time, as curious residents of West Berlin. The remainder of the graveyard, in the Mitte section of East Berlin, lay quiet, tranquil, shaded by trees, as if observing the travesty but unable to protest. The Church of Reconciliation was across from Marino's apartment building, a Gothic revival design dominated by a lofty spire that seemed to touch the clouds. The balance of the brick building was supported by a series of graceful arches, and it still stood proud and defiant in a nation that trampled the religious freedom the building represented. Fifty feet from the church, still bordering the road, was a row of nineteenth century townhouses, the cemetery sprawling behind them and then stretching several blocks south and east.

The city of East Berlin bordered half of West Berlin, but East German suburbs and countryside sprawled around the remainder, forming an island in an enemy sea. Marino wondered if the wall was being built on all borders, closing in West Berlin, trying to choke it, or force some sort of submission from the Allied nations in the West. It seemed the Communists always used West Berlin as a pawn in a global chess match. And then, after realizing how vulnerable the city was, a million thoughts raced through his mind. Could he get out? And if he could, would he be able to get back in? How would residents of West Berlin get food and clothes and other supplies? They had electricity – his clocks and lights were working – but for how long?

He looked across the way, to the church, and saw parishioners flocking to the sanctuary from the East, while small crowds of protestors were starting to form along intersecting streets in the West, all looking curiously at the barbed wire. He wondered what the rest of the world saw: West Berlin being walled in – or East Berliners kept out, denied the freedom the West enjoyed.

4

Kirstin Beck watched the workmen from the second-floor window of her townhouse. Tall and willowy, her blue eyes wide and bright, she was intelligent and attractive, with high cheekbones and long eyelashes. Although she had been married for eight years, many weren't sure why. Her husband Steiner was much older, a college professor and loyal Socialist, a stern, serious man who didn't seem suited to his younger wife.

The noise had started early, just after dawn. She had been fortunate, avoiding the soldiers after she tried to escape. She barely made it home in time, stuffing her pocketbook and satchel into a rubbish can and barging into the kitchen just as Steiner reached for the note she had left on the kitchen table. He seemed interested in it, unable to see what it was. She snatched it away before he got it.

If only she left one day earlier. She would have vanished, unseen by all, like thousands of others who crossed the border, merging into West Berlin, free to come and go as they pleased. Now she faced a serious dilemma. Her grandmother was alone. And she depended on Kirstin not only for essential needs, but for companionship. Although a neighbor or two would ensure she was cared for, Kirstin still worried. She had to send her grandmother a message, to tell her she was delayed – even if she didn't know for how long. And she had to get to West Berlin, not just because of what she was fleeing from, but because of what she was running to.

Kirstin watched with dread while more trucks arrived, praying it was temporary, that she could go to the West in a matter of minutes, or in the worst case, a matter of days. But as more troops and workers appeared, surveyors made lines where barriers would go and carpenters started driving posts into the ground. The barbed wire followed, strung along the ground, nailed to the posts, and then layered higher until it reached over six feet. The intent was clear – to make West Berlin a free island in a Communist sea, preventing those in East Berlin from escaping. But Kirstin Beck had to get to West Berlin. She just had to – for more reasons than her grandmother.

Somewhere near nine a.m., Steiner went to morning service at the Church of Reconciliation. The attendance was much less than normal, since many parishioners came from the French sector of West Berlin. Faithful and loyal to their church, the barbed wire on *Strelitzer Strasse* now blocked their way. Some stood at the barrier, where crowds were forming, and watched the soldiers curiously, shouting in protest. They seemed anxious and afraid – most had friends and relatives in the East they might never see again. And, even though the border had been temporarily closed several times before, it had never been blocked with concrete barriers and barbed wire.

An hour later, when the service ended and those attending filed from church, some went into the cemetery, getting as close to the workers as the soldiers allowed. Kirstin watched them, fearful of a confrontation. As the crowd continued to gather, she left her second-floor study, hurrying down the stairs and out her kitchen door. She crossed the cemetery grounds to join them, passing tombstones and graves, markers and mausoleums.

The workers continued installing posts and wrapping barbed wire around them, the fence rolling like a ribbon into the horizon, cutting the city in two. Some in the crowd merely observed, as if trying to determine the impact on their daily lives. Others were more agitated, sensing that something precious was about to be lost. Kirstin warily watched them, knowing at least one, or maybe more, were Stasi, the East German secret police. The Stasi were everywhere.

She heard some from the congregation whispering as she approached, and she wormed past them to the front of the crowd, standing beside an elderly gentleman, thin and balding with a white moustache. He was a frequent churchgoer.

"Good morning, Dr. Werner," she said.

"Kirstin, what's happening?" he asked, agitated.

"I think they're closing the border."

"But why?" he asked. "Only yesterday we could cross. What makes today different?"

"They don't want us fleeing to the West," she replied. She paused, watching the workmen, and added, "Or even visiting, it seems."

"But barbed wire?" he asked. "I just heard someone say it's to keep the Fascists out of East Berlin. That makes no sense at all. It's to keep us in, not to keep them out."

Kirstin knew her life was about to change forever – but only if she let it. She had to get to West Berlin. And somehow, she would. It would just be harder.

"We all have family and friends in West Berlin," Dr. Werner continued. "Will they just become memories?"

"We can't even contact them," Kirstin told him. "I tried the telephone, but it's disconnected."

"Then we can only communicate though letters."

"The Stasi will censor them," she said, making sure no one could hear her. "Or discard them."

"I have family in the West that I need to see," he said, as if wondering how he would accomplish that.

"And I have to help my grandmother. She's only six blocks away, but now it seems halfway around the world."

"What are they doing?" a familiar voice cried from behind them.

Kirstin turned to see Dieter Katz, a student and churchgoer. Small and slight with round spectacles and shaggy hair, he was sometimes too vocal in his opposition to the Socialist regime. But then, most of the young were. They hadn't lived through the war. They were brave and brash, somehow thinking they were invincible.

"They're building a fence to keep us from leaving," Werner told him.

"They can't," Katz cried, moving past them. "My girlfriend is in West Berlin. And so is my university."

"Be careful, Dieter," Dr. Werner whispered. "Don't let them hear you."

"I don't care if they hear me," Katz responded. He edged closer to the guards.

"Don't let them make an example of you," Dr. Werner advised. "They'll use any excuse to throw you in jail. They would like nothing better."

"I have no intention of going to jail," Katz informed them. He seemed to be studying the guards, their positions, the height of the barbed wire, what the workers were doing, as if accessing strengths and weaknesses.

"Dieter, I have a grandmother in the West," Kirstin said, trying to calm him. "She's old and frail and depends on me for everything. I'm sure there are many others in the same situation. The authorities will make provisions. They have to."

"And my daughters are in the West," Werner added. "So are

many sons and daughters, fathers and mothers. A solution will present itself. If it doesn't we'll find one."

"I'm not waiting," Katz murmured.

Kirstin realized he was about to do something he shouldn't, acting on emotion rather than logic. "Dieter, don't do anything you're going to regret," she warned.

"I can't let them do it," Dieter muttered angrily, eyeing the barbed wire.

"Dieter," Dr. Werner said harshly, moving closer to him,

Before anyone could restrain him, Dieter darted towards the newly built fence.

"Halt!" a guard commanded, leveling his rifle.

5

———

Dieter eluded the first guard, twisting around him, and dashed for the barbed wire. The second soldier aimed his rifle, prepared to fire, but risked hitting guards or workers if he did. As Dieter sprinted for the fence, a guard watching the workmen saw him coming. He raised his rifle over his head and flung it forward, the butt smacking Dieter on the side of the head. Dieter collapsed in a crumpled heap, sprawled on the ground. Conscious but dazed, he tried to rise, stumbling forward, when the guard hit him again, knocking him back to the ground.

"Stop," Kirstin pleaded as she ran toward him. "Leave him alone."

Another soldier stepped in front of her. When she tried to push past him, he blocked her path with his rifle. "Stay away!" he commanded.

She ignored him, trying to reach Dieter. The guard shoved her roughly and she stumbled sideways, struggling to maintain her balance but fell, banging her head against a tombstone. She attempted to rise, but winced trying to stand, and plopped back on the ground.

"Leave her alone," Steiner Beck said as he filtered through the crowd. "My wife was only trying to help. She means no harm."

Another soldier came towards them, a sergeant, his face stern, older than the other guards. He seemed to have a sense of responsibility, perhaps in command of the small group. Or maybe it was compassion. They were all German. Maybe they shouldn't be fighting. "What's going on?" he asked.

"This man ran for the border," a guard explained.

"And I hit him with my rifle to stop him," said the second soldier.

"What happened to her?" the sergeant asked, pointing to Kirstin.

"She tried to help the injured man," Steiner Beck interjected, speaking for her. "And this soldier shoved her to the ground."

The sergeant studied them for a moment, his eyes passing from Dieter Katz to Kirstin Beck and back again. Finally, after several moments had passed, he seemed to reach a decision. "Arrest them both," he ordered.

A soldier yanked Dieter Katz up and pinned his arms behind his back. He opened a set of handcuffs and placed them over Katz's wrists, clamping them shut. He then shoved him toward a nearby jeep.

The second soldier grabbed Kirstin's wrist, pulling her up. She cringed as she stood, favoring her left ankle.

"Be careful" Dr. Werner protested, moving to Kirstin's side. "She's hurt. Can you have some compassion?"

"I'll take her home and the doctor can care for her," Beck said, pointing to his townhouse. "We live right there. Arrest her later if you absolutely have to."

"I have no choice but to arrest her now," the sergeant said. "I don't care if she's hurt."

"Please, have some mercy," Beck pleaded. "It's a trying day for everyone. Let her go in peace."

The sergeant shrugged. "I don't have the authority to do that."

Beck studied him for a moment, a man young enough to be his son. "I agree the escapee committed a serious offense. And you should turn him over to authorities. But my wife did nothing."

"Steiner, stop," Kirstin said, glaring at the sergeant. "I'll go if I must."

The guard averted his gaze and looked beyond them, to a man approaching. Dressed in a gray suit with matching hat, he was handsome, his face finely formed, his hair black. Around thirty-five years of age, he filtered through the small crowd as the onlookers stepped aside.

He stopped in front of them and looked to Dieter Katz, sitting in the jeep, his head bruised and bleeding. He then turned to Kirstin Beck, standing awkwardly, a soldier holding her roughly by the elbow. "I'm Karl Hofer," he said, "from the Ministry of State Security." He removed his credentials from his pocket and showed them to the sergeant, "What's going on here?"

"That man tried to cross the border," the sergeant said, pointing to Katz. "But we stopped him, sir."

Hofer's gaze hadn't left Kirstin Beck, and it seemed as if he didn't want it to. "And what happened to this woman?"

"She tried to assist the fugitive -"

"After he was injured," Steiner interrupted. "But the guard pushed her and she fell and hurt her ankle."

"We plan to arrest her, too," the sergeant continued.

"And you are?" Hofer asked.

"Kirstin Beck," she said, trembling, knowing this man was someone she should fear.

"Mrs. Beck," Hofer continued, "surely you know it's wrong to aid a fugitive."

"I'm sorry, sir," she said. "I do know it's wrong." She lowered her eyes to the ground. "I acted on instinct, to care for someone who was hurt."

"I'll ensure nothing like this ever happens again," Steiner Beck said sternly.

"That may not be enough, Professor," Hofer said.

Kirstin cast a guarded glance toward Dr. Werner. The Stasi knew her husband. She wondered if they were only casual acquaintances, or more. Maybe much more.

Hofer studied her for a few moments, the silence awkward and frightening. "Well, Mrs. Beck," he said finally. "See that you never make this mistake again. Do you understand?"

"Yes, sir," she replied humbly. "I understand."

"Do you need medical assistance?" Hofer asked.

"I can help her," Dr. Werner offered. "I'm a doctor."

Hofer turned to the sergeant, as if Kirstin Beck was already forgotten.

"I'll go to *Rusche Strasse* with the prisoner," Hofer said. "Carry on here, sergeant."

As Hofer walked away, the soldier released his grasp on Kirstin. Werner and Steiner moved beside her, helping her stand.

"Take her," the sergeant said. "But let this be a warning."

"Thank you, sergeant," Steiner Beck said. "I assure you, she won't cause any more trouble."

As they started back to the house, Kirstin looked at the barbed wire fence, and then the apartment building behind it, nestled in West Berlin. She noticed a man on the third floor watching her as she watched him. It was a man she had seen several times when crossing the border to visit her grandmother, a man she often spoke to. She wondered how much he had seen. For a moment their eyes met, each understanding.

6

Tony Marino saw the crowd gather in the cemetery as parishioners watched the wall's construction after church services ended. At first, they only observed, probably as confused as he was by what was happening. But then a young man dart toward the barbed wire in a futile attempt to escape. A soldier slammed the butt of his rifle into the side of his head, and the young man fell to the ground. A woman with blond hair tried to help him but was shoved away, apparently hurting her ankle. Marino knew she had seen him watching. Their eyes met and she studied him as he studied her, wondering why fate had placed them on opposite sides of the wire, one enjoying the freedom the other was denied.

He wondered who they were, the cast of characters on the other side of the rapidly rising fence. He had seen the woman many times, passing from East to West, and had often spoke to her – just peasantries and casual conversation. They had never formally met, and he didn't know her name or anything about her, even though they were acquainted. But she was the only one he recognized; no one else in the crowd seemed familiar. He had never been to their church and he didn't even know the denomination, even though he lived nearby and had spent two months in West Berlin. But he only went to the East for research, usually at the State Library on *Unter den Linden*.

Marino turned on the radio, hoping for news. The announcer described the border closing, noncommittal on whether it was temporary or permanent. There seemed to be much confusion – even among authorities – about the free city's future. West Berlin had radio and electricity, and Marino had turned on the spigot – water flowed freely and disappeared down the drain. But what about food and basic necessities – clothes, soap, utensils – the items used daily that are taken for granted until we no longer have them?

He considered going to the American embassy, to see if they had the answers, if they could guarantee his safety in a free city surrounded by barbed wire, even though, and strangely enough, it wasn't to keep him in but to keep others out. He had no reason to stay in West Berlin; he could leave at any time. He was a historian, a writer of non-fiction and documentaries, commissioned to compile a history of Germany. But after two months, using Berlin as his base, his research still wasn't finished. He needed another month, with the ability to move freely about Berlin. He wasn't sure if his current credentials would let him do that.

He turned the radio off and tried the television, the image only a foot square, the cabinet three feet high with a speaker on the bottom. It was more like a piece of furniture, with a lace doily and a vase on top of it. The image was sketchy and the sound a bit garbled, but the station was still broadcasting. Berlin had three channels, two showing Sunday church services while the third offered news. He turned to the news channel and saw a reporter at *Potsdamer Platz*, a camera trained on the closed border. Marino watched for thirty minutes but learned little more than he already knew or could see from his apartment window. Workers were stringing barbed wire around the entire perimeter of West Berlin, creating a democratic island in a socialist sea. He looked at the clock and noted the time difference with New York. He called his editor anyway, knowing he would wake him up.

Ned Simpson, Senior Editor at Green Mansion Publishing, groggily answered the phone on the fifth ring. "Hello."

"Ned, it's Tony."

"What's the matter?" he asked, as if knowing there was little reason to call in the middle of the night. Actually, there was little reason to call at all.

"The East Germans closed the border."

Simpson sighed. "It isn't the first time," he said, "and it won't be the last."

"It's different this time," Marino told him. "There are guards everywhere and they're building barbed wire fences. All inter-secting streets are closed and so are the subway stations along the border. Turn on your radio."

"Hold on," Simpson said.

Marino heard hear him rustling around the room, followed by voices, presumably the radio. Then the voices were different, as if the channels changed.

"There's a brief mention on the news about the border being closed, but nothing about barbed wire fences."

"I'm telling you, Ned, it seems serious. No one will be able to cross."

"Do you still have water, sewer and electricity?"

"Yes."

"That's because the East needs western currency," Simpson told him. "They'll still provide services. How about the phone lines to the East?"

"I haven't tried."

"I'll bet they don't work."

"I'm not sure if I can get out, at least not now."

"Why would you want to get out?" Simpson asked in apparent disbelief. "This changes everything."

"What do you mean?"

"Put your research on hold," Simpson instructed. "You're watching history being made, and you're right in the middle of it. That's your new book – a first-hand account."

"I hadn't thought of that," Marino replied. He wondered how an editor could see commercial aspects in the misery of East Berlin, or the fear in West Berlin. But maybe that's why he wasn't an editor. "Anything else?"

"Yes," Simpson said. "Call your mother."

Marino heard the click of the receiver and then dial tone. He put the phone down and drank his coffee, listening to the radio and changing television channels. He wasn't getting much information. He waited a few more hours and then called the operator, gave her a Philadelphia phone number, and waited for the connection. He got it a moment later, a bit sketchy.

"Tony, I've been so worried," his mother said, the Italian accent thick even after a lifetime in the States.

"Why?" Tony asked. "Have you seen the news?"

"What news?" she asked. "I don't care about the news. I haven't heard from you? How am I supposed to know if you're all right?"

He rolled his eyes. Italian mothers were all the same. They loved their sons above all else – except making them feel guilty. "I just called you last Sunday," he reminded her.

"You can't call through the week?" she asked. "What do I have to do, wait until Sunday to talk to you. What if you call while I'm at church?"

"Listen, mom, there's a lot going on in Berlin. You'll see it on the television."

"What do you mean there's a lot going on?" she asked.

"The East Germans are building a fence around West

Berlin. It doesn't impact me, I'm fine. But a lot of people in the East can't get to family in the West."

"That's horrible," she said. "How can they separate families like that? Not that we're together, with you being so far away. What are you going to do? Are you coming home?"

"No, not just yet," he said. "I have a little more to do here. Is everything all right with you?"

"As well as it can be with my son halfway around the world."

"Are you getting the money I send?"

"Yes, I get the money," she replied. "But I would rather have my son."

"It won't be much longer, mom. Take care and I'll call you next Sunday."

"You be careful," she said. "Don't let anything happen. And I'll try not to worry myself sick."

He smiled, imagining the tiny woman on the other end of the phone. "I'll be fine," he said, "so don't worry. And I'll talk to you next week."

"Wait," she said abruptly, catching him before he hung up the phone.

"What's wrong?" he asked.

"Are you getting enough to eat?"

"Yes, Mom," he said, missing her more than he would admit. "I'm getting plenty to eat."

He hung up the phone, smiling faintly. His mother was different, totally devoted to her son, as if nothing else in life mattered. Someday he would have to tell her how much he appreciated it, how fortunate he was to have a mother like her. But at the same time, he wondered why her happiness depended on him. It was a tremendous burden for him to bear. He was not only responsible for his own happiness, but hers as well.

He again turned his attention to the television. There was

more coverage now, the morning gradually yielding to after-
noon. And his suspicions were correct. The border was closed;
the fence was being constructed around the entire city of West
Berlin. Essential services would continue, routes in and out of
West Berlin from West Germany would remain available. West
Berlin would survive. At least for now.

But what would happen to East Berlin?

7

Kirstin walked back to the house, hobbling on her injured ankle. She leaned against Dr. Werner while Steiner walked beside her, providing additional support.

"Are you in pain?" Steiner asked.

"No, it's just tender," Kirstin replied. "I'm sure it's fine."

"I don't think it's broken," Dr. Werner said, "but I'll take a closer look when we get back to the house."

As they neared the edge of the graveyard, Steiner dropped a few steps behind them and looked back at the barbed wire fence. "I had best stay near the border," he told them. "Just in case someone else tries to escape."

Kirstin turned, wondering why he suddenly found his fellow parishioners so interesting. It was as if he was watching them, just as he seemed to be watching her. "Be careful," she advised. "And don't let anyone do anything foolish."

Dr. Werner helped her to the house and led her into the parlor. He eased her onto the chair while he sat on an ottoman and lifted her left leg into his lap. He then tenderly flexed her toes and foot. "There's some swelling," he said, "but it's not broken. We'll put some ice on it."

29

"How long will it take to heal?"

"Three or four days at most. Aspirin will help with the pain."

"Thank you so much," she said. "I appreciate your help."

"I just wish I had my medical bag," he replied. "I could wrap your ankle with gauze for more support." He paused and thought for a moment. "Suppose I go home and get it. I'm only a few blocks away."

"I don't want to be a burden," she said.

"No burden at all," he said as he rose from the ottoman.

"Are you sure?"

"Yes, it's no problem," he said "I'll only be a few minutes." He started for the door, but paused after taking a few steps, turning to face her.

"Is something wrong?"

"Why do you think Dieter tried to escape?" he asked. "He never would have made it. He must have known that."

"I'm not sure," she said. "Anger or frustration, I suppose."

"He's fortunate they didn't shoot him. I don't understand why he'd take that chance, with such little hope of success."

"Especially since the closing could be temporary," she said.

"It doesn't look like temporary," Werner observed tentatively, as if gauging her reaction.

"No, it doesn't," she agreed, hesitating. She knew no one could be trusted. The Stasi mingled among the population. They could be anyone – your butcher or postman, even your doctor or minister.

"I may never see my daughters again," he said ruefully.

She studied him closely, wondering if he was ally or enemy. "If I only knew yesterday what I know today," she said evasively. "I have to get to the West."

"For your grandmother."

"Yes," she said, then added evasively, "But for so much more."

He looked at her, guarded. "It seems the West has something we all want," he said delicately. "Maybe we should have gone when we had the chance."

Her gaze met his, not flinching. "It can still be done," she said cryptically. "It'll just be harder."

His eyes widened, the cause not apparent. He was either suspicious, or thankful he found someone with similar views. "Perhaps," he said, and then after a moment added, "I had best get that bag."

Kirstin hobbled to the refrigerator. She opened the freezer door to get ice but found most of the cubes in the tray weren't frozen. She banged on the thermostat with her fist and heard a motor start to hum, hopefully lowering the temperature. After sorting through the trays, she collected what ice she could and wrapped it in a towel. Then she returned to the couch and propped her ankle on the ottoman, wrapping the ice around it.

As she waited for Dr. Werner, she reflected on current conditions. The border was closed, whether temporary or permanent, and she had to accept that. She also had to get to West Berlin, for a variety of reasons. And she had to do it soon. But she realized that, given the circumstances, she couldn't do it alone. She needed help. She needed someone that despised East Berlin as much as she did and wanted to get to the West. But they had to be careful. And they had to be cunning. Unlike Dieter Katz.

Ten minutes later, there was a rap on the door. "Come in," she called.

"I told you I wouldn't be long," Dr. Werner said, entering with his medical bag. He sat on the ottoman, opened his bag and withdrew a piece of gauze, about three feet long.

"Thank you for doing this," Kirstin said. "I'm sorry to bother you."

"It's no bother at all," he said. He lifted her leg and started wrapping the gauze around the arch of her foot, winding it across the top and then gradually over her swollen ankle. "Is this too tight?"

"No, it makes it feel better," she said.

"You just need to stay off it for a few days."

Kirstin decided to risk continuing their conversation. "Poor Dieter," she said. "I hope the Stasi aren't too hard on him."

"I do, too," he said, "but we both know that's unlikely."

"Only a day ago, he could have walked into West Berlin, as he did every day to go to school, but not come back. Just as so many others have done."

Dr. Werner nodded in agreement. "Yes, but who knew?"

"Maybe Dieter won't be so stupid the next time," she said, acting as if it was an absent-minded statement

"The next time?" Werner asked with disbelief. "Do you think he'll be foolish enough to try again?"

She was quiet for a moment, evaluating his reaction, before she replied. "I think once you've tasted freedom, it's very hard to lose it," she said delicately.

"Yes, it is," Werner replied ruefully. "Sometimes I wish... well, never mind."

Kirstin cast him an anxious glance. "Be careful what you say," she warned, glancing around an empty room. "The Stasi are everywhere – your neighbor or your friends." She paused a moment and then stressed, "They're even your family."

A vague awareness crept over Werner's face, as if he suddenly understood. "I suppose the State has expectations for a professor," he said, as if studying her reaction. "Educators instruct the young to ensure socialism is continually triumphed."

"Yes, they do," she said, "especially if they hope to continue teaching." She hesitated, the seconds passing, the tension rising. She wasn't sure she could trust him, but decided to take the chance. "Isn't it strange that a professor with no religious beliefs attends service every Sunday?"

8

————

Steiner Beck approached a square building recently built of gray stone, part of Stasi headquarters on *Rusche Strasse*. There were several similar buildings, a complex of government offices that all looked the same, scattered along the boulevard. A large mound of rubble sat across the street, covering most of the block, remnants of bombed buildings from the Second World War. He suspected that someday soon the rubble would be cleared, replaced by square gray buildings like the one he was about to enter.

It was a warm day, a bit humid, the air stinking of sulfur, smoke belched from the lofty chimneys of a nearby factory that left the area draped in a misty haze. The leaves of trees planted along the street wilted with the humidity, some of the upper branches dying from pollution. A bus passed, half-filled with passengers, followed by a handful of Trabant automobiles. Built in East German factories renovated after the war, they were famously unreliable, from faulty transmissions to defective carburetors.

Beck was a man that appreciated opportunity. And chaos

and confusion, which now ran rampant throughout East Berlin, created opportunity. He intended to use that to his advantage, to leverage his skills to become more than he already was. A respected college professor, adept at indoctrinating his students in the principles of socialism, he wanted to mold the minds of an entire nation, to think for those who couldn't, to define the principles upon which an entire regime was built. And now was his chance.

He entered the building, the lobby furnished with functional chairs and leafy potted plants, a counter at the far end of the room. He approached the receptionist, informed her of his appointment, and was directed to the third floor. After finding the elevator out of order, he climbed the stairs and went to an office door marked *Karl Hofer.* He knocked lightly.

A receptionist opened the door, a young woman with her hair tucked in a bun, wearing black glasses and a plain dress, and directed him to wait. He sat on a stark wooden bench, casually leafed through a magazine describing the State's five-year economic plan and waited. Thirty minutes later, after the time for his appointment came and went, he fidgeted anxiously, wondering if the Stasi officer ever intended to see him. A few minutes later, the receptionist came to get him.

"Mr. Hofer will see you know," she informed him.

She led him down a drab corridor, without pictures or decorations, brown carpet and beige walls. When they reached a door at the end of the hall she knocked, waited a few seconds, and then led Beck into the office.

He walked in, noticing a plaque on the wall behind the desk. In neat, cursive writing, it depicted the Stasi creed: *The Ministry of State Security is entrusted with the task of preventing or throttling at the earliest stage – using whatever means and methods may be necessary – all attempts to delay or hinder the victory of socialism.* On the far wall, by the window, was a smaller plaque which stated: *The past is the present. The future is the past.*

Karl Hofer sat behind an oak desk, a handsome man with piercing black eyes, a pile of papers placed haphazardly upon it. There was a small bust of Lenin, an ash tray filled with cigarette butts, and a map of the city, folded and creased, scattered over the remaining space. "Please, sit down, Professor," Hofer offered.

Beck sat in the straight-backed chair in front to the desk. It was uncomfortable, but he assumed it was meant to be. "I came, as you requested," he said.

Hofer studied the professor for a moment, not speaking, as if letting the tension mount. After a moment of silence, he spoke, softly and deliberately. "What are we going to do with Mrs. Beck?" he asked.

"I don't know what you mean," Beck replied. "If you refer to the fugitive, Dieter Katz, and any aid she gave him, I suggest it was only a natural reaction. She saw someone harmed and tried to assist."

Hofer lit a cigarette, took a drag and blew the smoke in Beck's direction. "It would be very foolish to assume that I'm stupid."

"No, sir, I would never do that."

Hofer took a folder from the pile on his desk and glanced at Beck with an arrogant smile. "The name on this dossier is Kirstin Beck," he said. "Would you like to know what's in it?"

"That's really not necessary, sir," Beck said, uncomfortable with the proposal.

"But I think it is," Hofer said smugly. He seemed to enjoy dictating the discussion. He opened the folder and looked at Beck, waiting for his reaction.

"I don't need to see what's in her file," Beck assured him.

Hofer ignored him and started to read. "Kirstin Beck was born on July 26th, 1929, in Mitte, not far from where she lives now. Her father was a soldier, killed in Italy in 1943, and her mother died in a British air raid in 1944. She is just over six percent Jewish." He paused, raising his eyes. "Did you know that?"

Beck shifted in his seat. "No, I didn't."

Hofer continued. "Her maternal grandmother, Gertrude Manstein lives on *Jasmunder Strasse* in West Berlin. Until the border was closed, Kirstin visited her daily."

"She was raised by her grandmother after her parents died," Beck said weakly. "They're very close."

Hofer scanned the documents, not acknowledging Beck. A few seconds later, he looked up. "There's so much information her," he said, laughing lightly. "Let see what else we might find."

"I understand what you want," Beck said. "And I'll ensure my wife doesn't cause any trouble."

Hofer ignored him. "What an amazing woman," he continued. "Mrs. Beck is employed as an editor, listens to American music on the radio – almost exclusively – and has an affinity for Patsy Cline, the Platters and Roy Orbison. What a shame that radio broadcasts from the West are no longer available."

"She'll miss them, I'm sure," Beck mumbled, thinking of the stack of American records she played constantly.

"Mrs. Beck also plays the piano, quite well apparently, and is well educated."

"She's very intelligent," Beck said, his heart sinking. He wondered what Hofer wanted. And how much he knew. "There's nothing for you to worry about," he then advised the Stasi agent. "I can control her."

Hofer continued reading. "Some mental problems through the years, I see." He looked up, his gaze meeting Beck's. "I wouldn't have guessed that. She has serious issues, doesn't she?"

"She's very fragile," Beck replied quietly. "But still strong in many ways."

Hofer returned the dossier, reading through the material. "Now this is interesting," he said, eyeing Beck with surprise. "Mrs. Beck has a birthmark, shaped like a strawberry, in her pelvic region."

Beck was appalled. "Yes, she does."

Hofer looked at him curiously for a moment. "I'm surprised you noticed," he said, "since it's covered by pubic hair."

"Is there anything you don't know?" Beck asked, angry and annoyed. "Anything you don't see or hear?"

Hofer cast him a cocky smile. "Very little, actually," he said. He leaned forward, as if sharing a secret. "You should see your file."

Beck shivered, knowing the veiled threat was intentional. Karl Hofer could be a dangerous enemy, but, he suspected, a powerful friend. "That's quite all right," he replied curtly. He never thought about the Stasi spying on him. They should have no reason to. But he knew they spied on everyone. "I'm quite aware of the routes my life has taken. The successes as well as the failures."

Hofer again began to read the dossier. "I didn't know that you met at the University," he continued. "You were a philosophy professor and she was your student. You started having an affair on November 6, 1952." He grinned and again leaned forward. "And I see she wasn't the only student you were having an affair with. Somehow that doesn't seem acceptable for a professor, does it?"

"Mr. Hofer, please, I think I've heard enough. You've made your intentions quite clear,"

"No, Mr. Beck, you haven't heard enough," Hofer said sternly. "There's much more here. Let me see... you married in 1953. Eight years of marital bliss, yet you have no children."

Beck was uncomfortable. "My wife isn't capable of having children."

"That's so sad," Hofer said, feigning pity. "And I can see why. It's all here."

"I told you," Beck insisted, "that I don't need to hear anymore."

"But you do, Mr. Beck," Hofer informed him. "You do. Apparently, Kirstin was raped by Russian soldiers after the fall of Berlin, even though she was barely sixteen. She gave birth to a baby girl on May 9, 1946, and the State put the child up for adoption. It was a very difficult birth, especially for one so young, and Kirstin can not have any more children." He looked at Beck, slowly shaking his head. "Heartbreaking."

"It is a tragic story," Beck said softly.

"Unfortunately, this is the root of our problem and why, in my opinion, your wife is so very dangerous."

"I don't understand," Beck stuttered, fearing the worst.

"Recently your wife decided to find the daughter she lost to adoption sixteen years ago," Hofer explained. "In violation of the State adoption agreement, I might add. This quest became an obsession, and she's relentless in her pursuit. She believes she found the child's family in West Berlin but has not yet approached them." He looked up from the papers, his eyes wide with surprise. "She's quite a detective! Apparently, she did locate the correct family. How interesting is that? But what a pity she'll never see her daughter."

"Please," Beck said, willing to beg if he needed to. "My wife is very delicate. She never really recovered from that whole ordeal, mentally or physically. She means no harm."

Hofer put the dossier back in the folder. "Tell me, Mr. Beck, was it really instinct that drove your wife to help the fugitive Dieter Katz? Or do they have much in common, both desperate to get to the West."

"No, it was instinct," Beck said. "She's a loyal Socialist."

Hofer leaned across the desk, his expression stern. "I don't believe you, Mr. Beck. I'm going to watch her very closely from this point forward. And you had better, too."

Beck leaned back in his chair, tired of the games Hofer played. He studied his apparent adversary closely for a moment, and then asked, "What's in it for me?"

9

Tony Marino drove his Volkswagen away from the apartment building, turned the corner, and continued three blocks through a residential area, a few restaurants and stores sprinkled among the townhouses and apartments. He went south and then east to *Invalidenstrasse*, a frequently used crossing between East and West Berlin. He parked close to the border, expecting to find turmoil and pandemonium, angry crowds with policeman controlling them, and a strong military presence. Instead, he found a handful of residents looking curiously at a closed border. Two policemen stood nearby, warily watching the concrete barriers, barbed wire fencing, and stone-faced guards as they paced to and fro. Marino observed for a few moments, expecting something to happen, but not sure what it would be. When nothing did, he approached a policeman.

"What's going on?" he asked.

"They're adding more strands of barbed wire," the policeman told him. "One of the East German border guards crossed over to the West a few blocks away. They want to make sure it doesn't happen again."

"A border guard escaped?" Marino asked, surprised.

"Yes, he was watching the workers," the policeman said. "Apparently, he waited until no other guards were near him, then he leaped over the barbed wire and ran into the West."

"The other guards didn't shoot him?"

"No, they didn't notice until it was too late." the policeman replied. "A photographer was there, too. I think he got some good shots."

"Those photos will be all over the newspapers."

"And make it a lot harder for anyone else to get out."

"Some are saying it's temporary," Marino said, "and that the border will be open in a few days. But it doesn't look temporary."

"No, it doesn't," the policeman agreed.

"Are we going to do anything about it?"

"Not that I know of."

"Have you been given any orders?" Marino asked.

"No, not really," he said. "Just monitor the situation."

"For what?"

The policeman shrugged. "I suppose I'll know when I see it."

"Have you seen any Americans?"

"No, I haven't. At least not yet."

"Do you think they'll fight?" Marino asked.

"I doubt it," the policeman replied. "The Russians control East Berlin. And I don't think anyone, American, British or French, can do anything about it."

Marino returned to his car and drove south, past hospitals and office buildings, and then over an arch bridge spanning the Spree River. He continued to the western side of the iconic Brandenburg Gate, which was located along the border in East Berlin. He saw nothing but a few policemen, some curious pedestrians and a reporter or two, one of whom had a photographer with him – all studying the newly constructed barrier and the East German guards behind it. In the distance, near *Pariser Platz,* was a large collection of soldiers, probably close to a hundred, all heavily armed and supported by troop trucks and staff cars.

Marino decided to wait and see if anything developed. He went to an outdoor café across the street, with wrought iron tables evenly spaced along the pavement, all offering a view of the intersection. He ordered coffee, readily available in West Berlin but non-existent in the East, and a croissant, fresh and warm with melted butter. He then waited, scribbling what he saw in a small notebook he always carried with him. When he had finished his coffee, he ordered another. And then, as an afterthought, he asked for another croissant.

An hour later, he finally saw signs of the Allies. A British jeep came down the street, two soldiers in the front seats, traveling faster than the rest of the afternoon traffic. They approached the border and screeched to a halt only a few feet from the barriers and barbed wire.

Marino hastily paid his bill and hurried into the street, waiting for a confrontation. At the very least, he expected the British to demand an explanation, to provoke the East German soldiers or the Russian advisors sprinkled among them. He walked over near the jeep, stopping twenty feet away, and waited.

The British soldiers studied the border – the barbed wire fence and the guards who patrolled it. Across the street, East German soldiers were scattered across the landscape, as if they expected to receive orders, but were tired of waiting for them. Some glared at the British, as if daring them to act, while others seemed oddly out of place, like they were assigned a task they were totally unprepared for – German against German.

The jeep remained for almost an hour, two British soldiers watching a hundred East Germans. Eventually Marino heard the motor start, watched the driver put the vehicle in gear, turn around, and speed down the boulevard. The crossing was again vacant, except for a few policemen and a handful of onlookers. Even the reporters who were there earlier had departed, searching for a story somewhere else.

Marino returned to the French sector, staying as close to the border as the geographical configuration allowed. He wanted to see West Berlin's reaction – the citizens, the soldiers, any politicians brave enough to show their faces – but instead, he found no reaction at all. It was almost as if the Allies didn't care. Eventually, by late afternoon, the size of the crowds increased, mainly youth, college students or slightly older, and in an act of defiance they taunted the East German soldiers who pretended to ignore them. It wasn't a military action, it wasn't even a police action, but it was an act of civil disobedience, as ineffective as it was. But at least a protest was registered. The guards ignored the crowd, obeying orders, as they always had and always would.

Marino arrived back at his apartment building just after 6 p.m. When he entered his flat, he went to the window and looked out on the graveyard. The border was fortified, the barbed wire in place, crossing the cemetery to leave a slice on the western side, the remainder in the East. The church dominated the landscape, an overwhelming structure of brick, sitting sacred and holy – a symbol of what might have been, but in many ways, no longer was.

He called Ned Simpson. "There's no Allied military presence at all," Marino told him. "They're letting it happen."

"Because they have no choice," Simpson said. "They can't start another world war over West Berlin."

"I would have expected something," Marino said. "Even an official protest."

"Did you see any altercations?"

"No, but I'm told an East German guard jumped over the

barbed wire while it was being constructed and ran into West Berlin. A photographer got a picture of it."

"Interesting," Simpson said. "I'll let you know if the photo shows up in the papers."

"I'm sure it will."

"Are you getting all of this?"

"What do you mean?"

"Your notes," Simpson replied. "I meant what I said. This is your new project. Put the history book on hold."

"I'm documenting everything I see," Marino assured him.

"Good," Simpson said. "We need to move quick on this. I want something published before anyone else. Do you understand?"

"Yes, Ned," Marino droned. "I understand."

"Then let's get started," Simpson told him. "And check in with me every few days."

"Will do."

When darkness arrived, he again went to the window. He could see armed guards patrolling the cemetery, walking in pairs, one guiding a German Shepherd. He looked at the townhouses beyond the graveyard, to the end unit, where a light was on in a second-floor room, the curtains open. The woman he saw earlier when the young man tried to escape – the same woman who had so often walked by his apartment building – now stood in the window. He went into the parlor and got a small pair of binoculars. When he returned, she was still there. He raised the binoculars to his eyes.

She was also peering through binoculars, watching him as he watched her,

He was startled, and he put the binoculars down. He felt like a criminal, peeping in someone's window. But then he realized the world had changed – suddenly and drastically. In the course of a single day, a barrier was built to prevent those in East Berlin from getting out. People were desperate for information, news of loved ones, any help they could get – for solace if nothing else. Tentatively, he raised the binoculars back to his eyes.

The woman was holding a sign. It read: *HELP ME.*

And then her light was extinguished.

10

Dieter Katz lay on a flimsy cot in a dank cell, a narrow window near the ceiling. His head had been shaved, his rations restricted, and although he had been in solitary confinement for several days, he had yet to be questioned by authorities. He realized how stupid he had been, darting across a graveyard littered with guards in a vain attempt to escape. One impulsive action had changed his entire life, a few seconds in two decades of existence. One day he was among the leaders in his class at the Technical University in West Berlin, and a few days later he was in a Stasi prison. He wondered about his parents, working a farm near the Polish border, so proud that their son had gone to the city to get an education. He knew they wouldn't be very proud of him now. But he swore that if he ever got out, he wouldn't waste his second chance.

He was still determined to get to West Berlin, even though it now seemed a dream, given his circumstances. But when the time was right, his girlfriend would help him, and maybe a few other trusted family and friends. He had no way of contacting them, not while he was jailed, but he would eventually get out. He just didn't know when.

Freedom, now so elusive, would have been so easy to obtain. He could cross from East to West and back again whenever he pleased. But he took it for granted. He thought it was a right. Now he realized he had no rights. No one in East Berlin had rights; they only thought they did. In reality, everyone contributed to the collective, the common goal to ensure socialism prevailed and prospered. And now he realized, supposedly contaminated by Western ways, that he was a menace to socialism because his thirst for freedom could never be quenched. He knew that, but more importantly, so did his captors.

It was on his fourth day of captivity that a guard came to get him, pulling him from his cot and shoving him into a bright hallway, the walls made of concrete. They walked to the end of the corridor, climbed two flights of stairs, and entered a conference room where two men sat at a table, one of whom was the Stasi agent who had arrested him.

"Dieter Katz," the agent said as he entered. "I am Karl Hofer from the Ministry of State Security and this is Klaus Bauer."

Katz nodded sullenly, but respectfully. He didn't know what to expect – a life in prison or freedom – but he realized these two men would make that determination.

"Do you know why you are here, Dieter Katz?" Karl Hofer asked.

"Yes, sir," Katz replied, trying not to sneer, but failing. "I'm being punished."

"Punished?" Hofer asked, apparently incredulous. "Why is that?"

"Because I tried to flee to the West."

"No, you're definitely not being punished," Hofer informed him sternly. "You would know if I chose to punish you, because you would never forget it. Nor would your family."

Katz tried not to cringe, to appear strong and defiant, but he wasn't successful. He wondered why the Stasi mentioned his family. Could his actions really bring harm to his parents or siblings or cousins?

"You're actually very fortunate," Hofer continued.

"Why is that?" Katz asked warily, trying not to show how afraid he was.

"Because I think you have a promising future in the Socialist Party," Hofer replied. "And I intend to work with you toward that goal. Mr. Bauer will assist me, acting on your behalf."

"I don't understand," Katz said as he looked at the two men, wondering if something horrible was about to happen.

"Mr. Bauer is the superintendent of a youth industrial school in Mitte, not far from your home. He's agreed to accept you as a pupil."

"I won't be punished?" Katz asked, unable to believe his good fortune.

"Not punished," Bauer clarified, "but rehabilitated. It's an opportunity most would envy."

Katz hesitated, his gaze shifting between the two men. "What do you mean by rehabilitated?" he asked, pronouncing the word with distaste.

"You'll be enrolled at our center," Bauer said, "and provided with a military-style education. We focus on discipline and enlightenment, while emphasizing the concepts of socialism."

"But only after a few more days in solitary confinement," Hofer interjected. "Solitude cleanses the mind."

Katz thought the school sounded more like a mental facility, where they somehow erased your memories and managed to replace them. He heard rumors places like that existed, but he had never believed them. "What's the curriculum?" he asked tentatively.

"We have a varied program reinforced by a regiment of regulations," Bauer said.

"To instill discipline, respect, and gratitude," Hofer added.

"In time you'll become an obedient member of the collective, making a contribution to society." He glanced at Bauer and smiled before turning his attention back to Katz. "You've only lost your way, Dieter Katz, prejudiced by decadent western ways. A mistake, to be certain, but fortunately we can correct that."

Katz hesitated. "But I don't want anything corrected," he said. "Can't I continue my education at the Technical University in West Berlin, just as I did before?"

"The past doesn't exist," Hofer said in a measured monotone. "It never did. Yesterday is continually rewritten to reinforce what is today. And tomorrow exists only through today's eyes. You see, Dieter Katz, there is only the present. The past is the present, and the future is the past. Therefore, today defines our entire universe of thought and action. You understand that, don't you?"

Katz was confused and afraid. "No, I don't."

"In time you will," Hofer informed him. "This fantasy you're immersed in, a past that reflects only what you want it to be, not necessarily what was, is the root of your problem. Fortunately for you, we can easily address that. Mr. Bauer has a wonderful success rate with similar cases."

"I'm not sure I'll ever change my beliefs," Katz said bravely, refusing to be intimidated.

"The seed of doubt has already been planted," Bauer remarked with a smug smile. "You said you're not sure. And I certainly understand that. Because you lived a lie, a fantasy created by Fascist propaganda. You can no longer distinguish what is real and what is not, what will be and what was."

"But in time you will," Hofer added.

"You're not making sense," Katz argued timidly.

Bauer shared a knowing glance with Hofer, and then turned to Katz. "To your damaged mind we make no sense," he said. "But in time we will."

Hofer rose from his chair and started toward the door. "You'll understand eventually," he said. "A gifted mind like yours will quickly grasp the truth. And I'm sure Mr. Bauer will take good care of you."

Hofer opened the door and walked out.

And Dieter Katz knew his life would never be the same.

11

Dr. Jacob Werner lived in a modern apartment building, constructed after the war. It was five stories high, a nondescript square built of steel and concrete, the design enhanced by large tiles under the windows, a different color for each – lime, cobalt, amber, and cream. Every apartment was identical – the same size with the same amenities. Rent was subsidized by the State, with most residents paying the same monthly fees. Although tenants held a variety of occupations, and Dr. Werner was a prominent physician, their pay was essentially equal, regardless of profession. Werner often thought of the long road he traveled, years of medical school and internships, and then serving in the army, for wages that equaled an unskilled factory worker.

He survived the Second World War, a captain in the medical corps assigned to the Russian front. He participated in the initial invasion of Russia, experienced the early successes, saw Moscow in the distance, an elusive goal that would never be reached. And then fortunes reversed, and he retreated with millions of others, participated in battles to save the homeland, including the final fight for Berlin. He survived the Russian victory, when the capital city of the Third Reich was destroyed and ransacked. He had been a good soldier and loyal Nazi. And now he tried to be a good Socialist.

He wasn't proud of what he had done, especially during the war, and he rarely discussed it. As the years passed he took solace in his faith and family, asking a benevolent God for forgiveness. Married to his wife Anna for forty years, they had raised two daughters, now grown, both of whom fled to the West. The oldest, Katrina, lived in Bonn and was employed as an economic analyst for the West German government, while the younger, Teressa, lived in West Berlin, where she worked as a nurse. Many of the young had fled East Berlin since the war, especially those with skilled occupations, the professionals, those that helped an economy to thrive and prosper. They wanted opportunity and freedom, the chance to use their talents to better their lives and the lives of their children, perhaps looking for a world that no longer existed under the rigid dogma of socialism.

Werner and his wife Anna had gone often to West Berlin to visit their daughter Terresa. Recently married to a West German policeman, she was expecting their first child – the Werners first grandchild. Now, if the border was closed permanently, he might never see his daughter again, especially with stricter guidelines expected for those in West Berlin who tried to visit the East. What should have been among the most exciting times of their lives, had become a tragedy.

"Has the professor's wife recovered from her injury?" asked his wife Anna, a compassionate woman, devoted to her husband, as they sat at the kitchen table for dinner. She had prepared pork, with some green beans and corn. There was a shortage of potatoes, but they made do. All of East Berlin made do.

"Yes, she was fortunate," Werner said between mouthfuls. "It was only a sprain."

"Why would a solder try to harm her?"

He hesitated, and then took a sip of water. "I don't know that he did," he replied. "The guards are as afraid as we are. They don't want to hurt other Germans."

"He shoved her so roughly," she said. "It certainly seemed like he wanted to hurt her. She could have banged her head harder against the tombstone or been injured more severely."

"Yes, she could have," he agreed. "But I still think it's difficult for everyone. Especially the way the border was closed."

"There was no warning," she said, her eyes misting as they now so often did. "How can I see Teressa, or our first grandchild when she arrives, if the State prohibits visitors from the West? And God only knows when we'll see Katrina."

"I know," he said softly. "I don't even want to think about it." He had little left in life except his family – no dreams or aspirations, no hopes for fame or fortune. He only wanted to enjoy his daughters and any grandchildren that might come. But with each day that passed, that seemed a remote possibility.

Anna placed her hand on her husband's and looked at him, pleading. "Jacob, I can't survive without my daughters. They're all I have in life. Please, we have to do something."

He tried to be strong but couldn't. "For now, we have to accept what is," he said, his voice trembling, "and not dream of what is not."

She removed her hand and looked at him angrily. "Why?" she snapped. "We have a right to enjoy our family, as families have done throughout history."

"But we can't change the world," he said. "We can only live in it."

"Why can't we live the way we want to, like others do."

"Anna," he said sternly. "We have to adjust."

She leaned forward, again holding his hand. "We can have a life with Katrina and Terresa, but only if we want it badly enough."

"What are you trying to say?"

She leaned back in the chair. "You know exactly what I'm trying to say."

"I told you, I can't change the world," he said.

"But why let the world change you?"

12

Kirstin Beck was better prepared the next time she communicated with her friend at the window in West Berlin. She had a small chalkboard, chalk, and an eraser staged by the window of her second bedroom, which she used as an office, editing books for universities, publishers, and the State.

Steiner was downstairs, either correcting papers from his classes or enjoying his radio programs, so she had to be careful, listening for his footsteps on the stairs. If she heard him, she would put the chalkboard behind a bookcase, or underneath a chair, and turn off the floor lamp by the window. Then she would grab a folder off her desk as she left the office, acting like she planned to do some editing. She often sat in the parlor, or lay in bed at night, and went through notes, so it wouldn't seem suspicious. In many ways they lived separate lives, but somehow did it together. She wondered if that was normal, even though she doubted it was.

It was just after 9 p.m. when she saw the light in the third-floor apartment in West Berlin. She waited anxiously, peering through her binoculars, hoping her new friend would appear. A few minutes later, she saw him at the window. She checked the border guards, to make sure they couldn't see her, and then held up her chalkboard. Written upon it was her name: *Kirstin*. She held it there for almost ten seconds, took it down, and hurriedly erased it. Then she put the binoculars to her eyes.

He was holding a large notepad. Sprawled across the page in dark marker was his name: *Tony*.

Excited, she put down the binoculars and scribbled a question on the chalkboard. *What do you do?* She held it there for a moment, waiting, and then put it down. She looked through the binoculars.

He was still writing. A few seconds later he lifted the pad: *Writer. You?*

She laughed, since they had a common bond, and wrote on the chalkboard. *Editor. Good fit.* She held it there for a moment, and then picked up the binoculars.

He was laughing, pointing at her. He wrote on his pad and held it up for her to see. *Funny. How can I help?*

She lowered the binoculars. She needed to be careful. The Stasi were everywhere – even in West Berlin. And she really didn't know this man. They had engaged in casual conversation when she went to see her grandmother, but nothing more – just two strangers being polite. But he was her only conduit to the West. He might be her only chance. She picked up the chalkboard, thought for a moment, and then wrote: *my grandmother is in West Berlin.* She held the board for a moment, breathless, and then lowered it. She picked up the binoculars.

He had already written his reply and was holding up the notebook. It said: *I will help.*

She heard a creak on the stairs, and then another. Steiner was coming. She shoved the chalkboard behind the bookcase, the binoculars, eraser, and chalk underneath the chair.

"Kirstin," he called. He was close, up the stairs and into the hall.

She didn't have time to turn off the light, or to hurry to her desk for a folder. She turned as she heard him enter the room.

"There you are," he said. "I thought you were going to listen to the radio with me."

"I am," she said, her heart pounding at her close escape. She walked toward her desk. "But I have work to do. I came to get one of my folders."

"What were you doing at the window?" he asked.

She shrugged. "Nothing," she replied casually. "I wanted to see the moon."

He walked toward the window and peered out. "There is no moon," he said, looking at her strangely. He hesitated a moment, his hands on the window sill, his eyes trained on the cemetery below. "What's going on?"

"What do you mean?" she asked, her heart skipping, knowing she needed an explanation.

"Outside."

She came back to the window and looked. When Steiner wasn't watching, she averted her gaze to Tony's apartment across the border. His light was out. When he realized she wasn't alone, he turned off the light so he couldn't be seen. He was probably still watching, cloaked in darkness.

"In the cemetery," Steiner continued, pointing to the right, behind the church.

She looked down into the graveyard and saw two soldiers wandering through the tombstones, scanning the area with flashlights. "What are they doing?" she asked.

"I don't know," he replied. "Maybe they're searching for someone."

She studied the tombstones and mausoleums but saw nothing unusual. "I don't see anyone," she said, hoping he stayed distracted. She didn't want him questioning her, or worse, noticing the chalkboard.

"I hope some fool didn't try to escape," he mumbled.

Her mind wandered to another foiled escape. "We still haven't heard from Dieter Katz," she said softly.

"Don't worry about Dieter Katz," he said testily. "I'm sure he's fine."

"It might be nice if his friends and family knew that."

"I'm going down there to see what's going on," he said, ignoring her.

"Steiner, don't," she warned, lightly touching his arm. "It's better to mind your own business. The less you see, the better you are."

He looked at her coldly. "We should have more courage than that," he said. "We should report what we see, regardless of what it is. Don't you agree?"

"Yes, of course," she stammered. "You're right, as always."

Then she turned out the lamp and breathed a sigh of relief.

13

Tony Marino was surprised when he saw the man enter Kirstin's room. He had assumed she was alone, although he wasn't sure why. The man had startled her, entering unexpectedly, and she seemed to frantically hide the chalkboard and binoculars. Marino wondered who he was – a husband, perhaps, even though he was much older, or even a father. But regardless of their relationship, she seemed to fear him. But why?

Marino had turned out the light as soon as he sensed she was in danger. It was all he could do to avoid having their communications discovered. But he still kept looking, the binoculars pressed to his face, as he stood in the shadows. He watched her interact with the man, just as he would watch a show on television or a play at the theater.

She needed help, something regarding a grandmother in West Berlin. It seemed a simple request. He could call the grandmother on the phone or stop by to visit, maybe run a few errands. But he didn't want any responsibility, no significant commitments. He just wasn't very good at it. There were no entanglements in his life, no one he had to care for, except his mom. And that's the way he wanted it. Even his romantic relationships didn't last long, and some had been with spectacular women, attractive, intelligent, loyal. But somehow, he always seemed to lose interest, just when it started to become serious. They were all wonderful women, with few faults, women most men would love and appreciate, devote their entire lives to. He knew there was nothing wrong with them. But there was something wrong with him. He just didn't know how to fix it.

He wondered if Kirstin could write her grandmother a letter, just to prove she was all right, even though the authorities screened outgoing mail from East Berlin. Or maybe the grandmother could visit West Berlin, although now it was very difficult. West Berliners needed visas and other documents – all very difficult to obtain – to travel to the East. Very few had them or would be able to get them, which is the way the Stasi wanted it.

Tony Marino was American. He could go to East Berlin whenever he chose if Kirstin needed him to, as he often did for research, although now there was a midnight curfew. He had probably been to the East three dozen times already, sometimes more than once a day. He assumed he could still cross the border, although he might be watched by the Stasi. But he had a good cover. He was a historian, and he was writing a history of Germany. He had two books in print, sales were good, and he was researching his third. He could even fill a briefcase with notes and take it with him. If searched by the East German police, it would only substantiate his claim.

But regardless of what he had to do, he already decided he would help Kirstin, the mysterious woman on the other side of the cemetery.

———

The following morning, Marino rolled out of bed just after 6 a.m., made a pot of coffee, and turned on the radio to catch the ball scores. The Phillies had lost to the Braves, seven to six. Lee Walls at shortstop had gone three for five for the Phils, but it wasn't enough to get the win. They seemed destined for a poor season, mired in last place in the National Division, Cincinnati in first. When his coffee was done, he poured a cup – black and hot – and walked to the window that faced the border.

He saw guards patrolling the barbed wire, and he studied them for a moment. They were young, barely men, but they were alert. He suspected the barbed wire was effective. It was intimidating, it was patrolled, and it was difficult to pass through. Over two thousand refugees had escaped from the East on the day before the border closed, at least as documented in the refugee centers. But there had only been forty-eight on the day the barbed wire was built. He suspected there would be fewer each day as the East Germans continued to fortify the border.

Construction of an actual wall had already begun in parts of the city. Twelve feet high, made of concrete blocks, the top contained a round pipe that made scaling it difficult. It was a formidable barrier. Guards patrolled its length, some with German Shepherd dogs, and the construction of wooden watch towers, systematically spaced along its length, had already begun. He assumed the wall would cross the entire city. It was only a matter of time.

As he scanned the graveyard, he suspected it had once been beautiful, the graves spaced evenly, trimmed shrubs and beds of beautiful flowers defining the rows, all anchored by majestic tombs, mausoleums, and family plots enclosed in ornate wrought iron railings. But now it was unkempt, littered, tombstones tilted at crooked angles, some of the trees and shrubs as dead as the cemetery's inhabitants. It was a home for ghosts and goblins, hideous and decrepit, a stark reminder of good days gone bad.

He looked at the church, the beautiful brickwork marred by crumbling mortar, streaked with soot from pollution the city produced – cars and buses and factory smokestacks. The row of townhouses, Kirstin's on the end, must also have once been beautiful. Now the paint on the windows was chipped and faded, some of the slate roof tiles broken, and even though the shrubs and gardens were obviously cared for, they were far from what they probably once were. The fourth unit from the end of the block was still partially destroyed from a war that ended sixteen years before, the roof collapsed into the structure, fallen bricks littering the back yard.

Tony Marino studied the stark urban landscape, a city dying and in decay, and considered what Kirstin had been trying to tell him. Suddenly he understood her motivation. She had a grandmother in West Berlin, and she wanted to see her. She feared the man she lived with, whoever he was and for whatever reason. She had visited West Berlin often, where a vibrant renewal reinvigorated a once destroyed metropolis, business and enterprises thriving, from factories to stores to restaurants. The differences between East and West were as a striking as the contrasts between summer and winter. He suspected Kirstin wanted to escape. Why wouldn't she? But she didn't want the man she lived with to know.

14

Steiner and Kirstin sat in the parlor, a song called *Smoke Gets in Your Eyes* by an American band called *The Platters* playing faintly in the background. Steiner had a pad of paper before him, his pen moving fluidly across the page as he worked on a lecture for his next class. Kirstin scanned a manuscript she had removed from a manila folder, a new assignment she received earlier in the day. It was written by a former military officer and espoused the glories of socialism, suggesting that more rigid discipline among the people could reap rewards in future five-year productivity plans. She scanned it quickly, saw it was littered with statistics and cross references, and frowned, knowing she had to do a lot of research to validate it.

She disliked most of the books and pamphlets she was assigned to edit. Literature was approved and published by the State, anything with a hint of ingenuity or favorable reference to capitalism or Western ways was heavily censored. She edited novels that trumpeted the success of socialism, or the tragedies that befell those who opposed it, or history books that rewrote the past to portray yesterdays filtered through a socialistic lens, and government pamphlets offering advice on everything from travel through the Eastern bloc of Communist countries to care for the cars produced in East German factories, most of which had poor operating histories. She could only imagine what it would be like to work for a Western publisher, editing great works of literature, or historical documentaries, biographies – anything that wasn't censored.

"At church services this week there was almost forty percent fewer attending than before the border was closed," Steiner said, looking up from his student's papers. "The rest of the congregation must have come from the West."

"How can the reverend replace them?" Kirstin asked, not really caring. She occasionally went to church; Steiner always did. She thought it strange, a man so dedicated to socialism yet so devoted to his faith. Unless he only pretended to be devoted to his faith.

"I don't know that he can," Steiner replied.

"Do you know what happened to Dieter Katz?" She had inquired about Katz's fate several times but had never received a satisfactory answer.

"He's enrolled in one of the youth industrial schools," he replied. "Although I'm not sure what trade he's learning."

Kirstin felt sorry for the young man. His potential was so great; he was a bright, industrious, energetic youth with a twinkle in his eyes and compassion in his heart. But he had made a foolish mistake and it changed his life. She only hoped it wasn't forever.

"I don't know much more than that," Steiner continued.

"He was a bright young man," Kirstin said softly, "with a promising future."

Steiner frowned. "He wasn't bright enough," he countered, "or he wouldn't have tried to cross the border."

"He did it for the woman he loves."

"No, he did it for the love of decadent Western ways, and that's why re-indoctrination was required."

Kirstin was quiet for a moment, hiding her opinion. It seemed that she and Steiner drifted farther apart by the day, their visions of life and how it should be lived, and governments and how they should serve the people, providing the wedge. After a moment, she decided to speak. "He wanted more than East Berlin can offer, like many others," she said softly. "What's so horrible about that."

Steiner put his pad of paper down, his lecture apparently completed, and started to grade students' papers, as if continuing the discussion would lead to words that shouldn't be spoken. After a few awkward moments, he said, "Closing the border was needed – a necessary step for the collective good. Now the State can focus on the present, because the past no longer exists."

She didn't reply. He had an annoying habit of spitting out State slogans, as if the dull mantras would come alive if repeated enough. It only took someone with the ability to think to realize they never would. The State ensured people were sheep, following their leaders with unwavering loyalty, not asking questions. Steiner saw himself as one of the shepherds, especially to his students, and she suspected he wanted much more – a broader audience. She then reflected on a time, which seemed a century ago, when she had been one of those students.

She wondered why their relationship had failed. They had been so happy after they married, with common interests and goals for brighter tomorrows. But somehow, it had all collapsed. Was it because of their age difference – Steiner was twenty years older – or was it his political beliefs, his undying support and fanatical belief in both socialism and the State. She wondered if they had once been in agreement, cogs on the same wheel, unwavering in thought and deed, although she knew she had drifted far from that description. Maybe they each changed, growing as people but in different directions. Or maybe their marriage failed because he was a Stasi informant and she couldn't trust him

She returned to her editing, red pen in hand, marking the passages with the shorthand she typically used, correcting punctuation and critiquing paragraphs. It was a dry text, as non-fiction often is. She much preferred fiction, even when written through the prism provided by the State.

"The border closing, though unexpected, was good for us, too," Steiner said softly but suddenly.

She realized the conversation had taken a turn; she could tell by his tone. The discussion had shifted to private matters, perhaps painful memories she didn't want revisited. "Why is that?" she asked dryly.

He put down his papers and looked at her, and for a moment she saw the love in his eyes she found when they first met, the touching, sincere gaze that said so much more than words ever could. The gaze that seemed to be absent for so many years. "The girl," he said softly.

She paused, waiting for more, but it never came. "Do you mean my daughter?" she asked quietly.

"Yes," he said, his tone sensitive and compassionate. "Maybe the border closing was a blessing. Maybe it's best not to know, to not open wounds that have long since healed."

"That's just it, Steiner," she told him. "The wounds never healed."

"But maybe they should," he said. "You risk hurting inno-cent people, especially a child. What if you have the wrong family and can't find her? What if you do find her and she rejects you? Isn't this better, leaving it all as it was – undisturbed."

She hesitated, but then replied. "I'm not complete as a person until I find her," she said, trying to explain. "Whether it's today, tomorrow or five years from now. I won't give up – like I did when the State took her away. I'll do everything I can to be reunited. And when we are, I'll make everything right."

Steiner frowned and returned to grading his papers, writing comments in the margins.

Kirstin watched him for a moment, knowing she had probably said too much. One simple statement – putting personal preference above the collective – was enough to make her an enemy of the State. She knew it and so did he. But she also knew he was more than a husband, not someone in whom to confide, not someone to share hopes and dreams, to love today and tomorrow.

He was Stasi.

15

Karl Hofer sat in a straight-backed chair in front of an oak desk covered with papers in a cramped office beside an empty classroom in Humboldt University, a prestigious college in East Berlin. A photograph of a woman, early thirties, blond hair and blue eyes, sat on the desk. He noticed the woman's smile was empty, even though she was posing for a photograph, and for a moment he wondered why.

"I'm obtaining information from several different sources," Steiner Beck told him. "A few church parishioners, several of my students, and two of the professors here at the University."

Hofer held up a hand, as if to stop Beck from speaking. "I don't want to know who your informants are," he said. "At least not yet."

"I'm trying to show how critical I've become to your operation," he said. "I offer valuable information to you and other Stasi leaders."

"I realize that," Hofer said. "And it's much appreciated. But I don't need to know your sources."

"Of course," Beck said, as if wanting to be so much more than he was. "I understand."

Hofer paused, his mind wandering to different matters. He reached across the desk and picked up Kirstin Beck's photograph and studied it closely. She was a beautiful woman, but in a natural way, as if she wasn't trying to be. For an instant he thought of her birthmark before returning the photo to its original position.

"Is something wrong?" Beck asked, a bit anxious.

Hofer shook his head. "No, not at all," he replied. "I was simply admiring the photograph. There's a slight resemblance to my wife. The hair is different, a shade lighter, and the smile is not as broad, but there are some similarities."

"It was taken last year," Beck offered. "In the summer. When times were simpler."

"Yes," Hofer replied, but he wasn't really listening. His mind was wandering to his own family, a wife and two small daughters. He never seemed to have enough time for them. "Professor Beck, can you give me your assessment of Dieter Katz?" he then asked.

Beck eyed Hofer warily. "I don't know him well," he admitted. "Only some casual conversation after church services."

"Is he a threat?"

"In what way?"

"Is he committed to socialism?"

Beck paused, as if considering the question, and then replied. "I think he's been tainted by Western ways."

Hofer considered his recent meeting with Dieter Katz, a young man barely twenty, vulnerable and afraid but trying to be brave. By the time Hofer turned twenty, he had endured enough hardship to last several lifetimes. During the final days of the war, he was a teenager forced into the army, given a WWI rifle that hadn't been fired in twenty years, and told to defend the Fatherland. He spent the last few weeks of the Third Reich running and hiding, avoiding approaching soldiers, not knowing how to fight and too afraid to try. Eventually he hid in a garbage dump, Russian soldiers passing him, and managed to survive until he surrendered to the Americans. He had never fired a shot. He often wondered if he was a coward, or if he had done what he had to, just to survive. Maybe now he overcompensated as a Stasi officer – or maybe he didn't. But he had decided long ago, buried in garbage with Russian soldiers only feet away, that he would never again be the hunted. He would only be the hunter.

"Mr. Hofer" Beck asked, interrupting his thoughts.

"Excuse me," Hofer said. "My mind wandered for a moment. So, in regard to Dieter Katz, is he tainted because he went to college in West Berlin?"

"I believe so," Beck replied. "I think we've discussed this topic before. A professor can very easily make impressions upon their pupils, develop their minds, direct their thoughts – sometimes lasting a lifetime. A professor is an authority figure, a symbol of wisdom, that students honor and respect. Given that relationship, a professor wields tremendous power and is invaluable to a socialistic society."

"And how is that power exercised?"

"By influencing thought," Beck answered, "and causing conclusions to be reached, manipulating the mind. For example, in the East, pupils are taught Communist principles, the value of socialistic societies, the equality of man – that we all deserve the same rewards. Western beliefs are far different."

Hofer was pensive, envisioning the professor interacting with his students. He also imagined a world he had never known. He knew fascism and socialism, but nothing else. "Give me an example of how you sway the minds of your students," he said. "I'm very interested."

Beck seemed to collect his thoughts for a moment, perhaps reflecting on his many years in the classroom and how he might present a particular topic. Or maybe he was only trying to impress the Stasi. "As an example," he said, "if we examine the most famous philosophers of ancient Greece, the discussion soon narrows to two – Aristotle and Plato. Aristotle, from Athens, preached the value of democratic principles, presenting in a logical form the importance of freedom and liberty. A Western instructor might applaud the logic developed by Aristotle. Plato, on the other hand, believed that the elite – an intellectually superior group known as the elders – should rule the masses, make decisions for them in the collective interest, knowing what's best for both the individual and society overall. I contend that Plato foresaw our form of government, where the best and the brightest protect and guide the average citizen, and we're all better for it. You and I, Mr. Hofer, are the elite. We're the shepherds; the citizens are the sheep."

Hofer studied the professor sitting before him, a firm believer of everything he taught. Beck served his purpose, protecting socialism, ensuring it would never be attacked from within. At least not by citizens who had sat in his classroom. "In your opinion," Hofer asked, "if Dieter Katz was allowed to attend Humboldt University, would he contaminate the other students with Western values?"

"Absolutely," Beck declared. "There's no doubt."

Hofer was pensive for a moment. "I tend to agree," he said finally. "I'm afraid, at a minimum, that Mr. Katz's educational pursuits must come to an end. He'll remain in the youth industrial school run by Mr. Becker."

"I think that would be best," Beck agreed.

Hofer looked out the smudged window at the college campus, the buildings that comprised it, and the students crossing the grounds to attend classes. "I've arrested three parishioners from your church in the last six months," he said.

"I'm aware of that," Beck said. "And may I remind you that it was done with my assistance."

"I managed to rehabilitate one," Hofer continued, ignoring Beck's comments. "Mr. Baumgartner, who I think will develop into a good Socialist. And I've decided to give Mr. Katz another opportunity to prove his potential. But the third, Mr. Abel, is so subversive he remains in his cell. Why do you think we've had problems with so many in that particular congregation?"

Beck shrugged. "I can't answer that," he admitted. "I'm a philosophy professor, not a psychiatrist. But I suspect that, since half of the parishioners were from West Berlin, they may have influenced the others."

"Who else in that congregation is a risk?"

"None that I know of."

"I think they need to be watched closely, don't you?" Hofer asked "Especially given the church's location to the border. I think others may have been impacted."

"I suppose that's possible."

Hofer leaned forward, closing the distance between them. "Just so we clearly understand each other," he said firmly. "If we have any more dissidents, I will hold you responsible." He paused, eyeing Beck coldly. "And that includes your wife."

16

Tony Marino drank his morning coffee and considered how much had happened since the border was closed. He was focused on Kirstin, how he could help her, and was so preoccupied he didn't turn on the radio to catch the baseball scores. She hadn't really asked for much, but he suspected she would once she trusted him. And when he thought about her predicament, he realized she really didn't have anyone else to turn to. He had never had anyone so dependent on him before, especially for their own survival. Or maybe he had, but never realized it.

If she wanted to escape from East Berlin, and he was fairly certain she did, he wondered how he could help her do it. He couldn't engage the guards or stage a rescue from a fortified enemy position. He wasn't qualified. He had some army training, but he had been an interpreter – accomplished in conversation not combat. He had to quickly develop the skills required, or instead outsmart the enemy, which had a far greater chance of success. He couldn't risk Kirstin's life or his own. It was a tremendous responsibility and, if he chose to shoulder it, he couldn't fail.

He got dressed, left his apartment, and climbed into his Volkswagen. He decided to drive along the border, looking for weaknesses he might be able to exploit, should a rescue attempt be attempted. If he didn't find a suitable location in the city proper, he could always try West Berlin's perimeter with East Germany, the city's western suburbs.

His mission took much of the day. He found heavy fortifications in East Berlin streets that interfaced with the West – some with concrete walls already constructed or in the process of being built. He got out of his car at one street in the British sector and walked to the edge of the newly constructed wall. He could hear dogs barking on the other side, close to where he was standing. He shivered at the thought of someone trying to scale the wall while German Shepherds attacked them, biting their feet and legs. He found other areas of the city fortified with rolls of barbed wire attached to makeshift posts, very much like the fortifications outside his apartment building. Although somewhat promising – at least he could see East Berlin through the barriers – they were also heavily guarded. He realized that most of the urban landscape, streets and buildings and boulevards, held little promise for escape.

He assumed that the hardest regions for the East to defend were natural areas like parks, the River Spree, even the cemetery that bordered his apartment building. The landscape offered some protection, trees and shrubs, and, in the case of the graveyard, so did tombstones and mausoleums. He could cut the barbed wire from West Berlin, even though it was guarded, if he had a distraction that diverted the guards' attention while he made a hole large enough for Kirstin to pass through.

Other escape options were more difficult and required more planning. Kirstin seemed anxious, as if she had to escape quickly or at least address her grandmother's plight. False passports, tunnels, and even sewer lines all offered interesting opportunities. Although a false passport was the most promising, it was also the most difficult. Marino had no diplomatic contacts willing to take risks, especially to provide a passport for someone they didn't know. The East Germans also maintained a meticulous record of all who entered East Berlin, allowing them to remain until midnight, when they were required to leave. A successful exit with a false passport meant there had to be a record of that person entering on the same day. And in this case, there wouldn't be. It was challenging proposition.

After evaluating a breach of the border fortifications, as well as alternative methods like fake passports or tunnels, he realized he had to talk to Kirstin. He could always go to East Berlin to meet her; he assumed his documents would still be accepted. But he would have to be careful. The Stasi might be watching him and he didn't want to endanger her.

She wasn't at the window that night. He paced the floor, anxiously waiting for her light to come on, wondering if something happened to her. What if the Stasi suspected her, or the older man in her house realized she was communicating with someone from the West? He tried not to get alarmed, recognizing she could easily have a social engagement, or maybe she worked odd shifts. There were dozens of legitimate explanations to explain her absence.

On the second night, he was rooted to the window, staring across the cemetery at the end townhouse. He sat in his darkened living room, sipping a beer, the radio on faintly in the background. As the evening passed, and no light in the upper floor of the townhouse was lit, he wondered how he could find out what happened to her.

On the third night, just after nine p.m., she appeared at the window. Marino hurriedly scribbled on his pad: *Are you all right?*

She wrote on the chalkboard and held it up: *Yes.*

He flipped the page on his pad. *Who is the man? Are you in danger?*

She put her chalkboard down and walked from the window. He kept the binoculars to his eyes, watching, waiting. He saw her cross the room, almost out of sight. He struggled to see but couldn't. He suspected she stood at a doorway, perhaps looking into the hall or speaking to someone in an adjoining room.

A few minutes later, she returned. She picked up the chalkboard, glanced back toward the hallway, jotted a note, and then held it up.

Marino put the binoculars to his eyes and read the board. It said: *Husband = Stasi.* He put the glasses down, shocked. Maybe he hadn't understood. He picked up his pad and wrote: *Man is husband who is Stasi. You are in danger?*

Her reply was short: *Yes.*

He wrote: *Do you want me to get you out?*

She wrote: *Yes.*

He had guessed correctly. She needed more than help with her grandmother. She wanted to escape. He wrote: *I can come to East. Can we meet?*

She put the chalkboard down and again walked across the room, but this time she disappeared from sight. He waited patiently, wondering what she was doing. Maybe her husband was downstairs, and she crept to the top of the steps, ensuring he wouldn't surprise her. Or maybe something had gone wrong. Three or four minutes passed, painfully slow, before she again appeared. She picked up the chalkboard and scribbled furiously.

Marino stared through the glasses, waiting for the board to be raised so he could see it. He watched as she wrote, looked over her shoulder toward the hall, and then finished. Finally, she held up the chalkboard. It read: *State Library rear of third floor. Monday 10 am. Please bring me a toothbrush.*

17

Kirstin seldom attended church services, but she did that Sunday. She sat in the pew beside her husband, listening as the pastor referenced the Bible, the State, the people, the border wall – which he referred to as the Anti-Fascist Protection Barrier – and how all interconnected. Her mind wandered as she listened, drifting to her upcoming meeting with Tony. He seemed like a good man. And he was attractive, bearing a faint resemblance to Elvis Presley. She tried to guess his last name, where he came from, if he was married, but couldn't, not from their limited conversations before the border closed. He said he was a writer. Did he write fiction or non-fiction, mysteries or thrillers? As she anticipated their meeting, she grew anxious. The Stasi planted agents in West Berlin; Tony could be a member of the secret police. Or he could just be a man who was willing to help.

She looked at her husband and noticed his gaze shifting to others in the congregation, perhaps measuring their enthusiasm for the sermon. She wondered if he was watching her, documenting her movements or recording critical statements she made of the State. Or was he ignoring her, giving her more freedom than he would ever allow his students. Maybe the Stasi watched her, too. They might know more about her than she realized or wanted to admit.

She thought about her grandmother, the only person in her life that she truly loved. She was worried about her. Her grandmother needed help, assistance that Kirstin had always provided but now no longer could. And then she thought of her daughter. She couldn't remember the tragic events that led to her birth; she suspected her mind blocked the images, a defense mechanism that helped her survive. Nor could she remember the months after the birth, when she barely spoke, her mind a kaleidoscope of unwanted images, a past she hoped to forget and a future she couldn't imagine. It took years before she was well, even though there would always be a hollowness in her heart, a void that couldn't be filled. But almost from the second she was fully recovered, she began to plot the search for her daughter. The path to find her had been difficult – tedious research, incomplete records, uncoopera-tive people. And then just when she planned to approach the adoptive parents, hoping to become part of her daugh-ter's life, the border was closed.

She saw Dieter Katz across the church, sitting quietly against the far wall. His hair was cut very short, or the Stasi had shaved his head. It made his ears look big, his round spectacles more pronounced. He stared vacantly forward, listening to the sermon, barely blinking. She wondered if he still planned to escape, but decided it depended on what the Stasi had done to him, what they wanted him to become, and how different that was from what he wanted to be.

When the sermon ended, Kirstin realized she hadn't heard a word of it. She had pretended to listen – facial expressions were important, especially if the Stasi were watching. But her mind had been in a million other places, which made her realize she could comfortably fit almost anywhere in the world except East Berlin.

As she walked out of the church with her husband, Dr. Werner was waiting for her. "Can I speak to you?" he whispered furtively, ensuring Steiner couldn't hear.

Kirstin wasn't sure what to think. When her husband stopped to talk to the pastor, she took a few steps toward the cemetery, avoiding parishioners who paused on the pavement, gathering in groups to discuss the sermon, or the shortages of coffee and potatoes. There were always shortages. She wondered if it was like that in the rest of the world.

"What is it?" she whispered.

"I need help," he said.

"What type of help?"

"I'm being falsely accused."

"Of what?" she asked.

He looked around, watching the others. "Someone claimed I made derogatory statements about the State."

"Who told you?"

"The Stasi, Karl Hofer. I intend to deny it, of course."

"Why would someone do that?"

"I'm not sure," he replied. "But I think they're trying to destroy me."

"How?" she asked, suddenly alarmed. "Especially if you did nothing wrong."

"They also claim I didn't pay for medications," he explained. "Supposedly the State provided them."

She knew Dr. Werner was a competent and highly respected physician, and she doubted the allegations were true. "What did you say?"

"Nothing yet," he said. "I received notice detailing the accusations, ordering me to report to Stasi headquarters."

"But that's absurd," Kirstin said, watching those around her. "Do you have any idea what they're talking about?"

"I think they're referring to samples," he told her. "The Council for Medication sometimes provides them to monitor patients' reactions." His face twisted with disgust. "Essentially, they use my patients to conduct experiments. But I don't remember ever being charged for them."

"When did this supposedly happen?"

"I'm not sure," he replied. "I get samples a few times a year. It could be recent, or it could have been years ago."

"You should have nothing to worry about," she assured him, although she wasn't as confident as she sounded. She wasn't sure if he told the truth and the State was about to destroy him, or if he was a Stasi agent seeking sympathy.

He moved closer. "That isn't how it works," he said nervously. "They make the accusation and then they invent the evidence."

"But it's not true," she insisted, her voice a bit too loud.

"The truth is what the State says is the truth," he said coldly. "Don't you realize that? You are what they say you are, because they create your image. Perception is reality. And the people will believe it. Because if they don't, the same will happen to them."

Kirstin was afraid, aware of the danger, but she decided to trust him, knowing she might regret it. "What can I do for you?"

He studied those nearby, eyeing them cautiously, and moved closer to Kirstin. "My wife and I have to get out of East Berlin," he whispered. "Quickly, before they come for me."

She made a promise she had no right to make, risking her life and his, and maybe even Tony's. "I'll help," she promised. "But whatever happens, don't tell my husband."

18

Dieter Katz exited the church and stood in a line of parishioners greeting the minister. He waited his turn, glancing toward the cemetery where Kirstin and Dr. Werner talked quietly. They seemed suspicious, whispering and watching people as they passed, and he wondered what they discussed. But he decided if there was anyone in East Berlin he could trust, it would be them. They had already helped him once. They might do it again.

"Dieter, it's good to see you again," Steiner Beck said as he approached. He glanced at Katz's forehead, still slightly bruised from the rifle butt. "No permanent scars, I hope."

"No, I'm well," Dieter said, trying not to sound bitter. He knew he had to be careful. He couldn't say or do anything that aroused suspicion.

"I didn't see your girlfriend, Eileen, at service today," Beck observed.

"I'm afraid she can't attend," Dieter informed him, wondering why Beck was so friendly. "She lives in the West, just a few blocks away."

"I wasn't aware of that," Beck said, nodding to an elderly

couple that passed. "It must be difficult when a relationship faces so many obstacles."

"The only obstacle is the wall," Katz said with an innocent shrug.

Beck moved closer. "The wall was built for a reason," he said sternly. "We don't want the Fascists to destroy our way of life."

Katz was quiet for a moment. He knew not to argue. It would only make it harder. "Yes, there are obstacles," he replied, "but we manage."

"Do you get to see her at all?" Beck probed.

"We spend some time together."

"That's good," Beck said. "At least she manages to visit."

"Yes, she does," Katz replied, feeling awkward and not wanting to say too much. Eileen had a Swiss passport, which enabled her to come to East Berlin. He didn't want that spoiled.

"Hopefully it all works out," Beck said, smiling vacantly. "If it doesn't, I'm sure the young women in East Berlin would appreciate an interesting man like you."

"I don't really care about any other women, Professor," Katz said softly.

"You might in time," Beck suggested. "But for now, immerse yourself in your studies. Will I see you in one of my classes at the University?"

"No, I'm afraid not," Dieter said, hiding his disappointment. "I'll be attending the industrial school here in Mitte."

"A new beginning," Beck remarked. "How fortunate for you. The school has a good reputation."

Katz knew not to complain or express displeasure with the State. And he knew it could be worse. He could still be in prison. "Yes, I am fortunate," he said. "I've already been told that when I graduate, I can expect an exciting career in politics, the military or the Stasi."

"I'm sure you'll serve the State in the way you're best

equipped," Beck offered as he turned to talk to another parishioner. "Maybe you found you're calling."

"Yes, perhaps," Katz said, nodding his goodbye.

Katz briefly praised the minister on his sermon, and then approached Kirstin and Dr. Werner. "I'm sorry to interrupt," he said. "I just wanted to thank you for helping me the day the border was closed."

"You would do the same for us," Kirstin said, eyeing him cautiously. "It's good to see you again."

Katz looked around furtively. When he was sure it was safe to speak, he said, "I know you've heard stories about people arrested by the Stasi. Many become fanatical defenders of the State." He paused and looked at each in turn. "I assure you, that I'm not."

Werner greeted a woman with her young daughter and then faced Katz. "I only wish we could have done more for you." He then studied Katz's face, where the rifle butt had bruised it. "I see your injury has healed. Just the last remnants of a bruise. Do you have any pain?"

"No," Katz said. "Although I did have headaches for a few days."

"What became of you?" Kirstin asked. "We haven't seen you for a few weeks."

"I was in prison," he replied, "kept in solitary confinement. My release was conditional on attending the industrial school."

"Which I'm sure you don't want to do," Kirstin said softly.

Katz was hesitant. It was difficult to identify who was Stasi and who was not. "I don't know if it's the best path for me," he said tentatively. "But I certainly appreciate the opportunity. Although I was a physics major at the Technical University in West Berlin. That seemed better suited for my ambitions."

"I'm sure you'll migrate to what you most enjoy," Dr. Werner said. "You're a bright young man. There are many options available to you."

"I'm not so sure," Katz frowned. He turned, ensuring no one was listening, and then continued. "Although I know which avenue to take, the street is currently closed. I have to find my way around it."

"Be careful," Kirstin warned.

He wasn't sure if she supported or opposed him, although he suspected the former. "I will," he replied. "Actually, we all should be careful." He turned to go, but hesitated. "We should discuss this further. The three of us. We seem to have much in common."

Dr. Werner's eyes widened briefly. "Of course, Dieter," he replied. "It's always a pleasure to see you."

"Yes, do take care of yourself," Kirstin said, apparently non-committal.

Katz turned and walked away. As he reached the pavement, he noticed a black sedan, a Trabant, parked sixty feet away on *Ackerstrasse*. There was a man sitting behind the wheel. He thought it was Karl Hofer, but he couldn't be sure.

19

Tony Marino entered the border crossing at the junction of *Friedrichstrasse* with *Zimmerstrasse* and *Mauerstrasse*. Known as Checkpoint Charlie, it was used by foreigners to access East Berlin. Marino passed through a gate on the western side, an American soldier giving his documents a cursory glance, crossed a strip of land between posts, and reported to a white shanty where the East German guards were located. He entered the building, found two soldiers sitting behind a counter, and presented his papers.

"Empty your pockets," the first guard said as the second scanned his documents.

Marino removed his wallet, a set of keys, some money, and a new toothbrush from his pockets and put everything on the counter, watching as the guard eyed the toothbrush. The subject of shortages, toothbrushes were no different than potatoes, coffee, cosmetics, or toilet paper. They were rarely found in East Berlin. For a moment he thought the guard would take it, but he didn't.

"You need receipts for everything you buy," the guard said, as he counted the money. He wrote some numbers in a ledger on the counter. "I've documented how much money you have. You'll return with the same amount, minus what you can prove with receipts. Do you understand?"

"Yes," Marino said. "I understand."

"Who is the toothbrush for?" the second guard asked.

"A friend," Marino replied.

"Do you cross the border often?"

"Yes, I do," Marino replied.

"Will you cross within the next seven days?"

"Yes, probably."

"At the same time?"

"Most likely."

The second guard looked at the first, sharing a strange glance. "Next time bring two new toothbrushes," he said. "We'll be on duty for the next seven days."

Even though the request was innocent, Marino realized it would help to have sympathetic guards. "I'll be sure to do that," he offered. "I'll probably pass through in a few days."

They returned his belongings and, as he put everything back into his pockets, they kept scanning his papers. After studying the stamps on his passport, they returned his documents and nodded toward the door.

"Thank you," Marino said as he exited.

He caught the S-bahn to *Unter den Linden*, watching the other passengers warily, wondering if any were Stasi and, if so, were they following him. When he reached the library ten minutes later, he was the only one to disembark. Still, he went in the opposite direction for one block, turned abruptly and walked in the other direction. It didn't seem he was being followed.

The library was a large, four-story building of neo-Baroque design, adjacent to Humboldt University and the State Opera House, with an equestrian statue of Frederick the Great by the building's entrance. The structure suffered damage from Allied bombings during the Second World War and had still not been entirely repaired. A domed reading room in the center of the building remained in ruins.

Marino entered, finding a dozen or so readers and researchers near the entrance. He made his way to the rear of the third floor, where Kirstin had indicated, took a book from the shelf, and sat down in one of two worn chairs behind an aisle of books on Babylonian history. He glanced at his watch. It was 10:07 a.m. He should have made more precise arrangements. It was a large library and he wasn't sure he was in the right place, but he decided to stay where he was. If she didn't appear by 10:20, he would wander around the third floor to look for her.

A few minutes later he sensed someone standing next to him. He didn't turn or acknowledge their presence. He simply continued reading the book in his lap, browsing through the pages.

"Tony?" a voice asked softly.

"Yes," he replied. "Kirstin?"

She sat down beside him and smiled. "Did you bring the toothbrush?"

He was surprised by her appearance. Even though they had spoken a few times, before the wall, when she had visited West Berlin, he hadn't noticed how attractive she was. She wore no cosmetics, or very little if she did, and had blue eyes and a smooth complexion, like porcelain. "Yes, here it is," he said, removing it from his pocket.

"There's a shortage," she explained. "I'm sorry I can't pay you for it."

"I know," he said. "The guards counted my money. It has to match when I return. But it's no problem. I wasn't expecting any money."

"Thank you so much."

"It's nice to finally meet you," he said. "It's much better seeing you in person than through binoculars."

"It is," she agreed, blushing a bit. "And I really appreciate your offer to help."

"It's nothing," he said. "You seemed a little desperate and I couldn't leave you stranded."

"That's very nice of you."

"Is this a good place to meet?" he asked.

She frowned. "It has good points and bad," she said.

He quickly scanned the area, wondering what might be wrong. "Should we meet somewhere else?"

"This works, I just have to be careful."

"If it's risky, we can find another location."

"It's the University," she explained.

"The adjacent buildings?"

"Yes, my husband is a professor there."

Marino was startled and started to rise. "We should go," he advised.

"No, it's all right," she said. "I know his schedule. He's in class."

"It's still risky to be this close."

"No, not really," she said. "He's a slave to routine. He hasn't left the classroom, or his office next to it, since the first day he taught there. Her brings his lunch every day except Wednesday, when he eats at the café across from the Opera House."

"That still doesn't sound safe," Marino said warily.

"Actually, it is," she continued. "If anyone sees me in the area, I can say I've come to visit him. And it provides you with an excuse, too. You can claim you're here to research."

"Are you sure you're comfortable?"

"Yes, it's all right."

He sat back in the chair, looked around the bookshelves, and listened intently for a moment. It seemed they were alone. "What can I do for your grandmother?" he asked.

She paused, as if capturing her thoughts. "I used to visit her daily," she said, "but I'm sure she knows why I haven't been there. She's in good health, but I did run errands for her, picking up groceries or her medicine. The neighbors are probably helping here, but I'm not certain."

He watched her closely, her expression sincere. She was worried. "Suppose I check up on her," he suggested. "Just to make sure everything's all right."

"Would you?" she asked.

"Of course. I'd be happy too."

"I would appreciate that very much," she said.

"No problem. What's her name?"

"Gertrude Manstein, and she lives at 16 *Jasmunder Strasse*."

"I'll visit her tomorrow."

"Thank you so much," she said. She leaned across the chair and gave him a light hug. "I've been so worried about her."

It felt good, her arms wrapped around him, even if briefly and only a friendly gesture. "I'm glad I can help. Is there anything else?"

Again she hesitated, as if she wanted to tell him something but didn't know where to start. After an awkward moment, she began. "Terrible things happened when the war ended and the Russians came, especially to young women like me."

He saw her eyes mist and suspected he was about to hear a very sad story. He didn't know if he wanted to. Confiding in someone forms attachments. He wasn't sure if he was ready for that. Or if he wanted it. "Are you sure you want to tell me this?" he asked.

"Yes," she said, her lip firm, as if she was trying to control herself. "It's important." She withdrew a handkerchief from her pocketbook and dabbed at her eyes. "When I was sixteen years old, I gave birth to a daughter."

Without even realizing it, he instinctively reached toward

89

her, taking her hand in his and gently caressing it. "Go on," he said softly.

"The State took her away, putting her up for adoption," she said, a tear falling on her cheek. "I couldn't protest."

"No, of course not," he said, trying to show compassion. "It must have been very difficult."

"I accepted what happened, or at least tried to," she said. "But as time passed, and she grew up without me, each day became more heart-wrenching than the last."

"I can't even imagine," he said, trying to support her. He tried to visualize what it would be like to lose the most precious person in your life. But he didn't want to.

"I spent years trying to find her," she continued, "and just before the border was closed, I located her in West Berlin. She lives just off the *Kurfürstendamm*."

"Did you contact her?"

"No," she said, shaking her head. "I couldn't. I never got the chance."

"What happened?"

"I planned to leave my husband, flee to West Berlin, and contact my daughter," she explained. "But when I tried to escape, soldiers were closing the border." She again dabbed at her eyes with her handkerchief. "Why didn't I leave one day earlier?"

20

D r. Jacob Werner shifted uncomfortably in a straight-backed chair. His pulse raced; his stomach was queasy. He was angry at his reaction, having served the Fuhrer so bravely in the war, but now crumbling under the Stasi's penetrating gaze. He felt as if his entire life was about to unravel, collapsing in a crumpled heap around him.

"More than one source has reported you to the authorities," Hofer was saying. "And unfortunately, your folder has landed on my desk."

"I have no idea what you're talking about," Werner argued, feeling tiny beads of perspiration on the back of his neck. "I am a loyal Socialist. And I've committed no crimes."

Hofer leaned back in the chair. "It's an interesting situation," he said. "I certainly can't defend you, not with so many witnesses."

"Who are these witnesses?" Werner asked testily. "I have a right to know."

Hofer chuckled. "You have no rights, Dr. Werner," he said pompously. "You never did."

Werner felt his face redden with anger. He struggled to

maintain his composure, knowing Hofer baited him, looking for any excuse to arrest him. "Please, tell me what was said," Werner requested. "I've been a loyal German my entire life. I fought for the Fuhrer. I embraced socialism. You at least owe me an explanation. Explain the allegation and I'll prove it false."

Hofer fingered the manila folder that contained Werner's file. "On the S-bahn, at *Rosenthaler Platz*, on Tuesday, August 25th, you made a comment about the Anti-Fascist Protection Barrier." He paused and raised his eyes to meet Werner's gaze.

"That makes no sense," Werner said, trying to remember anything he may have said, or when he might have been on the S-bahn.

Hofer continued. "You specifically said, that the barrier was a disgrace."

"I would not make that comment," Werner said. He was beginning to worry. It was something he might say. But he couldn't let Hofer know that,

"You claimed the barrier demonstrated the victory of capitalism over socialism," Hofer said icily, "because it kept Socialists from seeing the freedom and prosperity that capitalists enjoy."

Werner was pensive, reflecting on the date in question. It was twelve days after the border had been closed. He rarely rode the S-bahn, especially so close to his home. It could only have been to visit a patient, when he might have been rushed. A moment later, he remembered. He had gone with his wife to visit a friend of her aunt's, an elderly woman who wasn't feeling well. He had examined her, offering care.

"This is your opportunity to convince me of your innocence," Hofer said.

"I was on the S-bahn on the day in question," Werner admitted. "I was visiting a patient. But I have no recollection of making those comments."

"Really?" Hofer asked. "The witness who overheard them was quite distressed. It was reported immediately."

Werner remembered waiting for the S-bahn. He was talking to his wife – maybe he did mention the border wall. He ran the images of the street corner through his mind. No one stood out, just the normal stream of people getting on and off the tram. Then he remembered a group of Free German Youth, teenagers belonging to the organization created to reinforce the principles of socialism. But they were children, early teens at most. Could they have reported him? Good God, he thought. Children? He could do nothing but deny it.

"I don't recall ever saying that," he said, his voice trembling. He thought of the Second World War, surviving three years fighting the Russians, shivering through the coldest winters imaginable, starving, only to die because children accused him of betraying his country.

Hofer leaned across his desk. "I think you do."

Werner suspected he wasn't a very good liar. But he tried anyway. "No, I have no recollection."

"It's useless to deny," Hofer continued. "There are several more claims against you, from neighbors in your apartment building, friends who are concerned about you, strangers who worry you might do something to harm the State. And then of course, we have the financial accusation. Theft of state property is a horrendous criminal act."

Werner noticed his hands were trembling. He put them in his lap, hiding them from Hofer's view. "I have never stolen from the State."

"Apparently the Council for Medication doesn't agree," Hofer continued.

"I still don't understand their complaint."

"I find that hard to believe," Hofer said, shaking his head in pity. "Surely you're aware of your behavior."

"No, I'm not."

"You were given fifteen packets of medicine to combat severe headaches by the Council for Medication. Patients have verified they were given the medication, yet you made no reimbursement to the State."

Werner recalled the incident vividly. "They were free samples," he protested.

"Free to your patients, perhaps," Hofer clarified. "But you were aware the State expected reimbursement."

"No, I wasn't." Werner replied. "I get sample medications all the time and I've never made any payments."

Hofer rubbed his chin. "Maybe this is more serious than I thought," he said. "You never made payment?"

"I was never asked to," Werner declared.

"I'm not sure why," Hofer said. "Everyone knows payment is required. Maybe there's more than the incident documented."

"If I owe the State anything, I will gladly pay them," Werner said. He knew there was something else going on, he was caught in a spider's web, already convicted of a crime he didn't commit. It was clear the State considered him guilty of something. He just didn't know what.

Hofer sighed. "I'm afraid this is much worse than I thought," he said. "It places us both in a difficult situation."

"I already offered to remedy the situation," Werner said. "I'll reimburse the State, and I'll never make that mistake again."

Hofer slowly shook his head. "I'm afraid there's more," he said gravely.

"More what?"

"There are other accusations," Hofer informed him.

"Like what?" an incredulous Werner asked.

"Illegal sex acts."

"That's preposterous!" Werner exclaimed. "These are ridiculous charges."

Hofer shrugged. "Perhaps," he said. "It's sad actually. A man spends his entire life building an impeccable reputation. But it takes only minutes to destroy it."

Suddenly Werner understood. He was no longer trembling, no longer afraid. It was clear Hofer had a hidden agenda. He only needed to know what it was. "What is it that you want?" he asked.

Hofer relaxed, a slight smile curling his lips. "Cooperation is the preferred response," he said. "Hopefully we can clear up these allegations and you can return to your normal existence."

"Yes, I want to cooperate," Werner said, angry but anxious. "I'll do whatever I have to."

Hofer eyed him closely, letting a few tense moments of silence pass before he spoke. "Tell me about Kirstin Beck."

21

Jasmunder Strasse was a short street, only three or four blocks long and close to the cemetery. Like much of West Berlin, it was in the midst of renovation and rebuilding, economic growth driving the city's renaissance. Most of the street had been destroyed during the war and, as Tony Marino walked along the avenue, he passed new apartment buildings, each a bit different, some of brick, others of smooth cement painted different colors, and a few more faced with stucco. Balconies jutted from some of the newer buildings, decorated with potted plants that splashed color across the urban landscape.

Sixteen Jasmunder Strasse sat in a row of turn-of-the-century townhouses, ten narrow units in total. The last four, those closest to the intersection, had suffered damage during the war. They had been rebuilt, the bricks not quite matching, the window molding not as ornate, but they were functional, just a bit more modern, the material choices more frugal. As Marino glanced up and down the street, the new buildings outnumbering the old, he suspected the townhouses' days were numbered and it wouldn't be long before a developer bought them and demolished the buildings, using the space to build apartments that would house many more residents than currently lived there.

He approached Gertrude Manstein's residence, noticing the building was well-kept, a flower pot underneath a mailbox affixed to the brick. The front door was oak, the finish worn and weathered, and he lifted a brass knocker, tapping lightly. He waited patiently, and several moments later the door opened.

"Can I help you?" asked an elderly woman, probably past eighty. She gazed at him curiously, leaning on a wooden cane. She was tall and willowy, her eyes a bright blue, her hair long and straight and gray. The resemblance to Kirstin was remarkable.

"You must be Gertrude Manstein," Marino said, smiling.

"Yes, I am," she said, looking at him curiously. "Are you selling something?"

Marino laughed. "No, I'm not," he said. "I'm Tony Marino, an American, and a friend of your granddaughter. She asked me to look in on you."

"My goodness," she gasped, moving her hand over her heart. "Please come in. Is Kirstin all right?"

"Yes, she is," Marino said as he crossed the threshold. "She's doing well, but she's very concerned about you."

Gertrude led him into a dark parlor, the sun's rays that passed through the front window not providing much light. Behind the parlor was a dining room, an oak buffet against the far wall, a matching table with four chairs centered in the room. The kitchen was just past it, some light filtering in through windows above the kitchen sink.

"Please sit down," she said, leaning on her cane and motioning to a stuffed chair across from a sofa.

"Kirstin looks very much like you," Marino said as he sat down.

Gertrude smiled, apparently pleased with his observation. "Many people say that."

"She's very beautiful," he added, without thinking. "And so are you."

"Yes, she is," Gertrude said, chuckling. "And if I didn't know any better, I would think you were flirting with this old lady."

Marino laughed. "I'm sorry," he said. "Just an honest observation. I didn't mean any offense."

"And none was taken," Gertrude said. "Can I get you anything?"

"No, I'm fine," Tony said.

"Tell me about Kirstin," Gertrude asked anxiously. "I've been so worried about her."

"She's well physically," he said, but then paused, wondering how much more he should share. He decided to discuss everything except Kirstin's daughter, not knowing how much information the grandmother had.

"And emotionally?" Gertrude probed.

Marino studied the woman before him, her physical condition fragile but her mental faculties apparently unblemished. "I suppose I'll tell you everything," he said.

"I wish you would," Gertrude replied, her eyebrows knitted with concern. "I've been very worried about her."

Marino paused, choosing his words carefully. "Kirstin had planned to leave her husband and escape to the West," he informed her. "Unfortunately, on the night she chose to do that, the border was closed."

Gertrude sighed and slowly shook her head. "I'm not surprised at all," she said. "I knew she would leave him eventually. I just didn't know when."

"Are they happily married?" Tony asked, and then realized the answer was obvious. He rephrased his question. "Or, were they ever happily married?"

"Initially, I suppose they were," Gertrude said. "Although he was much older. I was against the marriage from the beginning. But when Kirstin made her choice, I supported her."

"Were you against it because of the age difference?"

Gertrude hesitated, but then spoke. "It was more than that. Kirstin was very fragile at the time. She was still recovering from..." She paused, as if searching for the right words, and then said, "From the effects of the war. Even though it was several years later."

"Do you think he took advantage of her?"

"Not so much that, but she was intimidated by authority. She always has been. Life hasn't been easy for Kirstin. Not then, and not now. But I almost felt like Steiner pressured her into the relationship. Nevertheless, they appeared to be very happy at the time."

"What happened?"

"As the years passed, they grew farther apart," she explained. "Until I wondered why they were even together. Now I wonder if I'll ever see her again."

"For now," Marino said, "I'm to make sure you have everything you need. And then we'll figure out what to do next."

"The neighbors have been taking care of me," she said. "They don't seem to mind, but I hate to impose."

"Suppose I come by once a week," Marino offered, "and I'll get your groceries and anything else you might need. Kirstin mentioned medicine?"

"Yes, there's a pharmacy around the corner. I need my prescriptions filled once each month. I have enough pills for two more weeks."

"How about groceries?"

"I have a list on the kitchen table."

Marino rose, went into the kitchen, and took the list. "I'll go pick these items up," he said. "Then maybe we can chat when I get back."

"Thank you so much," she said. "It's difficult without

Kirstin." She hesitated, her eyes misty. "And I miss her so much."

He looked at Gertrude, so frail, so alone, and he thought of his mother. He suddenly missed her very much, aware of her advancing age and that they were separated by several thousand miles. He was all she had. And she was entirely alone. As soon as he finished in Berlin, he would go back to Philly and spend some time with her. Maybe even bring her on his next trip. Then he laughed to himself. Or maybe not.

"Are you all right?" Gertrude asked, perhaps more intuitive than he would have thought.

"Yes, I am," he said. "I was just thinking of something."

"You look sad."

"No, I'm fine," he replied. "My thoughts just wandered for a moment." And then, for whatever reason, he found himself confiding in her. "I was thinking of my mother. She's all alone, too. In Philadelphia."

"You miss her, don't you?"

He looked at Gertrude. She was the type of woman that people liked to have in their lives. A good woman, kind and compassionate. "Yes," he said softly, "I do miss her."

"Then you should make plans to see her," Gertrude suggested. "Maybe for the holidays."

"Yes," Tony muttered. "That would be nice."

"And when will I see Kirstin?" Gertrude then asked abruptly.

Marino was quiet. He could see where everything was heading. He would help the grandmother, he would maintain contact with Kirstin, and he would help her escape from East Berlin. But only if he could make a commitment, if he could accept some responsibility. And for him, that might be the hardest thing of all.

22

Eileen Fischer was a tiny woman, barely five feet tall, with short brown hair and dark brown glasses. She had a Swiss passport, even though she was born in East Germany, just outside Leipzig. Like so much of the skilled work force, her family had escaped to West Berlin more than ten years before, eventually settling in Zurich. She had returned two years earlier and now attended the Technical University, majoring in world governments while living with an aunt in the French sector of West Berlin.

She took the S-bahn from her aunt's house to Checkpoint Charlie, exiting the tram at *Friedrichstrasse*, on the western side of the border. She entered the American guard shack, her Swiss passport attracting little attention, and exited a few minutes later. Then she walked across the border and into the shanty on the eastern side, handing her passport to the guard.

"Empty your purse and pockets, please," the guard requested as he wrote her name in a ledger.

She meticulously removed the items in her purse and placed them on the counter, and then laid the empty purse beside them. "I don't have anything in my pockets," she said.

The guard counted her money and wrote the amount in the ledger. "Be back before midnight and get receipts for whatever you purchase."

She picked up her personal effects – lipstick, rouge, a wallet, a small notebook with some of the pages torn out, a pencil, and a folded map. "I'll be sure to be back in time," she said as she turned toward the door.

"See that you are," the guard replied sternly.

As she left the shanty, she saw Dieter Katz standing on the corner, just past the intersection. She smiled when she saw him and waved.

He ran across the street, as if he couldn't wait to hold her. But he edged so close to the border zone that he attracted a guard's attention.

"Halt!" the guard commanded, pointing his rifle at Katz.

Katz froze, his eyes wide, and held up his hands. "I'm sorry," he said. "I won't come any closer."

"It's all right," Eileen said, hurrying toward the two. "He's waiting for me."

The guard wasn't convinced and the standoff continued. Katz didn't move, hands above his head, as the guard, barely old enough to shave, walked warily towards him.

"I didn't mean to get so close," Katz pleaded. He slowly started to walk backwards, hands still above his head.

"Don't move!" the guard ordered.

Katz stopped, frightened. "Please, I don't want any trouble."

Eileen Fischer realized she had to diffuse a situation no one wanted to escalate. She continued walking forward, her steps slow and measured, until she stood between the guard and Katz. "It was an honest mistake," she said, facing the guard. "No harm was intended."

Several seconds ticked by, no one moving. Then the guard slowly lowered his rifle, glaring at Katz as he did so. "That was stupid," he said. "You could have gotten killed."

"I won't do it again," Katz assured him as Eileen approached. "I promise."

"See that you don't," the guard said coldly. He turned and walked away, moving closer to the border fortifications.

Eileen ran the last few feet to Katz and hugged him. "You need to be more careful, darling," she hissed.

"I wasn't thinking," he said. "I was just so happy to see you."

She kissed him, tentatively at first and then a bit more hungrily, before pulling away. "I think I like your hair short," she said as she rubbed his close-cropped hair with her hand.

"It's military discipline," he said, rolling his eyes. "The cornerstone of the industrial school."

"It sounds so exciting," she joked.

"Come on," he said. "Let's go before the guard changes his mind."

They walked down the boulevard, two young lovers holding hands. They merged with other pedestrians, the S-bahn, cars and taxis passing on the street beside them. When they were a block from the border zone, and away from prying eyes and ears, they walked into a park and sat on a bench facing away from the boulevard, watching the birds sing from the trees.

"I've been so worried about you," Eileen said. "I came to see you at Stasi headquarters but they wouldn't let me in."

"No one ever told," he said, pulling her close. "Although I'm not surprised."

She kissed him on the lips. "It's all right. We're together now."

"I will never go back to prison," he told her. "No matter what happens."

"I understand," she said, softly stroking his cheek with her fingers. "I know how difficult it must have been."

"They're trying to indoctrinate me," he said.

"Indoctrinate you, how?"

"By convincing me that socialism, and life in East Berlin, is superior to capitalistic societies in the West."

"And is it?"

He shrugged. "Sometimes they're very convincing, and I want to believe them, I really do."

"But you don't?"

He hesitated, as if he wasn't sure. "It's been many years since you lived here," he reminded her. "You don't remember the shortages, the lines to buy food, the empty shelves."

"I heard on the radio that the shortages are temporary," she said. "It has something to do with trade agreements."

He sighed, as if digesting her explanation. "If that's true, why has there always been shortages?"

"I'm told toothpaste is available now," she said, "so maybe it's getting better."

"Toothpaste is, but toothbrushes aren't," he told her. "Tea is available, but coffee isn't. You don't have any shortages in the West?

"No, we don't," she admitted. "Although prices seem to be rising."

"Prices are fixed here, set by the government," he told her. "Just like everything else."

She paused, and then decided to change the subject. "How is your schooling?"

"It's different than the West," he said. "There's no exchange of ideas, no motivation to think or create. There are continual lectures, almost like brainwashing. It's stifling."

"I suppose that's how they control people," she said. "They don't want people to lead, they only want them to follow."

"Without asking questions," he added.

She hugged him again, wrapping her arms around him, and then kissed him, lingering. When she heard a noise, a twig snapping, she pulled away, giggling as an old man walked past them.

"We should find somewhere more private," he whispered.

They stood, holding hands, and walked towards the boulevard. The weather was pleasant for autumn, they were in love, and the world was theirs for the taking. Except he was confined to East Berlin, and she was free to come and go as she pleased.

"What are we going to do?" she asked, a hint of desperation in her voice.

"I'm going to escape," he replied, "so we can be together."

"Oh, Dieter, please be careful," she said. "Look what happened the last time you tried to get away. You almost had your skull fractured."

"It would have been worth it, if I escaped."

"But it's different now," she warned him. "Far more difficult."

"I'll still get through the border," he told her. "I just need to find the right location."

"Dieter, I don't think you realize what's going on," she said. "Border guards have orders to shoot those trying to escape. It isn't a game. People will die."

"I'll just have to be smarter than the guards."

"It isn't that easy," she insisted. "You know that. I don't want anything to happen to you."

"What do you suggest?"

She hesitated, not sure what to tell him. "Maybe if you had help," she suggested.

"What do you mean?"

"There would be less risk if you were with a group of people, with a detailed escape plan."

He smiled triumphantly. "I already thought of that."

She was surprised. "Are you actually planning to escape?"

"Yes, I am," he replied. "And we'll be together sooner than you ever imagined."

23

Tony Marino scanned the border from his apartment, ensured no guards were watching, and then held the notepad up to the window with a message scribbled upon it: *Grandmother well.* He waited, knowing Kirstin's reply would follow.

I miss her

He wrote: *Is daughter next?* Then he peered into her second-floor window through his binoculars.

She was still writing. After a few seconds, she held up her chalkboard. *Can you get me out?"*

He put down his glasses. He knew she wanted to escape; they had already discussed it. And he wanted to help her, he really did. But it was a tremendous undertaking. He would risk his life as well as hers. He thought about it a moment more, and then scribbled on his notepad. *Library tomorrow at 10 a.m.*

She put down her glasses and wrote a reply: *Yes.* A moment later, she turned off the light.

He sighed, watching the darkened room a moment more, and wondered whether to proceed. Each day he got deeper, even though he could stop at any time, walk away, leave Berlin if he had to. Or he could continue. For some strange, inexplicable reason, for he really had no idea what to do next, he decided to proceed. He sighed, moved away from the window, and turned on the radio. Maybe the Phillies won – for a change.

———

Marino brought two new toothbrushes to East Berlin and gave them to the border guards.

"You remembered," one of the guards said, a brief flicker of friendship on his otherwise stern face. He looked around, made sure no one was watching, and put the toothbrush in his pocket.

The second guard scooped up his toothbrush, nodding his thanks.

"I told you I would," Marino said. It wasn't much of a bribe, but it was all he could offer. He might never see these guards again, or their paths could cross at a critical time, when something as simple as a toothbrush made a huge difference. They both seemed appreciative and, for now, that was all he wanted.

He took the S-bahn to *Unter den Linden,* studied those that got on with him, and then eyed the remaining passengers: mothers, children, workers. He wondered if any were Stasi, and he walked up and down the car to see if anyone watched him. No one did. When the tram stopped near the library, four men got off with him, all younger, maybe college students. He merged with passing pedestrian, observing as the others went in different directions. It didn't seem as if anyone was following him. He walked up the steps to of the library, took a route to the third floor that was different from his last visit, but saw no one that seemed interested in what he was doing.

Kirstin was waiting when he arrived, sitting in the same chair she occupied the first time they met. When she saw him approach, she rose to greet him and gave him a quick hug.

"Thanks for checking on my grandmother," she said.

"She's doing well," he told her. "The neighbors are looking after her. I picked up some groceries while I was there, and I'll be sure to visit again next week."

She took his hand and grasped it tightly. "I really appreciate it."

"I'm glad I could help," he said. "And I enjoyed her company." He leaned forward, closer to her. "There's quite a resemblance."

She chuckled. "I've heard that my entire life," she said. "I suppose we do look alike."

"And your mother?"

She thought for a moment. "No, she looked more like her father. Dark hair, brown eyes. Not as tall and thin."

"We had an interesting chat," he said. "Your grandmother gave me some personal insights I can use in my book."

"Good, I'm glad you liked her," Kirstin said. She paused, glanced around the nearby aisles, and whispered, "Have you considered what I said?"

"About getting you out?"

"Yes," she replied. "Can you do it?"

"I'm not sure," he said. "But I did check areas where the landscape makes it difficult for guards to patrol."

"What did you find?"

"There are several locations we could use," he said. "But we'll have to move quickly. They're replacing the barbed wire with concrete walls."

"What do you suggest?"

"There's a park in the American sector," he told her. "The border is still barbed wire and it's lightly guarded. I can get you across there."

She hesitated, apparently considering his proposal. "It sounds dangerous," she said.

"It is," he agreed. "But everything is dangerous, no matter what we do."

"Can we use the cemetery instead?" she asked. "It still has barbed wire."

He hesitated. "Yes, I suppose," he replied. "But it's so close to your house. I thought it might be riskier."

"Why?" she asked.

"Your husband could be watching you."

"I suppose that's true," she admitted. "But I'm willing to take the risk."

"If it makes it easier for you, then we'll use the cemetery."

"It's more than just me," she said, cringing, as if worried about his reaction.

He was surprised. "Who else?" he asked.

"A friend and his wife, if that's all right," she said. "And perhaps one more, a college student – the boy who tried to cross the border the day it was closed."

"He seems a bit impulsive," Marino observed warily. "We have to be cautious."

"I will be," she assured him.

"Do you trust these people?"

She hesitated, but only briefly. "Yes, I think so."

He shifted in the chair, uncomfortable with her reply. "You need to be absolutely certain."

"I am," she confirmed. "They're good people. And they want to get out so badly. We should help them."

"I suppose," he said, still worried. "As long as it's manageable."

"But we need a better way to communicate," she said. "The chalkboard is difficult. My husband almost caught me twice."

"It's easy for me to come here," he said. "I give the guards toothbrushes and they don't hassle me. I can come every few days. Even more if I need to."

"That would be wonderful," she said, showing more enthusiasm than he expected. "But we can't meet at the library too often."

"I agree," he said. "Especially with your husband at the University."

"It's still a good location," she said. "I have a reason for being here and so do you."

"Do you ever visit your husband?" he asked.

She shook her head. "No, not like I used to." She turned, her eyes meeting his. "I'm afraid of what I might find."

It was an unusual statement. Was her husband having an affair? Or did she mean his ties to the Stasi. He decided not to pry. She would tell him if she wanted him to know. "Does he ever come to the library?" he asked.

"Not that I know of," she said. "But if he did, he would never come to this section."

"We should still choose another location," he suggested. "Just to vary where we meet so it's not too dangerous."

"I suppose once a week at the library is safe," she said. "But we have to be careful. Someone might be watching. The Stasi are everywhere."

"Next time we'll meet at a museum or a café," he suggested. "Think about it."

"I will," she said, looking at her watch. "I don't have much time. How long before we're ready to escape?"

He thought for a moment, visualizing the preparation. "A few days," he replied. "I have to survey the area and get some tools."

"How about Saturday night, around 2 a.m.?"

"Yes, I suppose we'll be ready by then."

"Good, I'll let the others know."

"Just be careful."

"I will," she replied, standing. "And now I had better go. Thank you so much for helping me."

"You're welcome," he said softly. "You would do the same for me."

"If our roles were reversed, I think I would."

He hesitated, wanting to share his emotions but wondering if he should. He rarely did, especially after only knowing someone for so short a time. But this was different. After a moment, he said, "There's so much more I want to know about you."

She smiled shyly, as if flattered. "In time you will," she said coyly.

He loved her smile. It was warm and genuine, not plastered on her face with no meaning behind it, like so many smiles in the modern world.

She gave him a quick hug. "I have to say goodbye."

"Wait," he hissed, as she started to walk away.

"What is it?" she asked, studying the empty aisles around her.

"Should I contact your daughter?"

She paused, as if she wasn't prepared. "Not just yet. Maybe if I don't make it on Saturday."

"Can you give me her information?"

She took a pen and piece of paper from her pocketbook and scribbled a name, address and telephone number on it. "I'm certain this is the family. But I never actually spoke to them."

He put the paper in his pocket without looking at it. He noticed her looking at him, not as she usually did. It was more like she was studying him, trying to make a determination. "What's wrong?"

"Nothing," she said, as she started to walk away. Then she stopped. "Are you sure you're not married?"

He laughed lightly. "No, not married," he said. Then he paused, hesitant to continue. He looked at her for a minute, tried to speak but couldn't. After a moment, he finally summoned the courage. "This is very hard very me. You're making me do things I wouldn't normally do."

"I don't understand," she asked, confusion etched on her face.

"I have issues," he said, struggling to get the words out, revealing a flaw he had never shared before. "I don't like commitment or responsibility. I never have. I just can't seem to deal with it, no matter how hard I try."

Her gaze never left his. "Why?" she asked simply, probing, perhaps wanting him to see what she already could.

He studied her closely, intimidated by how intuitive she seemed to be. And then he realized that she was vulnerable, too. Just like he was, although few would ever see it. "My mother was an Italian immigrant," he explained. "She raised me by herself, working two jobs, sometimes three. I never knew my father."

"Many women were single parents after the war," she countered.

"No, you don't understand," he explained. "This is different. My mother never remarried, rarely dated, everything she did was for me. I wrecked her life. And I won't wreck anyone else's."

She took his hand in hers, staring at him, her blue eyes soft and sincere. "I thought you were so intelligent," she said softly. "But now I don't think you're very smart at all."

"What do you mean?"

"You didn't wreck your mother's life," she told him. "You *are* your mother's life,"

24

Karl Hofer studied the man sitting across from him and evaluated his commitment. Hofer had dozens of informants, some better than others, a few superb. But they all had motives. Usually it was money, or better living conditions that a favored member of the Party enjoyed, or power – the ability to control others. And then occasionally there was the informant who betrayed family, friends and neighbors for the cause, because he truly believed socialism was the supreme form of government and any that deviated from it deserved to be identified and punished. Such a man sat before him.

"The subject doesn't have many friends," the informant was saying. "His select group of acquaintances are primarily family, a few of his patients. But he seems to be a private man."

Hofer glanced at the dossier on his desk, written words that described the life of a man as observed by others. "I don't think we should underestimate him," he warned. "He was decorated on the Eastern Front during the Second World War."

"But as a doctor, not a fighter."

"That doesn't diminish his courage," Hofer observed. He

briefly thought of his own experience during the war, forced to defend Berlin. But he hadn't. He hid from Russian soldiers in piles of garbage. "He stood at the gates to Moscow, and then walked every mile back to Berlin, under the onslaught of Russian forces."

"But he's not a model citizen," the informant replied, "which is why I brought his behavior to your attention."

"Dr. Werner had no incidents until recently," Hofer said, referring to the suspect. "His record is unblemished."

"Maybe his record was unblemished because no one ever observed him," the informant countered. "The man was a Nazi. He's not a Socialist and he never was. The evidence to support my conclusions has been mounting since the war ended. It's just gone unnoticed."

Hofer frowned. He glanced out the window, saw the sun's rays piercing the smog cast by a distant factory smokestack. He briefly thought of how nice it would be to spend time with his daughters, enjoying the afternoon, but then his eyes returned to the papers on his desk. "Yes, perhaps you're right," he said softly, knowing he controlled a man's fate. A man, perhaps, with more courage than he had.

"I've observed Werner both in private and in public," the informant continued. "I contend he's guilty. He's only trying to act normally because he suspects a trap."

Karl Hofer studied the dossier, lightly tapping his pen against the paper. "I'm sure he knows he's being watched."

"What's the basis of the most recent allegations?"

"Derogatory comments about socialism and the Anti-Fascist Protection Barrier."

"Is there more than one witness?" the informant asked.

"Several," Hofer said. "A youth group overheard comments on the S-bahn. One of them recognized the doctor and reported it to authorities."

"After I had suspicions of subversive behavior?" the informant asked.

"Yes."

"Doesn't it prove my assertions?"

"It might."

"Could he have been misunderstood?"

"Unlikely," Hofer replied. "I also interviewed one of his relatives who claimed Werner praised capitalism, West Berlin in particular, at a dinner party. Apparently, he contrasted the progress of West Berlin to the stagnation of East Berlin."

"That's a damning statement in itself," the informant remarked. "And clearly indicates a lack of understanding. Apparently, he doesn't know what socialism is. He only thinks he does."

Hofer briefly wondered if his conviction was as strong as his informant's. "But why not flee to West Berlin?" he asked. "He had the opportunity. Many of his patients were in the West."

"People are afraid of change," the informant said. "He's lived in the same residence for most of his adult life. And even though his daughters are in the West, his sister-in-law and her husband, to whom he is very close, live just around the corner."

"I find it interesting," Hofer mumbled, "the workings of the human mind. So many now act caged, just because of the wall, without realizing they were always caged. The gate had just been left open."

"What are your plans for Werner?"

"I want to squeeze him," Hofer said. "I want him to be afraid, to think imprisonment is only a step away. And then I want him observed, to see who he befriends and who he deserts. I think his behavior will be very revealing. And he'll provide us with names of other subversives."

"How do you intend to do that?"

"I created false charges against him," Hofer explained. "A

claim he didn't reimburse the State for medications, just to observe his reaction."

"What did he do?"

"He insisted he did nothing wrong."

"As I would expect."

"But I countered with something much more damaging," Hofer said. "I threatened him with evidence of sexual deviation – offering just a glimpse of what I can do to him and his reputation." He paused dramatically and added, "If I choose to."

"What was his reaction?"

"He was appalled and disgusted," Hofer said. "And he vehemently denied any wrongdoing."

The informant leaned back in the chair. "What's next?" he asked. "Do you keep toying with him, performing social experiments, or do you arrest him?"

"I'll apply more pressure," Hofer replied. "I'll produce witnesses, statements and victims."

"It'll totally destroy him."

"It's designed to."

"What's the objective?"

"Eventually he'll surrender and do whatever I ask," Hofer said. "He'll break, never as strong as he once was, and he'll submit, knowing I can still destroy him whenever I choose."

"What will you make him do?"

"He'll spy on whoever I tell him to – his patients, his neighbors, his family. He'll betray anyone and everyone, just to please me."

"That's brilliant," the informant said, glancing at his watch. He rose to leave. "I really must be going. I should have more information for you shortly."

"It's much appreciated, Professor," Hofer said.

"I'm pleased to serve," Steiner Beck replied.

Hofer watched as the professor walked toward the door, suspecting he couldn't be trusted, although he wasn't sure why.

Maybe because he was too ambitious. Or maybe it was something more, something he hadn't yet discovered.

Beck turned as he opened the door. "Is there anything else?

"Yes, "Hofer said, eyeing him sternly. "Initiate surveillance on your wife, too." He then paused dramatically and added, "Before I do."

25

"Hi, mom," Tony Marino said into the telephone. "How are you?"

"Tony, what's wrong?" his mother asked.

"Nothing's wrong. Why do you think something's wrong?"

"It's Thursday."

"Alright, so it's Thursday," he said.

"You only call on Sunday."

"But I wanted to call on Thursday to see how you're doing."

"What are you trying to do, give me a heart attack?" his mother asked. "You call on Sunday. When you call on Thursday, it makes me think something's wrong."

"Ma, nothing is wrong. I wanted to see how you were."

"Jesus, Mary and Joseph," she said, and he could imagine her making the sign of the cross as she said it. "You met a girl, didn't you?"

He hesitated. How did she know that? "No, I didn't meet a girl," he said, not wanting to discuss it. "I just wanted to see how you're doing."

"Who is she?"

"Mom, will you stop?"

"Is she Italian?"

"Mom, what are you doing? I called to see if you need anything."

"Is she at least Catholic? I don't know what I'd do if she wasn't Catholic. I'm going to call your Aunt Marie in Brooklyn and tell her. What's your girlfriend's name?"

"Kirstin," he said, without considering the impact of an admission to his Italian mother.

"It is a woman," she declared. "I knew it. Wait until I tell your aunt."

"I just called to see if you were all right," Marino said, feeling like his mother knew him better than he knew himself. "Ma, I have to go. Tell Aunt Marie I said hello. I'll call you on Sunday."

"Wait a minute," she said. "Are you starting another war?

He was confused. "What are you talking about?"

"In Berlin."

"No, I told you what happened. The East Germans are building a wall."

"President Kennedy said there might be a war," she told him. "He called up the reserves. Do you remember Joey Pinto, the boy that lived on Oregon Avenue? He was in the reserves. And the President made him go somewhere, I forget where it was, in case there's a war."

Marino couldn't imagine the United States going to war over Berlin. But worse had happened. "I didn't know that, mom. But there's no war here. At least not yet. There's a lot of tension, but no war."

"Tony, why don't you come home?"

"I'm not finished here yet."

"Come home, Tony," his mother repeated. "And bring Kirstin. She'll like it here."

He realized a thousand questions were about to be asked, so he thought it best to end the conversation. "Mom, I'll talk to you soon," he said.

"Call me Sunday," his mother said. "Just so I know you're all right."

He hung up the phone, wondering if issues in Berlin were about to take the global stage.

He left his apartment and got in his Volkswagen Beetle, looking for a hardware store. He found an industrial supply company on *Brunnenstrasse* and purchased metal shears capable of cutting barbed wire and thick leather gloves to protect his hands while he handled the metal shards. He also obtained a short shovel, should he need to dig any wire imbedded in the soil, and some rope to secure the wire after it was cut, to prevent injuring the refugees.

"Planning a robbery?" the clerk joked as he paid for the merchandise.

Marino chuckled. "I wish it was that simple," he said.

He left the hardware store and went to a men's clothing outlet where he got a pair of black pants, soft shoes, and a black turtle neck shirt. Even though the edge of the cemetery had little lighting, the dark clothes would minimize the risk of the guards seeing him. He stood at the register, paid the clerk once the tab was totaled, and went out to his car. He sat behind the wheel for a moment, wondering if he had forgotten anything, before driving home.

He returned at dusk, brought everything to his flat, and staged them near the door, prepared for Saturday night. He then turned out the lights and sat beside the window. Using his binoculars, he studied the barbed wire border that sliced the cemetery into segments. The northwest corner seemed the best location. It was dark and isolated, the barbed wire fence about thirty feet from the stone wall at the cemetery's edge, the entire length in West Berlin, along with tombstones and mausoleums. A wrought iron fence that defined the northern side of the graveyard ran from the northwest corner to the street, the adjacent property belonging to a clothing manufacturer. The church was a few hundred feet away, centered by the boulevard, a short expanse of lawn between it and the rowhouse where Kirstin lived.

As he studied the terrain, existing trees and shrubs, mausoleums and tombstones large enough to hide behind, he decided the best location to cut the wire was at the corner, where it was affixed to the wrought iron fence. There were tombstones on both sides of the barrier, providing cover for him in the West and the refugees in the East. Flanking the cemetery was the rear of a clothing manufacturer, the small factory only operating during the week. A vacant lot sat behind it, guards patrolling the border, but the wrought iron fence prevented them from entering the cemetery. On the Western side, abutting the barrier, was an old factory, a large brick building three stories high. A metal fabricator occupied the north end, the center was damaged, bombed during the war and never repaired, and the south segment, adjacent to his apartment building, was vacant.

Marino found the clothing company interesting. It also offered possibilities, a building with much activity during the week – trucks that made deliveries and picked up goods – but empty during the weekend. Separated from the barbed wire by a vacant strip, it really wasn't that far of a distance. He briefly thought of a tunnel, a method that spawned other successful escapes, but he lacked the resources to construct one, both financially and physically. And even though the clothing company offered the perfect location in the East, and the bombed factory did the same for the West, he knew nothing about digging a tunnel: soil removal, type of spoil, the water table, interior condition of the factory. Too much work and too many variables. Clearly the most logical choice was cutting the barbed wire in the cemetery and eluding the guards.

He put his binoculars down, moved away from the window and sat on a stuffed chair across from the television. On a table beside the chair was a folder with some of his notes. Laying on top of it was the piece of paper Kirstin had given him at the library. Scribbled on it was the name Lisette Haynor, her daughter. He suspected the story was heart-wrenching, a tale he would like to hear, one he could eventually tell in a novel instead of the non-fiction he normally wrote. And he suspected it was a story that Ned Simpson would like to sell.

He realized how much had changed in so little time. When Kirstin asked for help with her grandmother, he hadn't hesitated. It was a trivial request, only taking a few hours of his time. Next, he would locate her adopted daughter, something he never would have done only a few months before. But he willingly agreed, getting significant satisfaction in knowing he could change someone's life for the better. Just as Kirstin had, perhaps, changed his.

Marino saw her appear in her window later that evening, near 9 p.m. He scanned the barbed wire to ensure no guards were watching, and then peered through his binoculars. She was holding up her chalkboard, which said: *I like seeing you.*

He smiled and issued a written reply: *I like seeing you, too. Planning escape.*

She replied: *How's it going?*

He looked down at the border guards, walking back and forth in front of the barbed wire. One stopped, just below his window, and lit a cigarette. Marino stayed back, standing near the drapes, peeking from behind them.

A moment later, the guard looked up. He seemed to scan the apartment building, his gaze wandering among the many windows that faced the East. He took a drag of his cigarette, slowly exhaling the smoke.

Marino carefully moved the curtain, ensuring he could watch but not be seen. The guard still stood there, looking up. Marino couldn't tell if he was admiring the building or watching his apartment. He seemed transfixed, studying something that had caught his attention. Marino closed the drapes and waited.

After a minute has passed, he looked out again. The guard was slowly walking away, returning to his regular routine. Marino waited until he was a safe distance away and scribbled on his notepad: *NW corner closest to wrought iron fence.*

She watched with her binoculars and then set them down and wrote on the chalkboard: *Sat nite 2 am.*

He wrote a reply: *Yes.*

She jotted a note on her chalkboard and held it up for him to see: *Not sure how many.*

Marino put down his glasses. Not sure how many? He was fairly certain he could get Kirstin out, but he didn't know how many more. She told him four people at the library, and he was anxious about that. His stomach felt queasy, the responsibility and commitment he had shunned his entire life now unavoidable. Several people were entrusting their lives to him, a man they had never met, to execute a dangerous and potentially flawed plan. And he couldn't desert them. He realized what a damning indictment of socialism the escape actually was. Could capitalism, and the freedom the West offered, be worth the risk of imprisonment or death – just to escape from East Berlin? It was a sobering thought.

He held up his notepad: *all wear black.*

She replied a moment later: *yes.*

He knew the longer they communicated, the riskier it became. A border guard could glance up and see the messages they were exchanging, as one just almost had. He would stop after one last message. *Friday at noon to confirm.*

She scribbled a reply: *Yes, Olga's Café on Torstrasse.*

He saw her put the chalkboard away, and a second later the light was extinguished. He kept watching, saw her exit the room, framed by the light in the hallway. He didn't really have to see her on Friday. But he wanted to.

26

Kirstin Beck stepped into the tiny examination room, hoping to see Dr. Werner. She was alone, the room stark and cold, the paint peeling from the crown molding, the wall paper starting to fade. She had waited over two hours, and she now eyed the clock, knowing the facility would close shortly. Medical offices weren't open many hours, especially since doctors weren't compensated for any extra hours worked.

Ten minutes later, the door opened and Dr. Werner entered, holding a chart in his right hand. "Hello Kirstin," he said warmly. "I'm surprised to see you. I thought your ankle would have healed by now. Please, take off your shoe."

Kirstin did as she was told, listening closely. She heard no one outside the door, not even the nurse walking through the corridor. She again studied the room, ensuring there weren't any surveillance cameras. In the adjacent examining room, she could hear a child talking to her mother as she waited for the doctor, but nothing else. She assumed they were safe.

Dr. Werner tenderly moved her left ankle, twisting it gently. "Do you feel any pain?"

"I had to see you," Kirstin whispered. "It's important."

His body stiffened, as if surprised, but he recovered quickly, still holding her ankle. "What is it?"

"Saturday night at 2 a.m.," she said. "In the far corner of the cemetery, where the iron fence abuts the clothing company."

"I think the ankle is doing much better," he said loudly, should anyone be eavesdropping. He then whispered, "How many can I bring?"

"How many are there?"

"My wife and I and, if I could, her sister and her husband."

"We have to be very careful," she hissed. "Can you trust them?"

He hesitated, pensive for a moment. "Maybe I should just bring my wife."

"If you trust them, they can come," she said. "Just make sure everyone wears black."

"How will it happen?"

"Someone from the West will help us," she said. "He'll cut the barbed wire just before we get there. When the guards are distracted, we'll hurry through."

"I'll see you at 2 a.m."

"Can you get there without being seen?"

"Yes, I think so."

"Please be careful. And tell your wife and her sister to do the same."

"All right, Mrs. Beck, that should be all," he said loudly. "The ankle should be perfectly fine in a few more days."

Kirstin left the clinic and hurried to *Invalidenstrasse*. She walked six blocks, passing among pedestrians who paused to look in shop windows, periodically glancing at her watch. She reached the café just after 5 p.m., only a few minutes later than planned, and sat down at an outdoor table, waiting to order. A few minutes later, a young man with short hair and glasses came to her table.

"Mrs. Beck, I'm surprised to see you," said Dieter Katz.

"I remember you mentioned that you worked here," she said. "I was in the area and thought I would stop in."

"Thank you," he said, "it's nice to see you. What can I get you?"

She glanced at the adjacent tables, half were occupied. But no one seemed to pay any attention to her. But then, you could never be too sure. The Stasi were everywhere. "I suppose I'll have a coffee and *Pfannkuchen*."

"Coffee and *Pfannkuchen*," he repeated. "I'll be right back."

"Dieter," she said softly, lightly touching his arm.

He paused and looked at her, as if expecting her order to be changed. "Yes?"

She glanced around furtively, and then continued. "Saturday at 2 a.m. In the corner of the cemetery by the wrought iron fence, next to the clothing manufacturer."

His eyes widened in surprise, but he recovered quickly. He studied the other patrons for a moment, and then leaned closer. "How?" he whispered.

"A friend in the West will cut the wire," she said, her voice barely audible. "When the guards are distracted, we'll pass through. Is it just you?"

He paused, thinking for a moment. "I'll be bringing a friend."

"Do you trust him?"

"Yes," he said, and then noticed a customer trying to get his attention. "I'll be back in a moment."

He walked to a nearby table, spoke to man dressed in a suit, then went inside the café. He returned a few minutes later, put a slice of *Quarkkuchen* on the man's table, and then brought Kirstin's coffee and jelly-filled pastry.

"Here you are," he said loudly. Then he whispered, "My girlfriend will be there too, in the West, to help your friend."

Kirstin wasn't sure Tony would like that. It seemed a risk

that wasn't worth taking. "Are you sure she can be trusted?" she asked.

"Absolutely," he replied. "We love each other very much and only want to be together."

"What's her name?"

"Eileen Fischer," he said. "You may have met her at church services before the border was closed."

Kirstin vaguely remembered meeting her. She considered his request and, after a moment's thought, decided to proceed. Tony could use the help anyway. "She can meet a man named Tony in front of the apartment building at the edge of the cemetery, sometime before two."

"I'll let her know," he said. "She'll be thrilled."

"How will you tell her?" she asked. "We only have two more days."

"We have ways of communicating," he said. "They're safe."

Kirstin remembered Dieter's impulsive run for the border when the barbed wire was being strung. Just as she was wondering if she had made a mistake, he reassured her.

"Don't worry," he said. "I have no intention of confronting the Stasi again. Are others coming?"

"Yes, at least four," she said, "plus your friend. It could be our only chance. It gets harder every day."

He eyed the customers, making sure he wasn't attracting attention. "I understand."

"Can you get there without being seen?" she asked.

"Yes," he replied. "And I'll bring a gun, just in case we need it."

27

Tony Marino waited patiently in a booth toward the back of Olga's Café. It seemed a good location, quiet, most of the patrons sitting outside. He arrived early, didn't attract any attention, and ordered a glass of wine. He opened a folder and started to go through some notes – both for his book on the history of Germany and a timeline he kept on current events in Berlin for the documentary Ned Simpson wanted him to write.

Kirstin arrived a few minutes later. "Hello," she whispered as she sat across from him and gently squeezed his hand.

He smiled. "How are you?"

"A little nervous."

"You need to be very careful," he said. "Especially with the others coming."

"I told you there could be more than four."

"How many?"

"There are six besides me."

"Do you know them?"

"I know two fairly well," she said, "and I've met a third. But I don't even know who the others are. They're family and friends of friends."

"The total is seven, including you."

"Yes."

"And you're sure none are Stasi?" he asked.

"No one can ever be sure," she admitted. "But if, in the end, we change the lives of six people, it'll all be worth it."

He looked at her, brave and defiant, yet fragile and vulnerable. He admired her, wanting to help others so badly. There was a lot he could learn from her. "I suppose that's manageable," he said. "But we'll have to get them through the barbed wire quickly."

"There's something else," she said. "But I wanted to tell you in person."

"What?" he asked warily, suspecting complications.

"You'll have an assistant."

"What do you mean?"

"The girlfriend of one of the refugees is in the West," she said. "She wants to help."

"Do you think that's wise?" he asked. "We don't know if we can trust her."

"I was hesitant at first," she said. "But her boyfriend insisted she was safe. And she does live in West Berlin."

"A lot of informants are in West Berlin."

"That's true, but he wouldn't involve her if he didn't trust her," she said. "He spent a week in a Stasi prison. If anyone wants to avoid risk, it's him."

"I just hope he's right."

Kirsten paused, as if evaluating their strategy. She still held his hand, softly caressing it with his fingers. "I could always say we don't want her involved."

Marino hesitated, but then relented. "No, it's all right," he said. "As long as he trusts her, and you trust him. I can use the help anyway."

"She won't get in the way?"

"No," he said. "She can create some sort of diversion to keep the guards distracted."

"I knew you would think of something," she said with an impish grin.

———

Marino left the cafe in East Berlin far sooner than he wanted to, but Kirstin had to meet her publisher and couldn't stay. He returned to West Berlin, made some dinner and then glanced at his watch. It was 7:30 p.m. New York was six hours behind. He picked up the phone and called his publisher. The phone rang four times before someone answered.

"Ned Simpson."

"Ned, it's Tony."

"Tony, how are you? Is everything all right there?"

"Yes, same as last time I talked to you. Why?"

"Kennedy called up the reserves. People are talking about another war."

"I know, my mother told me," Marino said. "But you know as well as I do, that the world won't go to war over Berlin."

"I suppose not," Simpson said, although he didn't sound too certain. "Is the escape still on?"

"Yes, it's tomorrow night. It's gotten a bit more difficult, though."

"How so?"

"We're up to seven people."

"Seven? How did that happen?"

"Friends of friends, I suppose. Or cousins or sisters. You know how it goes."

"But that increases the danger," Ned said. "Do you trust them?"

"I don't even know them," Tony replied. "And there's little

risk for me. I'm in the West. As long as I don't get caught cutting the wire. It's the refugees that are in danger."

"If you pull this off, it'll make for a great story. Do you have enough material for the book yet?"

Tony sighed. It was always business with Ned. Somehow the human tragedy of seven people risking their lives had escaped him. It was about how many copies he could sell. "I suppose," he replied. "A short one."

"You can fatten it up, especially when you get into everyone's individual story. We'll need to make this one personal."

"Yes, I suppose," Marino replied.

"Are you ready?" he asked. "Do you have everything you need?"

"Yes, I have gloves and cutters. And I've been watching the guards. They have a certain routine. I should have several minutes to cut the wire."

"How exposed are the escapees?"

"There are mausoleums and tombstones on both sides of the barbed wire, some six feet high, that they can hide behind. They're exposed getting there, and then waiting to get out."

"I suppose not much can be done to mitigate that."

"I'll need some sort of diversion, but I'm not sure how to manage it. And there is a slight complication."

"What's that?"

"I'll have a helper," he said. "The girlfriend of one of the escapees is in West Berlin."

"That adds a good human-interest perspective," Ned said. "Two lovers, apart for too long, risking their lives to be together – and all of that nonsense. Make sure you stick that angle in the book. Can she help?"

"Yes, I think so," Marino replied. "I may be able to use her for the diversion."

"To do what?"

"I'm not sure," he admitted. "Maybe honk her car horn or

something like that. Anything that attracts the guard's attention for a few minutes."

"Just be careful," Simpson said. "Another day and it'll be over."

"I hope so."

"Do you remember the East German guard you told me about, the one that crossed the barbed wire?"

"Yes, a few days after the border closed."

"His photo was in *Life* magazine."

Marino was surprised. Maybe the world was paying attention. "That's great," he said. "At least people know what's going on over here."

"They sure do," Simpson said. "It has a lot of attention. And if you pull this off tomorrow night, your photo will be in *Life* magazine, too."

28

Kirstin lay in bed and stared at the ceiling, daring not to move. She could hear Steiner, breathing rhythmically beside her as the clock ticked on the nightstand next to the bed. She was worried; he came to bed later than normal, as if he intended to stay up half the night. But after he nodded off in the parlor while listening to the radio, she convinced him to go upstairs. He fell asleep quickly, and now she had to make sure she didn't wake him.

She waited until 1:20 a.m. and delicately slid from the mattress so he didn't stir. She moved slowly away from the bed, tiptoeing into the hall. When she reached the stairs, she waited. After a moment of silence, she assumed he still slept. She cautiously descended one step at a time and stayed close to the wall where the tread had more support and the boards were less likely to creak.

When she reached the bottom of the stairs she paused. It was still quiet. Stepping quietly across the parlor and into the kitchen, she went to the pantry. Her clothes and the satchel with her money and papers were hidden behind some boxes and cans. She gently took them out and removed her nightgown, hiding it behind a bag of flour. She dressed quickly, slinging the satchel over her shoulder. Her shoes were by the back door, a place where she often left them, and she put them on, lacing them quickly, ready to flee, ready to leave the husband she no longer loved and the life she had once shared with him.

There was no need to leave a note, not this time. Steiner couldn't follow her. He couldn't bully her or demand her return, like he could have done when she first tried to escape. Now they would never see each other again. For a moment she felt cruel, ending their relationship this way, but she knew if he had an inkling of her plans, he would turn her in to the Stasi. She briefly considered leaving the note anyway, the detailed description of how and why their relationship ended but realized it didn't really matter. Not that it ever did.

She eased open the back door and stepped outside. It was a cool evening, dark with little moonlight. There was a single streetlight in front of the church, but she could avoid it. She studied the guards near the wall. They slowly paced back and forth, patrolling the barbed wire. When they faced different directions, and weren't positioned to see her, she hurried across the expanse of lawn between her townhouse and the church, staying in the shadows so she couldn't be seen.

Mausoleums, trees and shrubs masked much of her view, but she could see the border from the corner of the church. Every twenty or thirty seconds, she saw a guard pass, first in one direction and then the other. She scanned the back of the church, saw nothing unusual, and hurried along the building to the far side of the cemetery. From tombstone to tombstone, shrub to shrub, mausoleum to mausoleum, she darted through the city of dead, stopping often, studying the terrain, ensuring the guards continued their patrol oblivious to her movement as she crept stealthily through the graveyard.

She stopped twenty feet from the iron fence that bordered

the clothing company. She could see the guards in the lot behind the building, marching along the barbed wire, similar to those in the cemetery. A few minutes passed while she marked their routine, counting their paces, when they turned, what they studied, and where they stopped.

Just as she stepped from behind a tombstone, moving furtively toward the barbed wire, she saw a guard behind the clothing company stop abruptly and turn. She froze, knowing he might be able to see her, and any motion she made would attract his attention.

The guard reached into his pocket and withdrew his cigarettes. He took one from the pack, put it in his mouth, and returned the pack to his pocket.

As he lit a match, distracted, Kirstin eased herself to the ground and lay motionless, waiting for him to resume his patrol.

He stayed where he was, staring into the night. He took a few steps toward her, paused, took a few more, and peered into the darkness.

She held her breath, watching as he came closer, barely sixty feet away. She had to stay still so he didn't see movement. And maybe if she did, he would leave and return to duty.

He kept observing, taking several steps closer, farther from his post at the barbed wire. Reaching to his belt, he removed a flashlight. He clicked it on, and the night was washed with a narrow stream of light. He trained the beam along the wrought iron fence, starting at the barbed wire and then gradually directing it toward the street.

Kirstin eased her torso behind a tombstone. She covered her face with her arm, leaving a small gap from which she could see. Daring to breathe, she lay still as the beam moved through the first few rows of graves.

"What's wrong?" the second guard called, fifty feet from the first.

"I thought I saw something," the first guard replied.

The second guard walked toward him. "What was it?"

"I'm not sure," the first guard said.

"Maybe it was an animal, or a tree branch blowing in the breeze," the second guard suggested.

The first guard waved the beam through the cemetery. He repeated the process, moving from one row of graves to the next, guiding the light deeper, probing, searching for something he wasn't sure he had seen.

"Do you see anything?" the second guard asked.

The first guard stopped waving the flashlight and trained it on the tombstone Kirstin hid behind. The light travelled over her legs, focused on the tombstone, and then passed over her again. The beam moved to the next tombstone, focused for a moment, and then the next, back and forth on either side of where she hid. Then it was extinguished and darkness returned. She lost sight of the guard and dared to raise her head, looking toward the barbed wire, hoping to find him back at his post, patrolling the border.

He was coming closer, twenty feet away, approaching the wrought iron fence.

"What did you find?" the second guard asked.

The first guard paused, feet from the fence, and studied the graveyard.

Kirstin kept her head covered with her arm, her body behind the tombstone. Seconds passed slowly, quietly, no one speaking. The guards could be coming closer, poised to point their flashlights at her and summon the soldiers in the cemetery. When she could no longer stand the suspense, she gently moved her arm and scanned the fence where the soldier had stood.

"I guess it was nothing," the guard called, walking away. A few moments later he was at his post, and the two returned to their routine.

Kirstin sighed with relief but remained where she was. She surveyed the cemetery and saw movement, furtive shadows darting toward the northwest corner. They must be the other refugees. The cemetery guards walked back and forth, from one end of the graveyard to the other, as if suspecting their night would be uneventful.

Twenty feet from the barbed wire, in the northwest corner of the cemetery, was a mausoleum with a broad stone base, a damaged statue upon it. As Kirstin crept toward it, she saw the others huddled behind it and surrounding tombstones. It was 1:50 a.m.

A few feet from the mausoleum, Dr. Werner hid in the darkness. He reached out his hand, guiding Kirstin toward him. His wife was next to him, and another couple, probably his sister-in-law and her husband, lay along the ground by a neighboring tombstone. No one spoke.

Kirstin sprawled along the ground, her heart racing from her narrow escape. She was afraid, as she suspected the others were. She closed her eyes, thinking of her daughter Lisette. If all went well, they would soon be together. And she would do it all a thousand times over again, regardless of the risk, if it led to Lisette.

A few minutes later, two more figures emerged from the darkness. Dr. Werner ensured the guards couldn't see him, and then waved as they approached. Dieter Katz slid up beside Kirstin. His friend waited with the doctor's companions.

It was 1:55 a.m. Seven people, shadows in the night, risking their lives for freedom, waited furtively in the cemetery as the seconds anxiously passed.

29

Marino went outside at 1 a.m. He needed to make sure he had enough time. He could be delayed – a guard stopping for a cigarette or reacting to a stray animal – and he couldn't take that chance. But he couldn't go too early, either. It increased the risk of a guard finding the breach in the border. As he left his apartment, he was trembling, having paced the floor for over an hour, mentally rehearsing what was about to occur, worried not so much for himself but for the seven souls who entrusted their lives to him.

He exited the apartment building and entered the alley next to the brick factory. He crept through the shadows until reaching the rear. Peeking around the corner, he saw the stone wall from the cemetery twenty feet in front of him. It ended at the wrought iron fence that split the graveyard from the clothing company. There were two guards in the empty lot, pacing with machine guns slung over the shoulders. And in the cemetery, past the stone wall and some scattered tombstones and mausoleums, two more guards patrolled the border, walking from the wrought iron fence to a wooden watchtower that was under construction but not yet functional.

Marino watched both sets of guards, studying their routine. When none were in a position to see him, he hurried to the wall and crawled over it. He slid on his stomach to a mausoleum. It stood six feet high, close to the barbed wire – maybe four feet away. He was ten feet from the wrought iron fence, barbed wire affixed to it, with a wooden post directly in front of him, coils of wire tacked to it.

The barbed wire was strung in rows across posts. Marino would cut the three lowest strands and tie them in place with rope. He could remove them just before the refugees were ready. They would crawl under the remaining strands, most of which would remain intact, scrambling to freedom before the guards saw them.

He watched the guards, waiting until they couldn't see him. He crawled to the wooden post and tied the lowest strand of barbed wire to the pole with rope. Then he cut the wire. It flexed but remained in place. He hurried back to the mausoleum and waited, knowing he had at least two more wires to cut to prepare for the escape.

He stayed low to the ground, observing the soldiers. For thirty seconds every four minutes, they couldn't see him – if they all maintained their routine. When he had the opportunity, he scurried back to the wooden post. He tied the second lowest strand with rope and cut the wire. It sprang but stayed in place. Scrambling back to the mausoleum, he waited and watched. When the guards faced different directions, he tied and cut the third lowest strand. He studied the wire, now tied securely, and estimated how long it would take to remove it once the guards were distracted, at least on the cemetery side, and how much time the refugees would need to crawl underneath it.

Satisfied his plan would work, he sneaked back to the wall. He lay in the shadows, then eased himself over it. Crawling on his hands and knees, he made his way back to the apartment building. He glanced at his watch. It was 1:20 a.m. He went to the front of the apartments, not far from the entrance, and hid behind a large shrub, waiting for Eileen Fischer.

Just after 1:35 a.m., a white Volkswagen with a dented fender arrived. The vehicle was parked on the side of the building and a young woman, dressed in black slacks and a pullover shirt, nervously exited the car.

"Eileen," Marino hissed.

She glanced furtively about to ensure no one was watching, and then made her way to where Tony was hiding. "Are you Tony?" she asked.

"Yes," he replied. "It's nice to meet you. I wish it were better circumstances,"

"Me too," she said. "But I'm thrilled to be a part of the escape. What do you need me to do?"

"I already cut the wire," he told her. "I just have to pull it out of the way."

"How much time do we have?"

"About twenty-five minutes."

"Have you been watching the guards?"

"Yes, I have," he said. "They pass more frequently than I thought."

"Will we have enough time to get Dieter out?"

"It's more than Dieter," he told her. "There are actually seven refugees."

Her eyes got large. "I had no idea," she said. "How much time will they need?"

"A few minutes at most," he replied. "But I timed the guards and we'll only have about thirty seconds every four minutes. Probably not enough time."

"Dieter said we need a distraction," she said.

"Yes, we do," he replied. "I thought you could honk your car horn."

She thought for a moment, as if considering his suggestion.

"Can you show me the border?" she asked.

They went to the edge of the apartment building and peeked through some shrubs at the short stone wall and the barbed wire behind it. The guards walked back and forth as they patrolled the area, their paths sometimes crossing, sometimes not. Occasionally they would stop and speak to each other for a few seconds before moving on.

"A loud noise might be worse," she offered. "The guards from the vacant lot might respond, too."

He glanced at the second set of guards. The wrought iron fence blocked them from coming into the graveyard, but if they were close enough to see what was happening, they could fire their machine guns.

"I know what might work," she said, as if suddenly struck with an idea. "I could shine my headlights on the guards."

Marino glanced at his watch, mindful of the time. "How would you do that?"

"I can drive down the street, but act like I'm going the wrong way," she explained. "I'll pull into that parking lot across from the watch tower and point my headlights at the guards. Then I can pretend my engine stalled. While they're distracted, the others can escape."

He was surprised. He hadn't expected her to make much of a contribution. Now he was glad she came. "That's a great idea," he said. "It should work well."

"I have to do it exactly at two, right?"

"Yes," he replied. "Do you have a watch? Our timing has to be perfect."

"I do," she said, rolling up the sleeve of her shirt. "What time do you have?"

"One forty-two and fifteen seconds."

"Hold on – let me adjust. How about now?"

"One forty-three exactly."

"Good," she said. "I better get ready. I'll pull my car out a minute before. Good luck."

30

Just before 2 a.m., Eileen Fischer drove down the street and turned into a parking lot next to the cemetery. She pulled up close to the barbed wire, pointing her headlights at the guards. Then she stopped, as if her engine stalled. She timed it perfectly. The guards were crossing paths when blinded by her headlights. They paused, holding their arms in front of their faces, hiding from the glare, trying to move closer to the barbed wire to assess any threat they might be facing.

Marino waited at the wall. When the headlights shined on the guards, and the soldiers in the vacant lot weren't facing him, he hopped over the stone wall and darted to the barbed wire. Figures approached, various shapes and sizes. They came closer, low to the ground, furtively moving forward and hiding behind tombstones, waiting for him to remove the barbed wire so they could dash to freedom in West Berlin.

The guards in the cemetery were distracted. The guards in the vacant lot were a hundred feet away. Marino hurried to the wooden post. He untied two strands of wire and they sprung from the post, dropping to the ground but still preventing passage for those anxiously waiting. He would have to pull the wire away and hold it while the refugees slid under the remainder.

"Hurry, Tony!" Kirstin hissed, only feet away.

The refugees came closer. As Marino untied the third rope, he heard the distant click of a switch. A bright searchlight came on, spilling light along the length of the barbed wire, momentarily blinding him. He rolled away, hiding behind a tombstone, knowing he was fully visible to all four guards – just as the seven refugees were.

"Halt!" came the command. "Halt or I'll shoot!"

He saw soldiers running through the swath of light. First two, and then more, others fanning across the graveyard. He hesitated, and then dove forward and started pulling away the barbed wire so the others could escape.

A shot was fired, and then another, and a bullet ricocheted off the fence. With trembling hands, he tugged at the wire, collecting all three strands, trying to free a path for the others to use.

A woman screamed. The refugees huddled close to the ground, avoiding the gunfire. A young man started crawling forward. His arm caught in the barbed wire, the shards catching his clothing. Marino tried to yank it free.

The guards in the vacant lot rapidly approached. A burst of machine gun fire shattered the night, an endless stream of bullets pinging off the fence and burrowing in the ground, sending tufts of soil skyward. A bullet bounced off a tombstone, skimming Marino's hand. He felt the stinging pain and pulled away, rolling backwards. He saw the refugees tentatively retreating.

"Stop!" a guard yelled.

"Run!" Marino yelled, afraid someone would be shot. "Hurry!"

He saw figures scurrying from the searchlights, scrambling across the graveyard. Soldiers sprinted toward them, confused in the darkness, using flashlights where the searchlight beam was blocked by shrubs or didn't fan out far enough.

"Stop or we'll shoot!" a soldier yelled. The voice came from a different direction, toward the street.

Marino saw the fleeing figures fade in the darkness. Soldier's images were distorted in the searchlight's glare, but he heard voices yelling, giving directions and shouting commands. He realized he couldn't stay where he was. He dove over the stone wall and crawled along its length for twenty feet before darting toward the apartments and ducking into the alley between the building and the factory.

The border was brightly lit. He could see the searchlight in the back of a jeep parked along the barbed wire, a troop truck beside it. Soldiers still came from the truck, fanning through the cemetery.

Eileen Fischer started her car, executed the turn, and sped down the street, parking at the corner of the apartment building. She climbed from the vehicle and ran down the alley to meet Marino.

He watched the disaster, wondering who, if any, would escape. He couldn't see the refugees any longer; the trees and shrubs in the cemetery hid them. He turned as Eileen Fischer breathlessly approached.

"What happened?" she asked frantically.

"I don't know," he said, his heart sinking.

"Did anyone escape?"

"No, they were close," he said, "but I didn't get the wire removed completely. They ran away when the light came on."

"Couldn't they race through?"

"The guards were shooting at us."

She started crying. "Did anyone get hurt?"

"I'm not sure," he said, feeling as horrible as she did. He looked back at the brightly lit border. "There were guards near the street, too. They were trapped."

"Our plan seemed so good," she moaned, tears rolling down her face. "How did it go so wrong?"

Marino peeked around the building, studying the chaos. Soldiers combed through the darkness, searching behind tombstones and mausoleums. He heard dogs barking and briefly saw a soldier with a German Shepherd pass before the searchlight. It was a sickening sight. He wondered how many escaped, if any.

"It's horrible," Eileen cried, briefly covering her eyes. "How did they know we were coming?"

A sickening realization swept over Marino. "Someone must have told them," he said gravely.

31

The refugees scattered. Dieter Katz and his friend sprinted toward the street. The doctor's group moved through the shrubbery, stumbling in the darkness, panicked and afraid. Kirstin could hear their footsteps, the sound growing dimmer, just as the noise from the approaching guards grew louder.

She scrambled from mausoleum to tombstone, her heart racing, her breathing labored. The guards fanned across the graveyard. They tried to flank the refugees, pinning them by the wrought iron fence on the far side of the cemetery. Kirstin angled toward the church, crossing rows of tombstones and darting toward the townhouses, hoping she could get home without being seen.

She covered half the distance when she saw two soldiers. They were just ahead of her. If she didn't change direction, they would see her. She hid among shrubs, creeping toward the church. The building hid any light from the street, offering darkened recesses in which to hide. She waited, evaluating her next move, when dogs started barking and she frantically searched for paths to escape, knowing they would find her scent and lead the soldiers directly to her.

"Over here," a guard called, the voice loud.

Two soldiers approached, thirty feet away. She lay flat, sliding under a row of bushes scattered along a winding lane. She covered her face and hair, barely breathing. They came closer, their boots crunching the grass, their bodies blocking the light cast by the searchlight.

"I thought I saw something over here," one of the guards said, waving a flashlight.

Kirstin could see their boots. They scanned their flashlights, the beams passing over tombstones and mausoleums, and then along the ground and through the bushes that bordered the lane.

"Get the dogs," a guard called to those near the border. "We don't want anyone to escape."

"How many were there?" the second guard asked.

"I couldn't tell. Five or six."

"And in the West?"

"I don't know," he said. "But someone cut the wire."

They took a step closer. Kirstin barely breathed. The flashlight beam passed across her shoe and then her calf, but no one noticed. The soldiers walked down the lane, methodically searching, poking through shrubs, combing through tombstones and mausoleums, as she buried her face in the dirt.

A woman screamed, not far away, on the other side of the church.

"They caught them," one of the soldiers said smugly. "Come on, let's go."

As soon as they passed, Kirstin slid from her hiding place. She crawled fifty feet and darted though shrubs and tombstones. Stopping frequently, she waited while flashlight beams bobbed and searchlights scanned. She moved quietly past the church and saw a troop truck in the street. Two people were being led to it, handcuffed – an older man and woman. But they weren't dressed in black clothes, like the refugees. They wore pajamas.

The barking dogs came closer. Kirstin had to hurry. She scampered through the graveyard, hiding, sometimes feet away from pursuing soldiers. She darted a few feet and hid again. Minutes later, seeming like decades, she reached a mausoleum along the side of the church, thirty or forty feet from her back door.

She had to cross an expanse of lawn to reach her house. There were shrubs along the cemetery fence, casting shadows that would conceal her. If she made it that far, she was sure she could get home. In the center of the lawn, a dark area stretched where street lights didn't reach, too far for the searchlight. Kirstin moved toward it and then crawled on her stomach, shimmying across the grass. Each time she heard voices, she stopped.

She reached the edge of the fence and looked toward the street. She could see another troop truck. Soldiers were leaving it, running toward the back of the church and into the cemetery. Two soldiers walked up the church steps, opened the door, and disappeared from view.

When she was ready to dash to her kitchen door, she saw Karl Hofer standing on the pavement. He was talking to a man, his back to her, the legs of his pajamas visible, his robe wrapped tightly around him. It was her husband, Steiner Beck.

She froze. Steiner must have woken with all the excitement and couldn't find her. Now he was telling Hofer. Her escape had failed, and soon she would be in Stasi custody, tortured until she told the truth. Unless she was very creative.

She hid behind the shrubs and moved forward slowly until she reached her kitchen door. With a cautious glance behind her, she hurried up the steps and into her house. She undressed and hid her satchel and clothes in the pantry. Then she pulled out her nightgown and slid it over her shoulders.

She wiped her face with a dish rag, not knowing how well she cleaned it. It would have to do – there wasn't time to do better. Then she ran into the parlor, took a jacket from the closet, and put it over her nightgown. She went out the kitchen door and retraced her steps, making her way back to the fence, across the open area to the mausoleum, changing course, and walking along the side of the church toward the pavement, pretending to innocently come from the graveyard.

32

"No, they live around the corner," Steiner Beck was saying as Kirstin approached. "They're not trying to escape. How could they, they're in their pajamas."

Karl Hofer looked at the elderly couple standing in the back of the troop truck. They were trembling, their eyes wide, bound in handcuffs. "Release them," he said to the two men guarding them.

The guard unlocked the handcuffs and the pair stood anxiously, hoping they wouldn't be arrested for wandering where they shouldn't have gone.

"You're free to go," Hofer called from across the street.

The two looked at each other, amazed at their good fortune, and hurried away. "Thank you, sir," the man called.

"Idiots!" Hofer said to the guards. "Who tries to escape in their pajamas!"

"Steiner, there you are," Kirstin said as she appeared from the side of the church.

"The missing Mrs. Beck has been found," Hofer said sarcastically.

"Where were you?" Steiner asked, studying her closely.

"I was behind the church, trying to see what all the soldiers were doing," she said.

"That's a good way to get shot," Hofer said, watching her curiously. He looked at the cemetery for a moment and then back to the Becks. "Excuse me, I need to find out what happened here."

"I was just behind the church," Steiner said as Hofer walked away. "And I didn't see you."

She hesitated but recovered quickly. "I went out the front door first," she said, "to see what the trucks were doing on the street. And then I went back in the house and watched from the kitchen window."

"I don't know how I didn't see you," Beck mumbled. "I searched everywhere."

"I've been walking around for the last few minutes," she said, hoping she wasn't weaving a web from which she couldn't escape. "The searchlight woke me and I came downstairs to see what happened."

He looked at her, the jacket wrapped around her night-gown, her naked calves disappearing into socks and shoes. "You should have woken me," he muttered.

"When did you get up?" she asked, ensuring her false timeline could be justified. "I must have still been in the house."

"The dogs woke me," he told her. "At first I thought it was one of the neighbors and tried to go back to sleep. When I couldn't, I rolled over and realized you weren't there."

"And then you came down?" she asked, breathless, watching him as he watched her, wondering if he knew.

"No, I called but you didn't answer," he replied. "I went to the edge of the steps and called again."

"I must have been out front," she said, fearing her feigned defense was about to unravel.

"I didn't see you," he said. "I went back to get my robe but kept calling you. Then I went out front, but you weren't there. Where were you?"

She thought as quickly as she could. "I stepped around back for a moment, trying to see what happened, but then I came back in the house through the kitchen."

"I was out in the street by then," he said, as if trying to visualize how they continually missed each other.

"I went back out toward the cemetery, behind the church, and then realized something was seriously wrong," she explained. "I was afraid to get caught up in the middle of it and was walking back to the house when I saw you and Mr. Hofer standing on the pavement."

Beck peered into the cemetery, patrolled by guards, some with dogs on leashes. "It looks like some damned fool tried to cross the border." Then he turned and looked at his wife, a curious expression pasted on his face. He touched her right cheek, rubbing it gently, and said, "There's dirt on your face. You must have brushed against something while you were outside."

Kirstin smiled faintly and pretended to study the scene unfolding before them. Steiner watched her closely, as if waiting for a reaction. She knew he didn't believe her. But she didn't know what he would do about it.

33

Karl Hofer walked down the pavement to the church steps, where he met an officer and two soldiers coming around the building. "How many?" he asked.

"We can't say for sure, sir," the officer replied. "Six, maybe more."

"And none were apprehended?"

"No, sir."

"Any witnesses?"

"Yes, a man and woman who claim to live nearby. We found them on the street, watching the proceedings."

"Where are they?"

"In the back of the troop truck."

"Not anymore," Hofer said, his irritation evident. "I released them."

"Why would you release them?" the officer asked.

"Because someone I trust told me they were good Socialists who had no information," Hofer replied gruffly. "Now show me where they cut the wire."

"This way, sir," the officer said. He led him between the

church and clothing company, and then into the sprawling graveyard beyond.

"Are you sure they're still not hiding somewhere?" Hofer asked. "Maybe they opened up one of the mausoleums, or they're lying in bushes."

"We've combed the entire area with dogs," the officer said. "And we found nothing."

"Expand the search to nearby streets."

"Yes, sir," the officer said. He turned to one of his soldiers. "Search a two-block area. Take ten men."

The officer led Hofer to the barbed wire, passing tombstones, some crooked and broken, mausoleums, some ornate others more modest. They wandered through the grounds until they reached the rear of the graveyard, close to the border. The barbed wire slivered across the cemetery, leaving the last row of graves and a short stone wall perched in West Berlin. A wrought iron fence defined the cemetery on their right, the barbed wire attached to it and then strung along the border. Workmen were already repairing the wire where it was cut for the foiled escape attempt.

"The wire was cut here," the officer said. "At this fence post and tied in place with rope, probably earlier in the evening. At the time of the escape, it appears as if someone from the West was untying the rope, prepared to remove the lower sections of wire."

"But you don't know for sure that it was cut from the West?"

"No, sir."

"Did anyone see the wire being cut?" Hofer asked.

"No, sir."

Hofer looked at the lot behind the clothing manufacturer, two guards patrolling the border. "Did they see anything?"

"One of the guards thought he saw movement about fifteen minutes before the attempted escape," the officer informed him. "But he couldn't tell if it was a person, an animal, or just a tree branch blowing in the breeze."

"Did he investigate?"

"Yes, sir, he did," the officer explained. "He came over to the iron fence and checked the area with his flashlight, but he didn't see anything suspicious."

Hofer nodded and studied the apartment building on the other side of the border. It was new, constructed after the war, concrete, steel and glass, four stories high. The design was unique, very modern, almost space-age, so different from the gray concrete squares being built in the East. For a moment, he wondered what it was like to live in such an apartment, what modern conveniences his wife might enjoy, what school his two daughters would attend and what they would learn. He tried to imagine the stores, where shelves were supposedly filled with a variety of products without long lines to purchase them. But then he dismissed the thought from his mind.

"Was the wire removed at all?" Hofer asked.

"Two strands were," the officer replied.

"Are you sure no one escaped?"

"We don't believe so," the officer replied. "Based on the position of the wire."

"But you don't know for certain?"

"No, sir."

"Did you obey my orders?"

"Yes, sir, we did. We had the searchlight staged to light the entire stretch of barbed wire."

"Yet you caught no one and you don't know if anyone escaped."

"No, sir," the officer replied. "But we're fairly certain no one escaped."

"Captain, I happen to know there were seven people who tried to escape," Hofer said. "And I know the wire was cut from the West. If I know that, you should too."

"Yes, sir. I'll order my men to be more diligent."

"There will be a next time," Hofer stressed. "And just as I did this time, I will tell you when and where." He paused and gave the captain a menacing stare. "Only the next time you will catch whoever tries to escape and put them in prison. And if you fail, I will put you in prison."

34

"I don't know what happened," Marino said frantically, holding the phone to his ear.

"Did anyone get away?" Ned Simpson asked. "Or were they all caught?"

"No one escaped to the West," Marino said. "But I couldn't see the cemetery. There were searchlights and soldiers, some with dogs. I was totally unprepared. I don't know why I thought I could do this."

"It makes a fantastic story, though."

Marino rolled his eyes. "Ned, don't you understand," he said. "People could have been killed. You don't know what the Stasi are like. They're brutal."

"What could we have done better?"

"I shouldn't have done it at all," Marino said, exasperated. "I write history books. I don't have the skills to rescue seven people from a Socialist country. Now I've got to think of a way to save them. I hope they're not in prison."

"The plan was good," Simpson said, as if ignoring him. "You found a weak point in the border and exploited it. Everything under your control went well."

"You wouldn't think so if you were there," Marino muttered. "It was absolute panic from the second the searchlight went on."

"Maybe you were betrayed."

Marino was quiet, hesitant. He didn't want to believe it was possible, but he knew it was. "But by whom?" he asked.

"One of the seven," Simpson suggested. "Or maybe Kirstin's husband. She said he was Stasi."

"Maybe," Marino said, biting a fingernail. He sighed, feeling defeated. He prayed no one was harmed or captured.

"When will you know?"

"I have to find Kirstin," he said, not thinking clearly. "Maybe I should go to the East."

"And do what?" Simpson asked. "Surrender? Listen to me, you're tired and you're shaken. Try to get some sleep. It'll all work out in the morning. What's going on out there now?"

Marino turned the light out and walked to the window, pulling the drape aside. "It's quieter. The searchlight is still on. And there's a man wearing a suit walking along the barbed wire. There's an officer with him."

"How about the search?"

"It looks like they stopped.," Marino related. "Workmen are repairing the barbed wire."

"What's going on at Kirstin's house?"

"It's dark."

"Maybe she's asleep."

"I don't see how," he said. "Wait a minute. They just turned the searchlight off and the truck is leaving. It's almost back to normal."

"We need another plan," Ned said. "Maybe we'll just focus on Kirstin. At least initially."

Marino thought for a moment. "What about fake passports?" he asked. "I've heard it worked for others. We just have to make sure they're from a neutral country. Maybe Sweden or Switzerland."

"We can probably manage one for Kirstin," Simpson said, "but definitely not the others. Do you have any political connections?"

"No, but I could try the embassy," Marino replied. He paused, unable to forgive himself for the disaster. "We're assuming she wasn't captured. What if she was?"

"Let's flush out this passport thing," Simpson said. "I have some contacts here. Let me talk to them. It's not as exciting as busting through the barbed wire, but it'll still attract readers."

"There has to be a way," Marino said as he walked away from the window and sat on the chair by the phone stand. "We just haven't found it."

"I'll talk to the executives here, too," Simpson said. "Maybe they have some ideas. Why don't you try to get some sleep?"

"That's not as easy as it sounds," Marino mumbled, wishing he could erase the escape from his memory.

"We'll think of something," Simpson assured him. "Is there anything else?"

Marino sighed, wishing his life could return to normal. "What did the Phillies do?" he asked.

"They lost, six to five. Still in last place."

"They're rebuilding," Marino said, trying to justify a horrible season. "They'll be better next year."

"They can't get much worse."

Marino was quiet for a moment. "Just like tonight."

"Maybe it didn't go as bad as you think," Simpson said. "Find out what you can and call me again tomorrow night."

"Will do," Marino said, hanging up the phone. He rubbed his eyes, willing away the tiredness. Maybe he would be able to sleep.

He got up and started for the bedroom but paused and walked to the window facing east. He pulled the drapes back and studied the end townhouse. Without giving it much thought, he turned on the floor lamp beside the window.

An instant later, the light came on in the second floor of the townhouse. He grabbed the binoculars and saw Kirstin standing there in a pale blue nightgown, looking frail and afraid. She held up the chalkboard. It read: *safe*.

When she was sure he had seen it, she turned out the light.

35

"This the first place they'll look!" Dr. Werner's wife, Anna, hissed in the darkness.

"We have no choice," Werner whispered. "We can't outrun them."

Anna's sister was trembling. "I'm so frightened," she said. "What made us think we could escape?"

"We knew it would be dangerous," her husband reminded them.

"And now we're hiding under the altar in the church," Anna said. "We'll never get away."

"Yes, we will," Dr. Werner assured them. "Just be quiet. We'll wait another hour and then make our way back home."

"If the Stasi don't find us first," Anna said.

"Hush!" Werner hissed.

The large oak doors of the church slowly swung open, the brass hinges squeaking in protest. Footsteps crossed the threshold, the boot heels echoing on the tiled floor. Then they stopped and it was quiet. Several seconds ticked by anxiously.

"It'll be much easier if you surrender," a voice called, echoing through the empty church.

It was quiet for a moment as the soldiers waited for a reply. When none was received, they tentatively took a few steps.

"We'll find you," a second soldier warned.

The fugitives dared not move. They huddled together under the altar, a long wooden box closed on three sides and wrapped in crimson cloth, giving the thrifty construction a regal appearance. It was in the cavity, only accessible from the back, that they hid, crammed into the cramped space, their hearts racing, praying that a merciful God would spare them the hell their capture would cause.

They heard footsteps travel down the aisle. They walked up one side and down the other, louder, pausing, then fainter. As the minutes passed, the footsteps covered most of the church, the soldiers probably searching the pews. It was then quiet, the guards perhaps assessing, before the door to a vacant room on one side of the alter opened. The refugees could hear them, murmured voices from the adjacent room. The soldiers emerged a few moments later, walked across the front of the altar, and entered the minister's quarters on the other side.

The refugees heard closet doors opening and boxes being moved. "They're searching the minister's wardrobe," Werner whispered.

"Just pray that they leave," Anna murmured, her face buried in her husband's shoulder.

A door slammed closed, the noise echoing through the chamber. Footsteps crossed the church, long and measured. They walked up three marble steps that led to the presbytery, slowly approaching the sanctity of the altar.

Anna's sister sobbed softly. The others dared not move or make a sound. The footsteps came closer, only a few feet away. A soldier took a few more steps and paused. They could almost feel his presence, standing in front of the altar. A few seconds later he tapped on the front, only an inch from where they huddled together. He moved his hand about the face, tapping in different places and then stopped, apparently satisfied the altar was solid.

"There's no one here," he said.

His partner didn't reply. Seconds eerily passed. The soldiers remained, not moving. The four fugitives dared to breathe, only inches away, separated from the enemy by the slim slab of wood.

"Ah!" Anna gasped, as a bayonet was thrust through the wood, the blade inches from her head.

The doors to the church swung open, squeaking on their hinges, masking her cry.

"Did you find anyone?" a voice called from the front of the church.

"No," the soldier nearest to the altar said. Seconds later the bayonet was yanked form the wood, its owner struggling to free it.

"Come with me," the soldier by the door ordered. "They want us to search the graveyard again. The dogs must have picked up a scent."

They heard the footsteps leave the presbytery, walking down the marble steps, and then grow fainter as they traveled down the center aisle. A few seconds later, the door closed.

"Be quiet and don't move," Werner whispered. "It might be a trap. They could still be here."

"How long do we have to stay?" Anna's sister asked.

"At least another hour," he replied.

———

A delivery truck was parked across the street from the church. The driver was absent, probably asleep in a nearby apartment. A troop truck was parked behind it. Karl Hofer's Trabant automobile sat in front of it. Soldiers had already checked the truck's cargo space, breaking a lock that secured it closed, and found it empty.

"I can't hold on much longer," a young man named Helmut gasped. He lay horizontally across the truck's undercarriage, hugging a rear axle. His feet rested in the upper wheel hub, his arms supported his body, elevated eighteen inches off the ground.

Dieter Katz clung to the axle's other side. "Hold on until they leave," he said. "It won't be long. The worst is past."

"My arms are weakening."

"You can do it," Katz said.

Minutes passed and still they held, afraid to touch the ground, terrified they would be seen. Finally, almost an hour after they found their hiding place, they heard voices.

"I want a full report in the morning," a man said as a car door opened.

"You'll get it, sir," a soldier replied. "We're finishing up now."

"See that I do," the man ordered. The door closed and the engine started. The car pulled away, turning right at the next street.

"Gather up the men," the soldier said, apparently talking to an underling.

"Yes, sir."

Dieter and Helmut hung there, arms aching. Several sets of footsteps pounded across the street. They heard men climbing into the back of the troop truck. Doors opened and a driver and passenger got in, closing the doors a few seconds later. The engine started and the truck backed up.

Dieter and Helmut knew how vulnerable they were. If the vehicle retreated too far, and its headlamps shined underneath the truck, they could be seen, clinging to the axle. They waited breathlessly. The beams inched closer. The truck stopped, the light less than a foot away. The driver turned the wheel and the truck pulled away, leaving them exhausted, their arms aching, as they gently lowered their strained bodies to the street.

36

Kirstin held Steiner's arm as they entered church the next morning. She hadn't slept the entire night, overwhelmed by the traumatic escape, her mind foggy. Initially, she was awake anticipating the escape. Then she was terrified, eluding border guards and barely returning in time to fool her husband – if she had really fooled him. She couldn't understand what went wrong. She was inches from freedom, a minute or less away, and it was unbearable to think she had been so close to the new life that still remained beyond her grasp.

She was thankful she didn't get caught, and she was amazed that she managed to elude the border guards. Soldiers came from all directions, preventing escape from the cemetery, but somehow, she weaved between them, like threading the eye of a needle, to return home safely. Now she wondered if the others were as fortunate as she was.

"I'm surprised you're attending church two weeks in a row," Steiner said. "That's unusual for you."

She hesitated, knowing how badly she wanted to see the faces of the other refugees at the service, and to thank a merciful God for letting her escape, but she couldn't tell him that. She could only look at him, smile sweetly, and say, "It gives me the opportunity to see friends I might not see otherwise."

"I'm sure they'll be here," he said softly.

As they walked down the aisle, searching for an empty pew, Kirstin's eyes wandered, searching those in attendance. She couldn't appear too obvious, so she only glanced from side to side, not moving her head. But she saw none of the faces she wanted to see.

She and Steiner sat on the left side, toward the front, only a few pews from the presbytery. When he took a hymnal and started to thumb through it, she took the opportunity to scan the room. She spotted Dieter Katz, sitting on the far side, in the back. He appeared unharmed and, when his eyes met hers, he nodded discretely. She sighed with relief, assuming his friend escaped with him.

The sermon started a moment later. Steiner looked up, giving the minister his attention, making it harder for her to study the parishioners. A few minutes later, when all kneeled, she used the distraction to look over her shoulder. She saw Dr. Werner and his wife, sitting in the center section, only a few pews away, looking very weary. He smiled faintly, nodding his head.

Kirstin assumed his relatives escaped, also. At first, she thought it strange. What were the odds that seven people, with ages spanning from twenty to sixty, could elude trained border guards who seemed to know they were coming? She realized it had to be a miracle, an act of God, and she was glad she came to church.

An hour later, when the service ended, Kirstin managed to slip away from Steiner, who enjoyed talking to parishioners after church, probably evaluating their commitment to socialism. She sought out Dr. Werner and his wife.

"Is everyone all right?" she whispered.

Werner nodded. "Yes, but we were terrified," he whispered.

"We hid in the church," added his wife, Anna. "Under the alter."

"All four of you got away?"

"Yes, although I don't know how," Werner said. "Anna was almost stabbed with a bayonet."

Kirstin's eyes were wide with alarm. "We're all so fortunate," she said softly. Her gaze shifted to Dieter Katz, who stood by the pavement, studying his watch. "I'll contact you soon," she said to the Werners, lightly touching each on the arm, and walked away.

"Dieter, how are your classes going?" she asked as she went over and stood next to him.

"As well as can be expected," he said. "Especially since it isn't my chosen field of study."

"Your friend also?" she asked, coding her true inquiry.

"Yes, he's in the same situation. We're both doing well and eager for the next challenge."

"I'll contact you," she whispered, leaning towards him.

"There you are, darling," Steiner said as he came to join them. "Dieter, how are you?"

"I'm doing well, Professor."

"Good, I'm glad to hear that. Are you ready, Kirstin?"

"Yes, of course," she said. "I'll see you next week, Dieter."

He nodded, smiling faintly, as they walked away.

"The minister said the escape attempt was made in the far corner of the cemetery," Steiner said. "They cut the barbed wire."

"Did they get to West Berlin?" she asked.

"No, apparently the guards were waiting for them."

"Was anyone injured?"

"Not that I know of," he replied. "And somehow, they all got away, frightened for their lives, I'm sure. Apparently, there were five or six of them."

"Hopefully they learned their lesson," she muttered, saying what she knew he would want to hear.

When they returned home, Kirstin worked in her garden, or at least pretended to. She was actually watching the barbed wire border and the guards patrolling it. They acted as if nothing was amiss, the events of the prior evening apparently a distant memory. She did notice that an additional row of barbed wire had been added to the existing, stretching the entire length of the cemetery.

She cleaned the house, started preparations for dinner, and listened to some of her records – Etta James, Ricky Nelson and Patsy Cline – doing whatever she could to waste the hours away until she could contact Tony. She needed to see him, spend more time with him than a few minutes in a secluded section of the library. Somehow, a casual acquaintance was becoming much more. It gave her strength and solace, a shoulder on which to lean.

After dinner, she and Steiner settled in the parlor and listened to the radio. They didn't have a television, few in the East did, but there were several radio programs that he enjoyed. It kept him occupied, as well as reading the newspaper. She tried to start a conversation on several occasions, but he was immersed in the paper and merely nodded or offered a brief reply. When darkness arrived, she slipped away and went upstairs.

She got the chalkboard out and wrote on it, stepped back from the window so the border guards couldn't see her, and looked to Tony's apartment. He was waiting for her. She held the chalkboard up: *Everyone is safe*

A moment later, she saw his reply: *Good. I was frantic.*

She put down her binoculars and wrote on the chalkboard. A few seconds later she raised it up: *Café across from art museum at 10 a.m.?*

His reply was quick: *Yes, that would be nice.*

She paused, listening for any movement on the stairway. Then she scribbled a reply. *Can you come to the East more often?*

He replied: *Yes, I would like that.*

She put down the binoculars, a faint smile on her face, and wrote: *I can't wait to see you.*

She heard a creak on the stairs, turned off the lamp, and hid the chalkboard. She grabbed a folder of papers from her desk and walked into the hallway, bumping into Steiner as she did so.

"I was just coming back downstairs," she said with a disarming smile.

37

"Did they all get away?" Ned Simpson asked.

"Yes," Marino replied. "I'm not sure how, but they did."

"That's good. I was worried. Anyway, it'll add a lot of suspense to the story. What's next?"

Marino slowly shook his head as he held the phone against his ear. "Tomorrow I'm going to East Berlin to meet Kirstin. I'll be going more often."

"Can you manage that?"

"Yes, I think so," he replied. "My documents are all in order."

"But everything's different now."

Marino thought for a moment. Ned was right. Everything was different. "I'll be careful," he promised.

"Just don't get stuck there," Simpson said. "You have a book to write."

"I need another plan," Marino said, ignoring him. "I have to help these people. Especially after failing them last night." After he made the statement, he couldn't believe he did. For someone who avoided commitment, the rescue of seven souls from a Communist country was a monumental undertaking.

"I have a contact at the Swiss embassy in New York," Simpson said. "I asked if he could get fake passports."

"What did he say?"

"He said he would look into it but made no promises."

"Do you tell him there were seven people?"

"Yes, I did," Simpson replied. "He'll help with the first passport. But he wants to see what happens before trying any others."

"That makes sense," Marino said. "We'll try to get Kirstin out and then help the rest."

"He's not sure how to get the passport to you," Simpson said. "He's afraid if he mails it, the East Germans will intercept it."

"Not if it's flown directly to West Berlin," Marino replied.

"I'll let him know," Simpson said. "I suppose there's some details to work out."

"He'll need her description," Marino told him, wary of the risk associated with their latest attempt. "She's tall and thin with shoulder length blond hair and blue eyes, an attractive woman."

"Got it," Simpson said. He hesitated, as if he wanted to say something but didn't. After an awkward moment, he continued. "Just be careful, Tony. And call me as soon as you get back from East Berlin."

———

There was a center for refugees from East Berlin at *Marienfelde*, in the American sector. Before going East to see Kirstin, Marino stopped at the center, introduced himself to a man behind a desk, and a few minutes later was talking to a young college student named Johann who had escaped a few days before.

"There are still a few options available," Johann said. "Fake passports did work, but the Stasi are cracking down, especially now. You have to register upon entering East Berlin. And you can't leave if there's no record you entered."

Marino was quiet for a moment. He had yet to consider all the details involved with a fake passport. How could Kirstin leave if there was no record she entered?

"You look confused," Johann observed.

"No, not confused," Marino said. "But a fake passport is more difficult than I thought, given all the documentation."

"I think the best approach is to feign ignorance," Johann advised. "Claim the guard made a mistake when the person entered. Or maybe you can go in and get them. When you come out, insist the guard failed to register both of you."

"I'll have to give it some thought," Marino said, not as enthusiastic about the passport as he was. "How about a tunnel? Is that viable?"

"For those who dare, I suppose it is," the student responded. "They're very dangerous. Some have caved in; others have flooded. But one or two have been successful."

"How did you escape?"

"There's a park on *Kiefholz Strasse*, in the American zone, where sections of barbed wire were hidden by trees and shrubs. I crawled through the underbrush, cut the wire, and shimmied through."

"Do you think that's still an option?"

The student shrugged. "I don't know," he said. "But I doubt it. I'm sure the fence has been repaired. And they probably cleared the underbrush and posted more guards. They might have even started the wall. They're building it throughout the city."

"I know," Marino said. "They're tightening a noose around the neck of East Belin."

"Each day gets harder," the student agreed. "How many are you trying to get out?"

"Seven. Any ideas?"

"Find a good location and dig a tunnel."

"That's good advice," Marino said, "except I don't know anything about tunnels."

"It's still your best option," Johann said. "But if you dig one, get as many people out as you can."

"Thanks," Marino said as he turned to leave. "I'll think about it."

"Good luck," Johann called as Marino started to walk away. "And consider the tunnel. You can find diggers here. Someone will volunteer."

Marino paused, knowing he might need to pursue that option. "Do you have a contact for me?" he asked.

The student took a business card from his wallet and scribbled some information on the back. "The card is for my dentist," he said. "You can disregard it. The man whose name is on the back will help you. I'll even schedule the meeting."

Marino left the refugee center and drove his Volkswagen to *Friedrichstrasse*, and then up to the vehicle barriers at Checkpoint Charlie, the only crossing permitting foreigner's access into East Berlin. He rolled down the window and showed the American guard his papers and was waved through. He stopped a hundred feet further and parked his vehicle so the East German guards could search it. Then he went in to the shanty to show border personnel his documentation. It was different than his other trips through the checkpoint, when a bored guard went through the formalities, explaining rules and regulations. This time the guard was vigilant, sitting upright, while a man in a suit with a pockmarked face stood a few feet behind him.

"What is the purpose of your visit?" the guard asked.

"I have some research to do."

"What sort of research?" the guard asked.

"I'm writing a book on German history," Marino replied. "I need access to library archives and different museums and landmarks."

The guard didn't seem impressed. "You have to be back by midnight, with the same amount of money, or with receipts to explain what you spent."

"I understand," Marino replied, collecting his documentation. He turned to go.

"Wait," ordered the man in the suit.

"Yes, sir?" Marino asked.

The man pointed through the window. "What did the guards find in your car?"

Marino turned and saw guards examining a box of candy he brought for Kirstin. "It's a box of chocolates," he explained. "They're for a friend."

"For a friend?" the man asked. "You said you were doing research."

"I am, "Marino replied, starting to feel uncomfortable. "But I'm also meeting a friend for lunch."

"Why do you need an automobile?" the man asked.

"There are also landmarks I want to visit."

"Give me your papers."

Marino did as he was told, wondering if a box of candy was worth so much trouble.

"These documents are several months old."

"I realize that," Marino explained. "I arrived in West Berlin a few months ago."

"Yes, but it's different now."

"Different how?" Marino asked, getting testy. "The same people that gave me permission then are those that would give me permission now."

"Maybe we should see," the man said. "Maybe I should

detain you and conduct an interrogation on what your real intentions are."

"I told you my intentions," Marino said.

"Really?" the man asked. "Are you going to research a book or look at landmarks? Or are you having lunch with a woman, someone you care enough about to bring a box of chocolates?"

"It's all of the above," Marino said.

The man leaned forward, studied him closely, and said, "Maybe you're an American spy."

"If I was a spy, I'd be smart enough to get into East Berlin without having to deal with you. Don't you think?"

The man looked at him sternly and returned his papers. "Be back by midnight. Or I'll come find you myself."

38

Dieter Katz saw Eileen Fischer exiting the East Berlin guard shack and then walking down *Friedrichstrasse.* Minutes before, she had disembarked from the S-bahn in West Berlin, passed through Checkpoint Charlie, and crossed the border into East Berlin. She looked good, dressed in Western clothes, jeans and a top, a bit of make-up dressing a face that really didn't need it, but not much – just some eye-shadow and lipstick. He hugged her.

"Oh Dieter, I'm so glad you're all right," she said, holding him tightly. "I've been so worried."

"I'm fine," he said. "It was horrible, very frightening, but I survived."

"I've been frantic," she said, kissing him.

He was about to reply when he saw a border guard approach, probably off duty. The man walked down the pavement like a handful of other pedestrians, innocently passing by, but Dieter didn't want him to overhear their conversation. When he saw the guard's face, he turned away.

"Quiet," he whispered in Eileen's ear. He released her, smiled, and spoke loudly, ensuring the guard could hear. "Let's get something to eat," he suggested. "And then maybe we can go to that theater in Mitte."

"That sounds nice," she said, seeming a bit confused.

The guard walked by, paused, and then turned. "Mr. Katz," he said. "It's good to see you."

"Hello, Mr. Frank," Dieter replied, and then nodded toward Eileen. "This is Eileen Fischer."

"Madam," the guard said, tipping his cap.

"It's nice to meet you," Eileen said, forcing a smile.

"You have a fine friend here," Mr. Frank said as continued on, crossing the street. "We think very highly of him."

"Who was that?" Eileen hissed.

"One of the instructors at the Industrial School," he replied.

"He's a border guard."

Katz shrugged. "I can't help that," he said. "I only know him as a teacher."

He took her hand and they walked down the pavement. When no one was near them, they continued their conversation.

"The others escaped, also," Dieter whispered. "No one was hurt, but no one made it to the West, either."

"We should have been better prepared," she said, glancing at a couple pushing a baby stroller. "It was too risky."

"It seemed a good plan," he said. "And the location worked well, a weak area in the barbed wire. I don't know how we failed."

"I suppose it doesn't matter," she said. "As long as you and the others are safe."

"We're all very fortunate," he said. "Guards were everywhere."

"What do you think happened?"

"I'm not sure," he said. "Maybe our timing was bad."

"Or maybe you were betrayed," she suggested.

He stopped, turning to look at her. "By whom?"

"I don't know," she admitted. "But doesn't it seem odd that a searchlight was turned on just as you were about to escape, and the cemetery was swarming with soldiers?"

"Yes, but no one was caught," he countered. "If the Stasi knew an escape was planned, we never would have gotten that far."

"How do you know that?" she asked. "Don't you think it's all too much of a coincidence?"

"No, I don't," he replied. "If anyone betrayed us, we would all be in prison."

"I'm not sure I agree," she muttered. "How did you get away?"

"My friend and I hid under a troop truck."

She sighed, as if wondering what he saw that she didn't. "It still makes no sense," she insisted. "Doesn't the very fact that there was a troop truck prove they knew someone was trying to escape?"

"The guards arrived as we were leaving," he explained. "They weren't waiting for us. It didn't seem like they were aware of an escape attempt until it was made."

"I don't know," she said, shrugging. "Maybe you weren't betrayed after all. I suppose you would have been trapped if they knew, but you weren't."

"And I'm not sure about the searchlight, either," he said. "Maybe it's always been there and I never noticed."

"I think it's unlikely," she said, as if still not convinced.

"Maybe we gave ourselves away," he offered. "They might have heard us or seen the man who cut the wire from the West."

"No, I talked to him after it happened," she said. "He's certain no one saw him."

"The guards had to have a reason to turn the light on," he said.

"I suppose they could have seen something," she said, "even an animal, and wanted to know what it was."

"I think that if they knew about the escape, they would have had soldiers hiding all over the graveyard. But they didn't."

"It just seems suspicious," she said. "You need to be careful."

"Do you trust the man in the West, the one that cut the wire?"

"I don't really know him," she replied. "I just met him that night. But he seemed to have everything planned out. He had already cut the wire when I got there."

"Would you work with him again?"

"Yes, of course. Why, are you planning another escape?"

"I won't stop until I'm successful," he said.

"What about the others, do you think they still want to escape?"

"Yes, I think so. I'll find out."

"Do you know them all?" she asked.

"Some of them," he said. "But not very well."

"You need to be wary of strangers," she warned. "You can't trust anyone."

"Yes, you're right."

"Do you want me to see if I can find out anything about them?" she asked.

He shook his head. "No, I don't think that's necessary." Then he hesitated, his eyes trained on hers. "At least not yet."

"It's no trouble," she offered. "I'll find out what I can. What are their names?"

"Here's the restaurant," he said, guiding her across the street. "We have so little time together. Let's enjoy it."

"I'm just think we need to be cautious," she said. "We very well could have been betrayed. We can't let that happen again."

"And we won't," he said, pausing at the restaurant entrance.

"Then let's discuss the other six people," she suggested.

"What are their backgrounds, their motivations, who they could have told, what reasons they might have to betray us."

"Let's have dinner," he suggested, "and we can continue the discussion on the way to the theater."

"The Stasi are everywhere, even among those planning to escape," she said, aggravated, "Why are you so reluctant to talk about those who were with you? Your life depends on their loyalty."

"And their lives depend on mine."

39
___

Tony Marino sat in Gertrude Manstein's parlor, enjoying a cup of tea. He had gone to the pharmacy to pick up her prescriptions and then delivered some groceries. Their casual conversation, originally focused on the present and the fabulous future Kirstin would have once she got to West Berlin, wandered to the past, offering images that neither wanted to see.

"It was the worst day of my life," Gertrude said sadly, a vacant look in her pale blue eyes.

"Kirstin told me about it briefly," Marino said. "I can't even imagine."

"I always felt responsible," she continued, the heavy burden she bore visible in the wrinkled recesses of her face. "I asked her to go to the store, just in case the owner had something to sell." She paused to sip her tea, her eyes misty. "There wasn't much to eat after the war. And whatever goods did reach Berlin were stolen by the Russians."

"You can't blame yourself," Marino said. "You were only trying to survive. Just like everyone else."

"It was in the afternoon," she continued. "In broad daylight.

She went to one store, only a few blocks away, and I went to another, farther, over on *Rheinsberger Strasse*. I waited in line for over an hour for a few turnips, some carrots, and a stale loaf of bread."

Marino felt his eyes misting as Gertrude described the day Kirstin was assaulted. "You had no way of knowing she was in danger," he said. "It was a simple afternoon trip to the grocery store."

"I knew something was wrong when I got home before she did," she said, her eyes still vacant. "I could feel it, an emptiness in the pit of my stomach."

"Mrs. Manstein, please," he urged. "We don't have to discuss this. It might be better to leave the nightmare undisturbed."

She sighed, wiping her eyes with a lace handkerchief. "No, I think it's something you should know, especially since you're helping Kirstin find her daughter."

"I just don't want you to get upset," he said. "We can talk about it some other time."

"No," she said. "Now would be best. I started the story; I should finish it."

"It's entirely up to you," he said. "You don't have to if you don't want to."

She shook her head and began where she left off. "I got the neighbor, Mr. Steuben. He was a nice man, old at the time, but probably near ninety when he died. He's the one that found her. She was lying in the rubble of a bombed building next to the grocery store. She had been brutally beaten, her clothes torn from her body." She looked at him, tears dripping down her face faster than she could catch them with her handkerchief. "What type of animal does that to a young girl?"

"There were many atrocities," Marino said, trying to ease the poor woman's pain, but feeling it almost as deeply as she did. "Many who suffered. It's a dark chapter that should never have been written."

"I can't forgive myself," she said. "And I never will."

He moved beside her, wrapping an arm around her, his eyes starting to mist. "But you're not to blame," he told her. "You had no way of knowing that would happen."

"No," she muttered, "I did. I knew what the Russians were like. And I should have known better."

"Please, Mrs. Manstein," Marino pleaded. "I'm sure Kirsten doesn't hold you in any way responsible."

"She was in the hospital for several weeks," she continued, politely ignoring him, "but she never really recovered. It was over a month before she even spoke. She just laid in her bed and cried, a crazed look in her eyes."

"I'm so sorry," Marino said, hugging her tightly. "But please, don't think about it, don't dwell on hell when you created heaven. Look at the fabulous person Kirstin became. You must be very proud."

Gertrude smiled, wiping the last few tears from her tired eyes. "Yes, I am," she said. "And she's had such a difficult life."

"But she became the person she is because of you."

"It's such a shame," she said, almost as if she couldn't hear him. "She was just recovering from her parents' deaths when the Russians raped her. And then she had to heal all over again."

"And then the baby came," he said quietly.

Gertrude nodded. "Yes," she said. "A beautiful, healthy little girl, a glimmer of light in never-ending darkness. But the State took her. They argued that Kirstin was a child herself, still traumatized, and incapable of caring for a baby. And none of the medical experts offered a very promising prognosis. Kirstin barely spoke, only a few words each day, and she was too frightened to function. In some respects, they were right. She couldn't care for herself let alone another human being."

"She might never have recovered if she didn't have a strong, loving woman like you to help her," Marino said.

"I would have raised the child, too," Gertrude said. "If they had let me. But sometimes I think it was better. Kirstin was too unhinged, too emotional. The child would have been a constant reminder of the assault. She never could have coped."

"She's very fortunate you're in her life," he said. "And she loves you above all else."

Gertrude smiled. "And I love her just as much," she said. "I miss her terribly."

"Hopefully you'll be reunited soon."

"I still think I should have petitioned the State for custody of the child" she said.

Marino studied the fragile woman sitting beside him, blaming herself for the destruction of lives that a global catastrophe spawned. "You did the best you could," he said softly. "And no one could ask for more."

"I hope you're right," she said. "It just doesn't seem like it was enough."

"Maybe it's time to reunite the family," Marino offered. "Smiles can replace the tears."

"That would be wonderful," Gertrude said, as if she couldn't believe it might happen. "It really would. I've thought of my great-granddaughter every day for the last sixteen years. I would love to meet her, to see the young lady she's become."

40

"There was an escape attempt last weekend," Karl Hofer said as he sat behind his desk. "In the cemetery behind the Church of Reconciliation."

"I wasn't aware of that," Dr. Werner said, feigning ignorance.

Hofer smiled smugly. "It was a very clumsy attempt," he remarked. "I wonder who was involved."

"I wouldn't know," Werner said, his heart beginning to race.

Hofer leaned forward, bridging the gap between them. "I think you do."

"I'm sorry, but I don't."

"Why the cemetery?"

"I don't know what you're talking about."

"Who's your friend in the West?"

"I have many friends in the West?"

"Which one cut the barbed wire?"

"I don't know anything about that."

"Who went with you?"

"I wasn't involved."

Hofer sat back, his face stern. "This is a friendly discussion,

Doctor Werner," he said. "The next one may not be."

"I have no information to give you," Werner said.

"Tell me about Kirstin Beck."

"She came to see me last week," Werner replied. "A follow-up for her injured ankle."

"And she's doing well?"

"Yes, she is."

"Is that the only time you've seen her since our last visit?"

"Yes."

"Really?"

"Yes."

"You've only seen Kirstin Beck once since I told you to watch her?"

"Yes, sir."

Hofer opened a folder on the desk in front of him. "I have documentation describing each occasion you've met Kirstin Beck."

Werner paused, wondering if a trap was being set. He could tell Hofer enjoyed questioning him, as if wondering who he would protect and who he might betray. "I'm telling you the truth," he insisted quietly, refusing to be intimidated.

"Last Sunday after church. What about that?" Hofer asked. "You spoke for several minutes. And were then joined by the dissident Dieter Katz."

"I did chat with them for a few minutes after the service," Werner admitted, "but it was an innocent conversation."

"You just told me you haven't seen her."

"It was nothing," Werner protested. "We talked for a few minutes. I don't even recall what was discussed."

"Another escape attempt, perhaps," Hofer said.

"No, that isn't true," Werner said with distaste.

"What did Dieter Katz say?" Hofer probed.

"He discussed his new school, or his courses, something like that. We only talked for a minute."

Hofer was quiet, as if gauging how uncomfortable Werner was. "It would benefit you to be more cooperative," he said. "Especially with the many accusations the State has received about you."

"I am innocent of all charges."

"Really?" Hofer asked in disbelief. "You never took pharmaceuticals? Because I have witnesses who said you did."

"I told you before," Werner said, unsuccessfully hiding his irritation. "I was provided with sample medications to give to patients, as I often was. And that's what I did. I gave them to patients."

"Without reimbursement to the State."

"There was no reimbursement required," Werner insisted. "There never has been."

"Just because you never provided reimbursement doesn't mean it wasn't required. Does it?"

"They were samples," Werner insisted. "The authorities gauge the drug's effectiveness by observing the patient. The program has been in use for many years."

"We shall see, Doctor Werner," Hofer said. "We shall see."

"Yes, you will see that I'm telling the truth."

"And I suppose you never made derogatory comments about the State," Hofer continued.

"I may have expressed my frustration that the border was closed," Werner said. "I don't remember. I have friends and family in the West, as well as many patients. Now I may never see them again. I'm as frustrated as the rest of East Berlin."

"You do realize this is only the beginning," Hofer threatened, apparently not convinced of his sincerity. "Once I have a suspect in my sights, they are always proven guilty of crimes against the State. One hundred percent of the time."

"I am innocent," Werner stated firmly.

Hofer closed the folder. "I want more information on Kirstin Beck. And you're going to get it for me."

41

"We have to be careful," Kirstin whispered. "The Stasi could be watching me."

Marino sat across from her, drinking a glass of wine. "Is it wise for us to meet?"

She shrugged. "We have to communicate," she said. "It's a chance we have to take."

"Have you noticed anyone following you?"

"No," she replied firmly. "They watch in other ways – using family or friends. They make those you trust betray you."

He studied those sitting nearby. "Maybe we shouldn't meet in public."

"It's all right," she told him. "I'm cautious."

He was satisfied with her response. She knew East Berlin, and the suffocating loss of freedom, better than he ever could. He leaned closer. "What happened Saturday night?" he asked.

"I'm not sure," she replied. "There were seven of us, hiding among the tombstones. We were crossing the border when the searchlight came on."

"And everyone got away?"

"Yes."

He was pensive for a moment. "Maybe it was more of a coincidence than a trap."

"I suppose," she agreed. "But coincidence or not, it was still frightening."

"I'm sure it was," he acknowledged. "Do you still want me to get you out?"

"Yes, but quickly," she said. "My husband is getting suspicious."

He tried to imagine the world she lived in, trapped in so many cages. "I can get you a fake passport."

She thought for a moment, as if evaluating the risks. "What about the others?"

He looked at her, innocent and pure but hardened by life. She was kind and compassionate, such a good person. He had so much to learn from her. "We'll find another way to get them out," he said. "You can help me when you get to the West."

"If I escape, how will we communicate with them?" she asked.

"I can come to the East or we can use Eileen Fischer."

She seemed wary of her chance for success. "The passport sounds dangerous," she said. "Almost as bad as slipping through the wire."

"We'll plan better this time," he promised.

"I still have to face the guards and explain why I was in the East. What if they ask questions I don't have answers to?"

"I'll prep you on what to expect," he said.

She took a deep breath, as if evaluating risk and reward – a lifetime in prison or seeing her grandmother and daughter. "I have to do it," she said softly. "I'm just afraid."

"I'll be with you," he said. "And I won't let anything happen."

"When will you have the passport?"

"In a few days," he replied. "I gave the best description of you I could. You may have to alter your appearance a bit to match the photograph."

"Can we just use my photograph?"

"We can," he said, "but that's just as risky. If we alter the document, the border guards may notice. And if we switch the photograph with one of yours, we would have to trust a stranger to do it, probably a local printer or government official. I'm not sure we should do that."

"I'm willing to try it," she said. "My grandmother needs me and ..." She paused, almost as if she was afraid to continue. "And I hope my daughter does, too."

He was quiet for a moment, trying to envision the world she lived in, mentally and physically. Especially after what her grandmother told him. She seemed so controlled, and he wondered how hard it was to offer that perception. Was she really more like an eggshell, strong in some ways but fragile in so many others? "I'm sure your daughter will want to be part of your life."

"I hope so," she said, as if daring to dream.

He watched for a moment as she sipped her wine. "If you don't mind me asking, how did you meet your husband?"

"In college," she replied. "I was his student. I think a psychiatrist would say I was in need of a father figure."

He laughed. "Perhaps," he said. "Or maybe there are other reasons. Do you love him?"

"He has his moments."

He realized she hadn't answered his question. Or maybe she did, but with a veiled response. "Will you regret leaving him?" he probed.

"No," she said. "He's become a stranger. And he has been for several years."

"Are you sure he suspects something?"

"Yes," she replied. "I'm positive."

"Do you think he'll do anything about it?"

She hesitated, but then replied. "Not just yet. I don't think he wants to believe what he already knows."

"Isn't that dangerous?" he asked. "What if he does believe it?"

"Then the risk increases greatly," she told him. "He'll know when he threads minor incidents together that are individually innocent but collectively difficult to explain. And he seems to get closer every day."

"Will he have you arrested?"

"He won't hesitate," she replied. "At least I don't think he will."

He was quiet for a moment, reflecting on the passport. It posed a unique set of dangers, very different than the attempted escape at the cemetery. But he had to get her out of East Berlin.

"You're thinking," she said. "Is that good or bad?"

"I'm trying to find the best way to escape," he said. "I've talked to people at the refugee center in West Berlin and I'm studying different methods they used."

"I heard someone swam across the river," she said. "I could never do that."

"Most found weaknesses in the border, like we did at the cemetery," he explained. "They're usually in parks, areas with trees and shrubs. But the police are closing those gaps."

"And now a wall is replacing the barbed wire," she said. "It gets more difficult every day."

"Let's hope the passport works," he said.

She glanced at her watch and then studied the patrons for a moment. "I had better go," she said. "I have to see my publisher. We shouldn't stay in the same place together for too long anyway. Can we meet at the library later?"

"Yes, of course," he replied. "If you think it's safe."

"It is," she said. "Steiner will be in class."

"I'll drive along the border while you're with your publisher," he said. "Just to see what it looks like from this side."

"I'll meet you at the library," she said. Then she hesitated, as if unsure of what the future held. "If you want me to."

He looked at her, the blue eyes so warm and inviting, yet somehow so afraid, and he realized he didn't want her to leave at all. "Can't you just stay?" he asked, almost sounding desperate. "We can spend the day together."

She smiled, as if she liked his reply. "I have to see my publisher every day," she told him. "It'll arouse suspicion if I don't. I collect my assignments and drop off what I've completed."

"You don't work in their office?"

She shook her head. "No, I don't think anyone does."

"All right then," he said. "I'll see you at three." He didn't get out of the chair, even though he said he was leaving. He wanted to stay. And he wanted her to stay.

"I'll only be gone an hour or so," she said, as if reading his thoughts. "I'll see you soon. And if you can drive me back near my house afterwards, I can stay longer."

"That would be nice," he said. He then regretted saying it, knowing it suggested more than a business arrangement, although she didn't seem to mind.

She studied him for a moment, smiling. "Yes, it will be nice," she said softly, lightly caressing his hand.

42

Marino went back to his car, wondering what it was like to be Kirstin Beck. She was trapped in a life she didn't want and dependent on him, a total stranger, to escape. It had become much more than a story for his next book. It was personal; he cared about her. Tony Marino, a man who avoided commitment and responsibility, was mired in a mess few would want. He was falling in love with a married woman, whether he wanted to admit it or not, who was trying to escape from a Communist country to find a daughter lost to adoption, who she had never before seen, and to care for a grandmother no one else could help. The situation was complicated by her husband, a Stasi informant or, worse yet, a Stasi agent. Yet Marino drove forward, convinced he could somehow put all the pieces together. The man who shunned commitment and responsibility was disappearing into a murky mist of yesterdays. And a different man was emerging to replace him.

He left the café a few minutes after Kirstin and drove towards the border. The concrete wall was rising rapidly throughout the city, replacing the barbed wire initially used to seal the border. He continued to the Mitte section of East

Berlin, adjacent to where his apartment building was, drove past the Reunification Church and cemetery – site of their last escape attempt – and then past Kirstin's townhouse, the end in the row.

There was a stark contrast between East and West Berlin, the same city that somehow seemed continents apart, and Marino found it fascinating. The West was rebuilding, ruins from the Second World War disappearing as capitalism thrived and businesses were born, enriching the city's residents with jobs and products to purchase. In the East, hampered by socialistic dogmas, much of the city still lay in ruins. Modern buildings were constructed at a fraction of the pace in the West, and they all looked the same, designed with little imagination, as if mirroring the political system that stifled differing thoughts and views. Residents had no hope of advancement, no chance for a better life for their children, regardless of how hard they worked. It seemed unusual to him, but it represented a society many in the world were willing to fight for. And some would even die for.

He found no border weaknesses to exploit, so he drove to the library, parked his car and entered the building. He was wary of the location, so close to the University where Steiner Beck was now teaching, but there were so many people in the area – students, teachers, businessmen, soldiers, housewives – that they offered a human camouflage not available if he met Kirstin in a deserted park.

He went in the library and made his way to the history section. He found books relevant to his research and sat at a table to scribble some notes pertinent to the Russian attack on Berlin. It was a military advance that started near Moscow, pushing ever westward, inch by inch, yard by yard until the Russians had re-taken what was theirs and pushed into the enemy's territory. After four long years of intense combat and many millions of deaths, they destroyed the city of Berlin. The

Nazi regime crumbled with it, caught in a vice, the Russians in the East, the American, Brits and French in the West.

It marked the end of one evil empire, but also birthed a new one. The Russian Communists took control of all nations they occupied and became enemies of the West. Marino had fought them in the army – indirectly, of course, through his work as a translator – but he had still fought Communism just the same. And he was still fighting Communism in Berlin, not on the battlefield but in a subtler way, trying to help Kirstin Beck escape a repressive regime. Sometimes he wondered if he helped her because she exposed his own weaknesses, forcing him to confront and combat them. If he could win the battle with his own demons, then he could win the battle for Kirstin in East Berlin. He just had to be more cautious, more cunning, and remember that he risked other people's lives – not just his own.

Kirstin appeared in the library just before three. He had finished his research and was sitting on a different bench, along the exterior wall of the third floor, enjoying the sunlight that streamed in the window.

"Do you think it's safe?" she asked. "Sitting in front of a window?"

He studied her closely, gaining a new respect, and remembered where he was. "No, I suppose it isn't."

"Let's move," she suggested. "We can sit behind those shelves."

They walked thirty feet away, past rows of shelves to a back wall, hidden among stacks of books that were piled on the floor, waiting to be catalogued.

"Is this better?" he asked.

She nodded and sat down, putting her pocketbook on the floor.

"Do you understand what we have to do with the passport?" he asked.

"Yes, I just hope the description is close. I know how dangerous it is trying to cross the border."

Marino thought of his difficulties while entering, even with the proper documentation. "If it isn't right, we won't do it," he assured her.

She paused, as if she wanted to say something but knew she shouldn't, although she did anyway. "Why no wife?"

He smiled, pleased she was so interested. It was almost as if she was planning the rest of her life and he would be part of it. "I told you before," he said, "that I have problems with commitment. No wife, no kids, no house or mortgage, no car, no debts. Just free to come and go."

"And I came along and spoiled everything," she said, smiling. "Didn't I?"

"What do you mean?"

"Now you're mired in commitment – to me, my grandmother, my daughter, to six other people who are trying to escape."

He smiled faintly, since he had the same thoughts only an hour ago. "Yes, I suppose it's a little different now," he admitted.

"Your whole life has changed," she said softly. "It's very easy for me to see. Not as easy for you."

"I'm just trying to help you," he said. "I wouldn't call that commitment."

"Did you go see my grandmother this week?"

"Yes, I did," he replied. "I got her some groceries – just some milk and coffee and vegetables. And I went over to the butcher and got some fresh meat." He smiled, reflecting on his visit. "Then I took her out to lunch at the café on the corner. She seemed to really enjoy it."

"I'm sure she did," Kirstin said, as if proving her point without him realizing it. "And you committed to visit me once every week, didn't you?"

"Yes, I suppose."

She lightly took his hand in hers. "And how many times a week do you see me now?"

He hesitated, aware of the point she was trying to make. "The first time I came, we agreed on once each week. Then it was twice. But I'm sure, going forward, it'll be three. Four if we can get away with it." He started laughing. "I suppose this commitment stuff isn't so bad, after all."

She leaned over, kissed him on the cheek, and then pulled away, glancing around to ensure they hadn't been seen. "What type of books do you write?" she asked, changing the subject.

"Mainly histories of nations," he replied. "I did France and Belgium so far."

"What are you working on now?"

"A history of Germany. I'm almost finished."

"Do you need a good editor?"

He laughed, realizing she was asking if their current relationship could ever be permanent. "Yes, I do," he replied. "But first we have to get you out of East Berlin. And then I have to teach you something that's very important."

"What is that?" she asked curiously.

"Baseball," he replied.

43

Kirstin stayed at the library longer than planned, and she didn't get home until after 7 p.m. She knew she needed an explanation for Steiner, so she stopped at a grocery store on the way home and purchased a few items.

"Where were you?' Steiner asked when she entered the house. He was sitting in the parlor, his schoolwork before him, the radio playing lightly in the background.

"I got a few things at the store," she said. "But I waited in line for over an hour."

"I hope it was worth it," he mumbled, not paying much attention.

"They had chicken," she said as she walked into the kitchen. "There was a shortage last week."

"Wonderful," he called sarcastically from the parlor.

She emptied her shopping bag on the table and put the cabbage, turnips, and chicken in the refrigerator, cans of vegetables in the pantry along with a loaf of bread. She couldn't find coffee or potatoes or desserts, although she savored the chocolate Tony had brought her and hid the remainder behind some canned goods. He had also given her a bottle of perfume and she smiled, thinking beyond East Berlin, daring to dream of a life with no shortages. She liked Tony, he was a good man. And he seemed to like her. But she had a tangled web to unweave. She had to find Lisette and establish a relationship with her daughter. That was her priority, as it should be. As it always should have been.

After she put the groceries away, she returned to the parlor. Steiner hadn't moved; he still sat in his favorite chair, a floor lamp lit behind it, going over his lesson for the following day. The radio program didn't distract him, a talk show proclaiming the evils of democracy, a political program he listened to often. She wondered what world he lived in, to think socialism was such a success. Maybe he needed to stand in lines at the grocery store and endure the constant shortages: potatoes, coffee, bananas, toothbrushes, perfume – it never seemed to end. And as soon as a long-absent product arrived on the shelves, another disappeared.

"Are you working on your lessons?" she asked as she sat across from him, wondering if he even noticed her absence.

"Yes," he murmured. "I have a lot to do. Some of my classes were canceled last week. I have to make up for it."

"Why were they canceled?" she asked. "There wasn't a holiday."

"Renovations," he replied. "They're modernizing the building."

She was alarmed but tried to hide the shock on her face. She had just spent three hours in the library with another man, a block away from where Steiner was supposed to be. If his classroom was being renovated, where was he? "What did they do to cause classes to be canceled?" she asked, trying to seem only mildly interested.

"They painted rooms and replaced some statues," he said. "It only took a week, maybe a few days longer. I held classes on some of the days."

Kirstin's mind was racing. Where had he been for the last week, if not in his classroom? She decided to gradually ask the question, trying not to seem suspicious. "What statues did they remove?" she asked.

"There were busts of German historical figures in the corridor," he explained. "While they painted my classroom, the busts were replaced."

"Who was removed?"

"Nietzsche, Wagner, Hindenburg, Ludendorff, Bismarck – I don't know who the others were."

"Isn't that our history?"

"The past is the present," he muttered, mouthing a Party slogan. "And the future is the past. The statues are gone now."

"What statutes replaced them?"

"Lenin, Stalin, Honecker, Marx."

She was disgusted. A major cornerstone of socialism was to erase the past so no comparison to the present existed. "Were did you go while they painted your classroom?" she asked. "Did you stay in your office?"

"Yes, for part of the time," he said. "And I went to the library for a few days."

Kirstin felt like she was going to be sick. She studied him closely, but he didn't look up from his papers. He acted as he normally did and gave no indication anything was wrong. She started to relax. The library was a huge building. They could have been there at the same time, yet not have seen each other. She decided to probe a bit farther. "Were you at the library today?" she asked.

"No, this was last week," he said. "I'm catching up this week."

She decided not to press him. If he had seen her, she would have known by now. Unless he knew she was guilty of something and was setting a trap. That seemed far more likely. Especially with how suspicious he was after the failed escape, when he wiped the dirt from her face. She had to remember he was Stasi, clever and cunning, an accomplished liar. She could never outsmart him.

"What's the matter?" he asked, suddenly looking up from his papers.

"Nothing," she replied with a shrug. She had to ensure he didn't suspect her more than he already did. She decided to change the subject. "Did you eat anything?"

"No, I've been waiting for you."

"I'll get something ready," she said, rising from her chair and leaving the room. She had been gone almost eight hours and he hadn't even noticed.

Or had he?

44

Karl Hofer reviewed a dossier describing escape attempts since the border had been closed. Some attempts were ingenious, innovative, and he was somewhat envious at the courage, planning, or intellect that had gone into developing them. Others were founded on pure adrenalin, an almost daredevil attempt to cross the border, often against insurmountable odds. Curiously, some were successful. He wondered what drove people to take such incredible risks, knowing they might lose their lives, only for a taste of freedom. Or what they thought freedom was. Maybe West Berlin was worse than East Berlin. Or maybe it wasn't. Sometimes he wondered also.

As he leafed through the pages, he found that some attempts had similarities, while others were unique. The most common methods involved eluding guards in parks and cemeteries, landscapes that presented challenges to patrol. Most were like the thwarted escape at the Reconciliation Church in Mitte – very little planning or preparation required, simply sliding under, or cutting through, the barbed wire at the most opportune moment. Concrete walls currently under construction would provide additional protection from these escapes – a formidable barrier, heavily guarded, that was virtually impregnable.

He noted that some escapees had crawled through sewers to find freedom in the West. Sewer pipes were the last interconnection between East and West that offered unmolested crossings; primarily providing a source of revenue for cash-strapped East Berlin. But once the escape path was discovered by the Stasi, they ordered grates installed at all manholes, welded in place, preventing access. It was another route eliminated just as, one by one, they all would be.

He continued reading, awed that some refugees tried to swim across the River Spree and other waterways scattered through the city. It seemed to him, that this was the most difficult of all attempts. Not only was a skill required, since it wasn't easy to swim across a river, but the potential escapee was visible from the river banks while the attempt was made. His data showed far more apprehended than those successful. In addition, all guards had been ordered to shoot to kill, if necessary. A corpse or two would offer a strong deterrent for future attempts.

In the days immediately after the border was closed, many refugees fled to the West using fake passports. But once the Stasi identified the vulnerability, multiple processes were implimented to eliminate future successes: rigid documentation of when foreigners entered East Berlin, limiting their stay to one day, and comparing entries to exits. Although it was difficult to gauge the continued success of these attempts, he suspected there were few. Lastly, the list identified risk takers, those who drove cars or trucks or trains through barriers at the border, typically through established checkpoints. Some survived, others didn't.

As security tightened, the more obvious escape paths were closing. Even the number of attempts were dwindling, since most were unsuccessful, at least according to Stasi agents stationed in West Berlin, some of whom were imbedded in the refugee center. Hofer's superiors had instructed him to eliminate escapes, even though each attempt was more innovative and daring, as if freedom was the most precious commodity on the planet, like flies to a spider.

Hofer closed the folder and left his office, walking down the stark corridors of Stasi headquarters. The walls were littered with plaques of Stasi slogans, hanging where portraits or landscapes might be placed in the business world. He left the building, taking an exit that led to the concrete parking garage. On the second level he found his Trabant, climbed in and turned the key in the ignition. The engine didn't start. He cursed and tried again, but nothing happened. He waited a moment, accustomed to the vehicle's idiosyncrasies, and tried it again. The motor coughed and spit and sputtered but then turned over. He put the car in gear and left the garage.

He drove through the streets of East Berlin, headed to the cemetery, site of the recent escape attempt. It took about twenty minutes, traffic on the city streets sparse during late morning. Once he reached his destination, he pulled his car up to the row of townhouses that flanked the Reconciliation Church, parking in front of the first one. He exited the vehicle and walked up the steps to the end unit and tapped on the door. A moment later it opened.

Kirstin Beck stood in the entrance, a bit surprised, but seemed to recover quickly. "What can I do for you, Mr. Hofer?" she asked.

"You remember me, Mrs. Beck?"

"Yes, of course I do," she said. "From the day the border was closed. And the failed escape attempt last week."

"We've made tremendous progress since then," he said. "Most areas of the city have progressed from strands of barbed wire to concrete barriers. That should keep the Western Imperialists out, don't you think?"

"Yes, I suppose," she said, although her face showed disagreement.

"May I come in, Mrs. Beck?" he asked. "I have a delicate matter to discuss with you."

"Of course," she said, opening the door. She led him into the parlor where he sat in the chair next to the radio. She sat across from him.

"I've come to ask for your help, Mrs. Beck," he said, watching her curiously, like a biological specimen.

She looked at him warily, as if suspecting a trap. "I'm not sure how I can help you, Mr. Hofer."

"It's actually a simple request," he said, shifting in his chair. "I'm seeking information about the escape attempt that was made last Saturday."

She shrugged and eyed him warily. "I really don't know anything about it," she said.

"Tell me what you do know," he said with a forced smile. "That's a good place to start."

She hesitated, as if remembering the events of that evening. "I woke when the searchlight came on," she said. "I was disoriented at first, wondering what was going on."

"And what did you do?"

"I checked to see if Steiner was awake, but he still slept soundly."

"And then what did you do, Mrs. Beck?"

"I looked out the window but couldn't tell where the light was coming from. After a moment I came downstairs to see what was happening."

"You went out the front door, into the street?"

"Yes, at first I did."

"What did you see outside?" he asked. He knew exactly what she had said on the night of the escape attempt. He was curious to see if her story was still the same.

"I didn't see anyone but guards."

"Did you stay out front, in the street?"

"No, I went around to the back of the house," she said, speaking very deliberately, as if reliving every step she had taken – or every step she said she had taken.

"Is that when I saw you on the pavement?"

"No, I had gone back into the house, through the kitchen," she replied. "A few moments later I went out again and looked behind the church."

"Yes, I know," he said, springing a trap to see if he snared her. "Your husband told me." He paused, waiting for her reaction.

"I didn't see anyone trying to escape," she said, not giving any indication she found his statement unusual, even though he mentioned discussing the issue with her husband. "I only saw border guards, some with dogs."

"What concerns me," he said, "is that the attempt occurred in the cemetery behind the church."

"I don't understand," she said, seeming confused.

"I'm inclined to think that the perpetrators were parishioners."

"Why?"

"They're most likely to have seen the weakness in the border fence."

"Someone visiting the cemetery may have, also," she pointed out.

"Perhaps," he said, eyeing her closely. "Or perhaps not."

"I don't know how I can help you, Mr. Hofer," she said with a sigh. "I've told you everything I know."

Karl Hofer stood, as if to go, and then paused. "Dr. Werner and Dieter Katz," he then stated firmly.

"What about them?"

"I want you to watch them."

"And why would I do that?"

"Because I told you to," he said sternly.

"What exactly am I supposed to watch?" she asked as she led him to the door.

"Everything," he said. "And whatever you see and hear, you will report to me."

"And what if I don't?"

"You'll never make contact with Lisette Haynor," he said coldly. "But if you agree to help me, you might."

45

"Mom, it's not a relationship," Marino said into the telephone. "I'm only trying to help her."

"Tony, do you think I don't know what's going on?" his mother scolded. "I know you better than you know yourself. And don't try to tell me differently."

"But I'm telling you the truth," he said, even though his heart was telling him otherwise.

"I think you care about this woman," his mother insisted.

Marino was quiet. His mother had a knack for being right, but he wasn't sure how. "I'll see what happens," he said softly. "She's a nice person, attractive on many different levels."

"You'll see," his mother said. "I'm right and you know it. You haven't realized it yet, but you will."

He smiled, imagining her face as she talked on the phone. "I'll let you know what happens," he said.

"Is she coming with you on Thanksgiving?"

"Thanksgiving?" he asked. "What are you talking about?"

"I'm making dinner," she said, as if he should have already known. "Just like I always do."

He rolled his eyes. "Mom, I'm not sure if I can be there for Thanksgiving. There's a lot going on right now."

"You need to find a way," she said, as if nothing on the planet could possibly be more important than her cooking. "And bring your lady friend. Your aunt and uncle are coming from Brooklyn. They'll want to meet her."

"But mom -"

"I'm making a wonderful dinner, you'll see," she said. "It's not just turkey. I'm making pasta, too. With my own special sauce. Your lady friend will love it. I bet she never had a nice Italian dinner."

Tony smiled, wishing he could give his mother a hug and a kiss. "I'll call you in a few days, mom."

"Tell her about Thanksgiving," she said. "She won't want to miss it."

Tony checked the mail after he hung up the phone. His package arrived from the U.S., a plain shipping envelope, a bit tattered, but it made it. He tore the edge and opened it, retrieving the passport along with a note that said: *If this doesn't work, I have another idea. Ned.*

Marino wondered what the cryptic message meant but assumed he would find out soon enough. He examined the passport closely. It was Swiss, red with a little white cross in the upper right, the color and texture authentic. He opened it and looked at the photo that depicted Kirstin Beck. The hair was about right, the face more angular, the eyes not as bright. There was a resemblance, especially for someone who had never seen her, and the height and weight were accurate. It was actually very well-done. It might work, unless given detailed scrutiny. He studied it a moment more, evaluating which route offered more risk: a passport photo that didn't perfectly match its owner, or doctoring the passport to replace the photo with a real one. He finally decided that if he was with Kirstin when she crossed the border, and the guards accepted his explanation as to why she wasn't registered when she entered East Berlin, they might only scan her passport. And a Swiss passport was safer than an American passport, since she spoke limited English.

He left his apartment for an appointment with Eileen Fischer, girlfriend of Dieter Katz. They met at a café on *Ackerstrasse*, a few blocks from his apartment building. Since the weather was pleasant, they sat at an outside table and ordered lunch: beef roulade, mash and gravy, and some red cabbage.

"I don't know what happened," Eileen said, referring to the failed escape. "We seemed to have everything well organized."

"It's hard to say," Marino replied. "Maybe we accidentally alerted the guards."

"Do you think it was the distraction?" Eileen asked. "Maybe they got suspicious when the car headlamps were pointed at them."

Marino was thoughtful for a moment. "I suppose we'll never know," he said.

"They also could have seen one of the refugees near the barbed wire," she suggested.

Marino hadn't considered one of the escapees attracting the guards' attention. Maybe someone stood or happened to move when one of the guards was looking in their direction. "That's possible," he said. "I suppose we should be thankful no one was captured or hurt."

Eileen was silent for a moment, as if wondering whether to continue the discussion. After a moment of silence, she spoke. "I told Dieter someone could have betrayed us," she said delicately. "Even though it's a distasteful scenario."

Marino was pensive, watching a young boy walk past the café, a stack of newspapers under his arm. "I think you're right," he said. "It's something we should consider."

"Dieter was adamant," she told him. "He claimed to trust

even those he didn't know, whoever the other escapees were, because they all had the same objective."

"The problem is," Marino said, "it doesn't have to be one of the escapees. They could tell a friend or relative, and they in turn could inform the Stasi."

"It might be best not to reveal the details of anything else we plan," she suggested. "At least not until the last minute."

"That's probably a good idea."

Eileen sipped her wine and, for a moment, seemed to study those at adjacent tables. Then she whispered, "What's next? We can't rest until we get them out."

He briefly considered keeping his plan a secret but realized there was no reason why he should. But he did decide not to reveal Kirstin's identity. "I have a fake Swiss passport," he told her, "compliments of an American friend."

"Only one passport?" Eileen asked. "What about the others?"

"We'll try it with my friend first," he said. "If it works, I'll get passports for the others."

"It'll be difficult," she said. "You cross the border, just as I do. Sometimes it's hard even for us."

"I realize that," he agreed.

"Do you expect her to just walk across?"

"That's the plan," he said.

"How will you explain the documentation?" she asked. "The guards won't have a record of her entering East Berlin."

"I have a diversion planned," he said. "A simple explanation meant to confuse them."

"Will you be with her?"

"Yes, I'll go over and get her," he said. "I'll give my passport to the guards first, tell them some story to create confusion, and then she'll pass through with me. I'm hoping the guards will examine my documents, but not pay much attention to hers."

"You might try passing through just after shift change," she suggested. "You can claim the guards on duty when you entered didn't properly document your arrival."

"That's an excellent idea," he said, as his plan began to formulate. "They've even make mistakes as I go back and forth, so an error is certainly plausible. But I'm still worried about the passport."

"Is it that bad?"

"No, it's authentic – the texture of the cover, the paper, the styling. The description – height and weight – is also accurate. But it's hard to describe someone over the telephone and have a picture imbedded in a document that's a perfect match."

"Does the photo resemble her at all?"

"Yes, to an extent," he replied. "It's a blond with blue eyes, shoulder length hair."

Eileen laughed. "That description fits half the women in East Berlin."

"That's what I'm hoping for," Marino said, smiling. "Confusion."

After a moment, the smile faded from Eileen's face and she leaned toward him. "What if it doesn't work?"

"I don't even want to think about it."

"You'll cross at *Friedrichstrasse,* at Checkpoint Charlie?"

"Yes, we have to," he said. "That's the crossing for foreign nationals."

"Can I tell Dieter?"

He thought for a moment. If they really were betrayed, it wasn't worth the risk. But the most likely suspects were friends of friends or unknown relatives, rather than the main players. "Yes, I suppose," he said finally, "if he doesn't know already. But he mustn't tell anyone."

"Is there another plan, just in case?"

"Yes, there is, but it gets significantly harder."

"I thought you were a writer," Eileen said.

"I am," he said. "And a Philadelphia Phillies fan."

"What's that?" she asked, confused.

"Baseball," he said. He studied the perplexed look on her face. "Never mind. It's a game. Why did you ask if I was a writer?"

"Because I don't understand why you're developing escape plans," she replied.

"Actually, I'm not," he said. "I met some refugees at the center and learned quite a bit from them. It seems that the easy escape paths – oversights in border protection – are now almost non-existent. Especially since the barbed wire is being replaced by a concrete wall."

"There are still canals and rivers for those who can swim."

"They're more closely patrolled now," he said. "There are boats and additional guards on the river banks. It might still be doable for strong swimmers, but not for the average person."

"What other options are there?"

"A few groups of college students with relatives in the East built tunnels. Some have worked; others haven't."

She seemed surprised. "Where would we even start?"

"I'm not sure," he admitted, "We need people to do the digging, and again, it would have to be people we could trust, and a suitable location on each side of the border. We would also need money."

"To pay the diggers?" she asked.

"And for supplies," he said. "Then there's the excavated material. Where will we put it all? It's a big operation."

"I'm willing to help," she said, but then smiled sheepishly. "But I don't have any money and I can't miss too many college classes."

"Thanks," he said. "I need all the help I can get." He then paused, pensive, knowing a tunnel was a monumental undertaking, far riskier than their last attempt. "Let's hope the passport works."

46

Marino returned to the refugee center and again met with Johann, the college student who had escaped from East Berlin. After a few minutes of pleasantries in the main office lobby, an older man entered, a bit stooped, with gray hair and round spectacles.

"This is Otto," Johann said.

Marino shook the man's hand. "I'm Tony Marino."

"He's the American I told you about," Johann said.

"Thanks for agreeing to see me," Marino said.

"It's my pleasure," Otto replied. "Please, come with me."

Johann walked toward the exit. "I'll let you two discuss business," he said with a wave.

"Thanks, Johann," Marino called as Otto led him into a nearby office.

The room was functional, a desk with some metal filing cabinets, and a small oval table flanked by two leather chairs. Otto guided him to the table and Marino sat down.

"Johann told me about the passport," Otto said. "It's not as easy as it was when the border first closed."

"I've been told it's difficult," Marino said. "But I see no other option."

"It's crucial to convince the guards that, whoever you are bringing out, entered East Berlin earlier that day but wasn't properly registered."

"I think I have a plan," Marino said. "I go to the East often, and I've developed a rapport with some of the guards. I actually brought them toothbrushes once."

"But don't assume they'll help you," Otto warned. "Regardless of how friendly they are."

"No, I don't," Marino said. "But I thought my friend and I could exit East Berlin just as the shifts changed. I could claim a familiarity with the day shift guards and explain to the afternoon shift that a mistake was made documenting my friend's entry. She'll pretend to be my fiancée."

Otto was quiet for a moment, perhaps considering Marino's chance for success. "It might work," he said with a slight shrug. "We had a refugee here last week who crossed the border with her sister-in-law's passport. The guard barely checked her documents and never verified she entered East Berlin earlier in the day. He merely waved her through."

"I hope we get the same guard," Marino said enthusiastically.

Otto smiled. "If only it were that simple."

"Assuming we are successful," Marino then said, "can you help my friend get documented as a West Berliner?"

"Yes, I think so," Otto said. "We do it all the time."

"Thank you so much," Marino said, "I appreciate it."

"What are your plans if your friend isn't successful?"

Marino paused, wondering how much information to reveal. After an awkward moment, he continued. "I would try a tunnel," he said.

Otto studied him for a moment, perhaps searching for

sincerity. "A tunnel takes money," he advised him, "as well as the right people."

"I think I can get the money," Marino said.

"Good," Otto replied. "Because I can get the right people."

———

Marino returned to his apartment and called New York. As he was waiting for his connection, he wondered if the Stasi bugged the phones. They probably did, but he doubted they were sophisticated enough to trace the call. At least he had never heard any suspicious noises on the line or saw unusual activity on the street outside of his apartment.

"How's the passport?" Ned Simpson asked when he answered the phone.

"The photo isn't perfect," Marino said. "Not that I expected it to be."

"We did the best we could with the description you gave me."

"I know," he replied. "I'm not faulting you. But I have to be careful. We're putting her life in danger."

"If it's too risky, don't try it," Simpson suggested. "Find someone to alter the passport with her photo."

"That's just as dangerous."

"We can always try something else."

Marino thought for a moment, picturing the guards during his different border crossings. Some were very diligent. Others barely looked at his passport, as Otto had indicated. "I suppose it depends on the guards," he said. "Some are very observant."

"Don't take unnecessary risks," Simpson said. "Be prepared to back out if you have to."

"We can always leave, say we forgot something and claim we'll return shortly."

"Will you be with her?"

"Yes," Marino said. "I'll provide my passport first, so maybe they'll ask me all the questions."

"When are you going to do this?"

"Probably tomorrow around 6 p.m., just after shift change for the guards."

"Call me when you get back to the West."

"I will," Marino said.

"And good luck to you."

"Thanks," Marino said. "Before you go, what was your message about? The note you sent with the passport."

The phone line was quiet for a moment, Simpson apparently thinking. "Try the passport," he said. "If that doesn't work, we'll talk."

"Talk about what?"

"Just another idea," he said. "One that'll sell a lot of books."

Marino was quiet. He was interested in saving lives, not selling a lot of books. Although he had to admit it sounded good. "I'll call you tomorrow."

He hung up the phone and went into the kitchen for dinner. He heated up some vegetable soup and cooked some Bratwurst and sauerkraut, washing it down with a *Frisches* beer. The American military channel was on the radio and he listened patiently, waiting for the ball scores. Not surprisingly, the Phils lost again. They got walloped by the Dodgers, ten to nothing. But with only a few games left, it really didn't matter. They would probably finish with the worst record in baseball. Maybe it was time to think about next year.

He missed Philly – his mom and her mouth-watering Italian cooking, her homemade pasta and spaghetti sauce, the bar on Shunk Street, just off of Broad, where he would stop for a few beers, the Mummer's Day Parade on New Year's Day. Philadelphia was like no other city in the world. You knew your neighbors like you knew your own family. Everyone was friends

– close, tight-knit. Just like it should be. That's what America was all about.

After he finished his second beer, he sat next to the window, tablet and binoculars in hand, waiting for Kirstin to appear. When he saw the light come on in her window, he checked the border guards to make sure they couldn't see him and held up his pad. It read: *Have passport. Meet tomorrow at 6 p.m.*

When he put the tablet down and picked up his binoculars, he saw her writing on the chalkboard. She held it up. *Where?*

He tore his last written page from the tablet and scribbled on the next. *"Berlin Café – on Friedrichstrasse."*

He put his pad down, again checked the border guards, and peered through his binoculars, waiting until she held up her chalkboard. It read: *I'll be there.*

A second later, her light went out and she vanished from view. He waited, watching the room, but saw only darkness. And then, a few minutes later, he saw two silhouettes by the window.

47

"What are you doing?" Steiner asked.

"I was getting some papers," Kirstin replied.

"Standing by the window in a dark room?" he asked suspiciously.

"I was checking to see if the wall was finished."

"It's been done for days," he said. "You know that."

She felt beads of sweat on the back of her neck. "But they're still building the watch tower."

"Why did you turn the light out when I walked in?" he asked, glaring at her.

She tried to think of an excuse but couldn't. She walked toward him, so he wouldn't come near the bookshelf and find the chalkboard shoved behind it.

He stood in the doorway. His face was stern, his eyes accusing, as if he caught her doing something she shouldn't be doing. "Kirstin," he scolded. "I asked you a question."

She smiled, her heart racing, trying to act normally. "It was easier to see outside with the light out."

He walked to the window, eyeing her strangely. He stood at the sill and glanced out. A lone guard walked the wall. It was about twelve feet high with a circular top that made scaling it more difficult.

Kirstin moved behind him and looked out. Tony's light was still on, and he stood at the window, binoculars to his eyes. She had to distract Steiner; she had to do something to get him away from the window.

"There's nothing to see," he muttered. "No workmen, just a single guard." He turned to face her. "I don't know what you were looking at."

"I told you," she said, trying to hold his attention until Tony turned off his light. "I wanted to see if they were done. And they are. At least with the wall."

"But you knew they were done," he countered.

"I assumed they were," she said, babbling to keep his eyes trained on her, and not out the window. "But I wanted to see if they're putting barbed wire on the top."

"If they were, it would have been done already."

"It looks like the watchtower will be done soon, too," she continued. "Maybe then they won't have guards patrolling the wall. They can watch from the tower."

"I'm sure they'll have both. Why wouldn't they?"

"Yes, I suppose you're right."

He turned again, looking out the window. "I suppose part of the graveyard will always be in the West," he said. "It's strange, and a little morbid."

She saw the light go out in Tony's apartment and breathed a sigh of relief. She started for the hallway, trying to get Steiner away from the window

"Where are you going?"

"Downstairs," she replied. "I was going to sit with you while you listened to the radio."

"What about your papers?"

"I forgot," she said, laughing lightly, but knowing she was acting suspiciously. "And that's what I came up here for." She grabbed a folder from her desk, using the light that filtered in from the hallway, and left the room.

A few seconds later, Steiner followed her down the steps. When they were sitting in their respective chairs, and the radio volume was lowered just a bit, he looked up from his schoolwork. "Don't forget about dinner tomorrow night."

She couldn't hide her surprise. "What dinner?"

He frowned. "I thought I told you," he said.

"I don't remember any dinner."

"Yes, it's at the college," he said. He paused, pensive. "I was sure it was tomorrow. But maybe not. Didn't I tell you?"

"No," she replied. "You never mentioned it."

"I'll find out for sure."

She tried to think of an excuse, a reason why she couldn't go, but she really couldn't. It was easy to slip out of the house with little notice. She could claim she was going shopping, that a friend told her something scarce had suddenly become available: bananas or cosmetics or coffee. But it was difficult to pre-arrange anything, especially to avoid a social function that had apparently been planned for some time.

"You look annoyed," he said.

"No, not annoyed," she replied, trying to appear nonchalant. "Just surprised. And I'm wondering what to wear. Maybe that blue dress."

"I'll let you know tomorrow," he said as he went back to his papers.

Kirstin opened her folder, withdrew a sheet of paper, and pretended to read it. If she went to the dinner, she had no way of contacting Tony. But if she didn't go, Steiner would know something was wrong. He was already suspicious, and with valid reasons. He wasn't sure about her whereabouts during the failed escape, he could have seen her in the library while his classroom was being remodeled, and now he caught her standing at the window in the dark – staring at nothing.

He was cunning and probably prepared a trap, waiting for her to walk into it so he could keep her caged and controlled. It must be an intricate plan, drenched in deceit, waiting for when she least expected it. She knew she couldn't trust him. And she probably never could.

48

Just before noon, Kirstin Beck stepped into the Church of Reconciliation and sat in the rear pew on the left side. The church was empty, as expected for a weekday, and she took a moment to admire the awe-inspiring interior, something she had never done during Sunday service. She sat quietly and thought about her conversation with Karl Hofer, demanding cooperation or she would never see her daughter. She wondered how he knew about Lisette – from government records or had Steiner told him. Or maybe it was both.

She kneeled and was deep in prayer when she heard the door open. A moment later Dr. Werner appeared and sat in the pew in front of her. He opened a Bible, thumbing through the pages.

"Dieter should be here shortly," she whispered.

The doctor gave no indication he heard her. He simply sat, immersed in the Scriptures, occasionally glancing up at the altar. It seemed he suspected someone may have seen them come in and he didn't want to arouse suspicion, pretending he was only there to worship.

Five minutes later, the door opened again. Dieter Katz came

down the center aisle and entered the last pew, moving a few feet from Kirstin. "I'm sorry I'm late," he whispered.

Kirstin scanned the church, studying the pews and presbytery, ensuring they were alone. "We shouldn't stay too long," she said. "Are you both sure no one saw you?"

"Yes, I was careful," Werner replied.

"I was, too," Katz added. "I circled the block, just to be sure I wasn't followed."

"Good," Kirstin said, satisfied they were safe. "I wanted to share the progress made on our escape attempts."

"We have to hurry," Werner hissed. "The Stasi are still threatening me. And it gets worse every day."

"It's not much better for me," Katz said. "The sooner we do something the better."

"We'll make another attempt," Kirstin told them, "but using a different tactic."

"Which is what?" Werner asked, looking nervously at the entrance.

"I have a fake Swiss passport," Kirstin said. "I'm going to try to cross the border tomorrow night."

"What about us?" Katz protested.

"We have to get out, too," Werner echoed.

"If I'm successful, then you'll follow."

"But how?" Katz asked. "We can't even communicate."

"Yes, we can," she said. "I'll help from the West and Eileen and my American friend can take messages back and forth."

Werner and Katz were silent for a moment, weighing risks and rewards. Werner finally spoke: "Do you think this passport will work?"

"I don't know," Kirstin admitted. "But it's worth trying."

"It's not as easy as it was just a few weeks ago," Katz warned her. "The guards are better at finding false documents."

"And all visitors to the East are registered," Werner added.

"How will you explain that there's no record of your entry into the East?"

She hesitated, knowing he identified the most critical element of the proposed escape. "I'm not sure," she replied. "But my American friend seems to have a solution."

"It's too dangerous," Katz said. "There must be an easier way."

"It's all we have right now," Kirstin said, wondering if she was already too late. "But I think the American is developing other methods."

"The concrete wall has only been built through the city proper," Katz said. "Maybe we can escape through the suburbs where there's still barbed wire."

"We'll keep that as an option," Kirstin assured him.

"Who is this American?" Katz asked. "Is it the man Eileen met?"

"Yes, it is," Kirstin replied.

"Do we have to pay him?" Katz asked suspiciously.

She thought for a moment, wondering what motivated Marino. "No, he never mentioned money," she said. "But he is a writer. He may publish an article or a book about our exploits."

"And profit from our misery," Katz said with disgust.

"No, he's not like that," Kirstin replied. "But telling stories is in his blood. He won't be able to resist writing about it."

"It doesn't matter," Werner said. "As long as he gets us out."

"I agree," Katz said reluctantly. "But I don't necessarily like it."

"He's a good man," Kirstin assured them. "And I think he'll help us all escape."

"You're sure?" Katz asked.

"Yes, I'm positive."

"And our families, too?" Werner asked.

"Yes, everyone," Kirstin replied. "I'm not sure how, but I'm confident he will."

"There are six of us," Katz reminded her.

She paused, thinking of all who might want to escape, should a method be available.

"Make a list of friends and family that want to get out, also," she requested. "Assuming I'm successful tomorrow night, we'll start planning the next escape."

"It's too many people for fake passports," Katz countered.

Kirstin hesitated, knowing he was right. But she had faith in Tony. "He has another plan. It just isn't ready yet."

"What is it?" Werner asked. "I'm desperate."

"I'm not sure," she admitted. "But trust me. I won't let you down. The second I'm free, I'll work to free you."

"How will we know you made it?" Katz asked.

She thought for a moment. "We'll meet at Frieda's Café on *Anklamer Strasse*, day after tomorrow at noon. If I'm not there, it means I escaped."

"Or it means you were caught," Katz said ominously.

49

S hortly after 2 p.m., Steiner Beck sat in the office behind his classroom. He had another class to teach at 2:20, so he used the time to relax, sitting quietly, drinking a glass of soda since coffee wasn't available. For a moment, he thought about Kirstin's behavior the evening before, standing in the dark, looking out the window. Although he wasn't sure what she was doing, he could tell she didn't want him to know what it was. But he was determined to find out.

He grabbed the black telephone perched on his desk, put the receiver to his ear, and dialed the number to his house. On the fourth ring, it was answered.

"Hello?" Kirstin asked.

"Hello, darling," he said. "What are you doing?

"I'm editing, as usual," she replied. "How is your day?"

"I just finished a class and have a short break before my next one."

"Did you find out about the dinner?"

"Yes, I did."

"And?"

"It's being held at the college, in the cafeteria. Apparently, there's quite a crowd attending – even rumors the Minister of Education will be there."

"What's it for?" she asked.

"Some celebration, I'm told. It seems the school met its five-year targets for curriculum revisions. They'll probably have speeches and awards during dinner."

"I wish you would have told me it was tonight," she said, her irritation evident.

"Tonight?" Steiner asked. "Did I say tonight?"

"Yes," she replied. "That's what you said last night."

"No, darling, the dinner isn't tonight," he clarified. "It's tomorrow night."

"Fine," she said, sounding relieved. "What shall I wear?"

"Maybe the blue dress," he replied. "You always look good in that. And wear your hair up. I like it better that way."

"All right, I will," she replied. "What time will you be home?"

He hesitated, thinking about the rest of his day. "I suppose near six. Why, what are you cooking for dinner?"

"I'm not sure," she replied. "Probably sauerbraten. There's a shortage of potatoes, so maybe some cabbage or turnips with it."

"That should be fine."

"Do you mind eating later?" she asked.

"Why?" he asked. "Can't we eat when I get home?"

"I'm not sure I'll be here," she said. "Kappel Grocers may have some bananas and the Berlin Department Store might have stockings and cosmetics. I was going to wait in the queues."

He thought her response unusual – just like her recent behavior. She normally shopped during the day, early morning, if possible. Why would she shop in the evening? "Won't every-thing be gone by then?" he asked.

"One of the other editors told me they're late deliveries," she explained. "I don't want to miss them."

"All right," he replied. "What time will you be home?"

"I'm not sure, maybe half past seven, eight at the latest."

He was annoyed, and he didn't really care if her excuse was valid or not. "Why don't you have dinner with me and then run errands?" he asked.

"I don't want to miss anything," she explained. "It'll be gone if I wait too long."

"Just try to be home when I get there," he said warily, wondering why shopping was so important. "I can do without bananas and you can do without stockings and make-up."

"I'll see," she said softly. "But I'll have dinner prepared even if I'm not here. If you're hungry, you can heat it up."

"Fine," he said curtly.

"Goodbye," she replied.

He hung up the phone and looked across the desk.

"This promises to be an interesting evening," said Karl Hofer, seated in a chair across from Steiner Beck.

50

Otto, the administrator at the refugee center in *Marienfelde*, arranged the meeting. And when Martino entered the lobby the next morning, he found a young man waiting for him. He was in his early twenties, average height and weight, blonde hair parted on the left and green eyes. "I'm Tony Marino," he said, his hand outstretched.

The young man shook it firmly. "Josef Kramer," he replied. "I believe you may have an interesting proposition for me."

"Possibly," Marino replied. "You're a student?"

"Yes, in the structural engineering program at the Technical University," Kramer replied.

The door opened and a man entered, middle-aged. He nodded, walked past them, and went into an adjacent hallway. Marino scanned the lobby, searching for somewhere private, but didn't find it. He looked out the window to a café across the street.

"Would you like a cup of coffee?" Marino asked, motioning to the café.

"Sure," Kramer replied, and followed him to the door.

They sat at an outdoor table, the autumn weather pleasant,

and watched pedestrians passing by. They each ordered coffee and a croissant, and then continued the conversation.

"I'm told you're trying to get several refugees across the border," Kramer said.

"I am," Marino acknowledged. "And I was told you have a similar interest."

"I do," Kramer replied. "I also have a method that might be successful."

"And what is that?"

"A tunnel," Kramer replied.

"I assume you'll use your engineering expertise to build it," Marino said. "I want to ensure it's safe."

"It's not that difficult to dig a tunnel," Kramer informed him.

Marino smiled. "I'm not sure I would agree," he said. "I couldn't do it. You make it sound easier than it is."

Kramer seemed to appreciate the compliment. "I suppose it does take some skill."

"What would your design entail?"

Kramer sipped his coffee, took a bite from his croissant, and then chewed thoughtfully. For a moment he studied a delivery truck across the street, unloading crates of fresh fruit for a grocery store. "We obviously need a starting point and an end point – both as close to the border as possible."

"Would one hundred fifty feet work?" Marino asked. "Two hundred at the most?"

"Easily."

"How would it be built?"

"That depends," Kramer said. "There are factors that impact construction – soil consistency, is there a road above the tunnel – variables like that. And it costs money."

"I know you need material," Marino said. "And I suppose the diggers would be paid?"

"Not necessarily," Kramer replied evasively.

Marino considered his options. If he was able to finance tunnel construction, and people volunteered to dig it, then they should try to get as many people as possible out of East Berlin. "Volunteers would certainly help control the cost. I assume we can trust them?"

"I'll make sure we can.," Kramer replied. "But even if they volunteer, it'll still be expensive. We'll need wooden posts, plywood, lights."

"Electricity," Marino interjected.

"Yes, or multiple flashlights," Kramer said. "We'll also need some sort of ventilation, maybe two small fans blowing air in and out, tools for the excavation and a place to put the soil. We'll have a lot of excavated material."

"What size will the tunnel be?"

"About three feet square, maybe fifteen feet deep."

Marino thought for a moment. It was a huge undertaking. But if he could find the money, he would try it. There were so many people he could help, so many families he could reunite. He looked at his watch, adjusted the hours to Philadelphia time, and let his mind wander to the Phillies game. Maybe they were winning. "Do you follow American baseball?" he asked.

Kramer shrugged, surprised by the question. "No, sorry," he said. "I don't know anything about it."

"I'm a Philadelphia Phillies fan," Marino told him. "Obsessed with the game."

Kramer smiled, as if suspecting a joke. "Is that important?"

"No, not really," Marino said. "But if we build a tunnel, we'll be spending a lot of time together. And I don't have anyone to talk to about baseball – the teams, my favorite players, the World Series."

Kramer laughed. "I suppose I can learn."

"Or I can learn soccer," Marino said with a shrug. "But it doesn't matter. There's always the radio." He paused and sipped his coffee, visualizing the operation, before again focusing on their objective. "Let's say I have a location and I can get money for material. How much would you need?"

Kramer rubbed his chin, mentally calculating costs. "I'm not sure," he said. "Probably twenty or thirty thousand marks."

Marino was surprised. "That's a lot of money for braces and shovels," he said warily. "Is that with volunteers, or does it include pay for the diggers, yourself included?"

"No pay," Kramer said. "The diggers won't ask for money, nor will I. They have loved ones in the East that they want to get out. For me, it's my cousin. He'll be difficult to rescue, a definite risk, but it's a condition for me."

"You'll do it as long as your cousin is among the escapees?" Marino asked, for clarification.

"And his family," Kramer insisted. "And that's not negotiable."

"I understand," Marino said, calculating how many people would have access to the tunnel. "I need to get six or seven out."

Kramer thought for a moment. "Between those you want to help, my friends and family, and the volunteers' loved ones, we're probably talking about thirty people, maybe more."

"Is that doable?"

"Who knows?" Kramer said as he shrugged and smiled. "We'll be the first to try."

51

"I'm helping Kirstin escape in a few hours," Marino said into the telephone.

"Be careful," Ned Simpson cautioned. "If you suspect anything is wrong, don't do it."

"I won't," Marino replied. "It's not worth it."

"Do you have any other ideas?"

"Yes, the administrator at the refugee center recommended a tunnel expert to me."

"A tunnel would make a great story," Simpson said. "Especially with a bit about all of the refugees' lives – you know, their motivation for fleeing socialism and all of that."

"It would make a good book," Marino was forced to admit.

What's your motivation?" Simpson asked. "I understand the girl, you're probably falling for her and don't even realize it. But what about the others?"

Marino was quiet for a moment, contemplative. He had never been very good at helping anyone, but now he was trying. The refugees relied on him, they trusted him, and their only path to success led through him. It was satisfying, very rewarding, and he was sure it would feel even better when as many refugees as possible were standing in West Berlin. He was changing, and he felt better for it. Maybe the escape attempts helped him as much as the refugees. "I want to make their lives better," he said softly.

Simpson let out a low whistle. "Tony, Tony, Tony," he chuckled. "This broad really hooked you, didn't she?"

"No, it's not that at all," Marino replied defensively. "It's just something I have to do."

"If you say so," Simpson said, as if it wasn't the answer he expected. After an awkward moment passed, he continued. "What's involved with the tunnel?"

"We need money for supplies: wood, tools, and equipment like lights and fans. And we have to finalize locations."

"How much money do they need?"

"Thirty thousand marks for supplies, which leaves nothing for those that dig the tunnel."

"How many will be digging?"

"Probably six, maybe eight."

"Do they want to be paid?"

"Supposedly not," Marino told him. "They just want access to the tunnel. They have friends and family in the East who want to escape."

Simpson paused, as if considering what Green Mansion Publishing could get out of the situation. "If we build the tunnel, and everything works as planned, how many would escape?"

Marino assumed Kramer gave him minimal numbers. It would probably be higher, especially once people knew about it. "I would guess between thirty and forty."

Simpson whistled again. "That would be an amazing escape. And a fantastic book. How long will it take you to write it?"

"I don't know," Marino replied. "I haven't even thought about it."

"If you write the book as they dig the tunnel, like a documentary, and only have to write the ending when the escape occurs, can you have it to me a month afterwards?"

"I'm not sure, Ned. That's a tight schedule. I have to interview everyone after the escape."

"Start thinking about it now. And include the failed escape at the cemetery and whatever happens with the fake passport. I really think we're on to something."

Marino paused, reflective. "I don't want to use them as props for a story," he said reluctantly. "They're desperate."

"I don't see it like that," Simpson countered. "You'll be giving the free world a look at a Socialistic society, complete with all of its failures, and how desperate people are to escape it. They'll do anything to get to the West, to obtain their freedom. No one will ever again dispute the superiority of democracy over socialism. It's a classic story of good versus evil."

"Isn't that a bit dramatic?" Marino asked.

"No, I don't think it is. People will risk their lives to escape socialism. The world needs to know that. You have to write this book. It's the opportunity of a lifetime."

Marino still wasn't convinced. "I agree it's a good story," he admitted, "one that has to be told. But I feel like I'm profiting from someone else's misery."

"I'll tell you what," Simpson offered. "If you agree to write the book, Green Mansion Publishing will provide thirty thousand marks for the supplies needed for the tunnel. And I'll throw in another thirty thousand for the diggers when the tunnel is finished and everyone escapes."

Marino was shocked. "Sixty thousand marks?" he asked. "That's a lot of money. Almost three years pay for the average worker."

"I'll get it back from book sales," Simpson said nonchalantly. "And you'll be a rich man from the royalties, I promise you."

Marino was pensive, it seemed like a good situation – everyone got what they wanted. "All right, I'll do it."

"There's just two conditions," Simpson clarified.

"What are they?"

"You submit a completed draft one month after the escape that includes some personal stories of the refugees – you can change the names."

"Agreed."

"I want a photographer to document progress, take photos of the tunnel and the refugees."

"I'm not sure I can agree to that."

"Why?"

"The refugees have friends and relatives in the East," Marino explained. "We may be putting their lives in danger."

"What about this," Simpson proposed. "We won't use their real names and we won't show faces. If there's a face shot, we'll blur it out for the book."

"Agreed."

52

M arino went to the Berlin Café just before six p.m. He ordered wine, which wasn't available, but somehow coffee was. It wasn't as fresh as coffee in the West, but he drank it anyway.

His entry into East Berlin had been non-eventful, as it should be with an American passport. The guards had nothing to fear. No one was trying to escape into East Berlin; they were only trying to get out. It would be different when he left with Kirstin. Guards would examine their documents closely, challenging the missing record of Kirstin's entry, and demand answers they might not be able to provide.

When six p.m. arrived and Kirstin had not, Marino got anxious, studying the nearby streets, looking a block ahead to the border. He saw nothing unusual. He suspected if she was delayed, or she couldn't come, it was because of her husband. She was convinced he was Stasi, and Marino wondered if he had anything to do with their first failed escape attempt.

Stasi informers were frightening. They were family, friends, even children, who reported what they saw or heard – or worse yet, what they thought they saw or heard. They informed on random people, friends and family, strangers, even policeman who didn't seem totally committed to the socialist agenda. He looked at those around him, an elderly couple at a nearby table, a policeman enjoying the cup of coffee that was so rarely available, two parents with young children having dinner. Were any of them Stasi?

He expanded his observations, watching people walk down the street, young and old, single and in pairs, a small group of teenagers. Could they be trusted? Were any watching him while they passed? Had any circled the block, finding him suspicious, sitting alone and drinking coffee, which was so treasured in East Berlin? Or maybe the couple sitting on a bench across the street, waiting for the S-bahn, were really watching him. How could he know? He wondered how anyone lived in the East without losing their minds. Maybe you got used to it, the gradual loss of freedom until you didn't have any at all.

He saw Kirstin approach fifteen minutes later. She walked towards him, glancing over her shoulder as if fearful of being followed, watching those around her. She was trying to be cautious, at least that's how it seemed, but in doing so she actually looked suspicious. He could tell she walked in a world she had never before travelled.

She sat beside him, smiled, and briefly studied those around her. "I'm sorry I'm late," she whispered.

"Don't worry," he said. "We have time. I want to cross just after the guards change shifts."

"Is that important?"

"Yes," he said. "I suspect they'll be reviewing records from the prior shift. We'll have to explain why you're not registered as having entered East Berlin."

"What are you going to say?"

"That you're my fiancée, we came in an hour ago to have dinner with friends, and that the prior guards failed to document your entry."

"Why would they do that?"

"I'm going to claim they were distracted because I gave them toothbrushes, per a prior agreement, and they were so thankful they neglected their duties."

"Do you think it'll work?" Kirstin asked, her voice trembling.

"We'll see," Marino said. "I suspect they don't care who enters but are much more interested in who exits."

"Should we go now?" she asked anxiously.

"Yes, I suppose," he said, eyeing his watch. "We're cutting it close."

They rose from the table and strolled down *Friedrichstrasse* to Checkpoint Charlie. She put her hand on his elbow, as if trying to prove they were more than friends, or perhaps subconsciously showing that she thought they were. It was hard not to develop feelings for someone when you shared a nightmare, one dependent, the other so committed. He smiled – how had he changed from totally non-committal to totally committed? It got complicated when the person you were helping was attractive on so many levels, an intelligent match devoted to the written word. She was almost a mirror image of him: West versus East, man versus woman. And she was apparently available, trapped in a marriage that had long ago ended. But it was a potentially dangerous situation. They needed logic to succeed, not emotion.

As they approached the crossing they saw guards holding a young woman, around thirty, with blond hair. They came closer, watching the scene unfold.

"No, you'll remain here," a guard was saying. "At least until we prove your passport is valid."

"I assure you, my documents are in order," the young woman said angrily. "I am a Swiss citizen."

Tony looked at Kirstin warily. "Let's wait a minute," he said.

He glanced at his watch. It was six-thirty, just when they

planned to cross. A blonde woman about thirty years of age, with a Swiss passport, was being challenged by the border guards. Kirstin was blond, about thirty years old, and had a fake Swiss passport. Something wasn't right, but he didn't know what. The whole scene was surreal, almost a dream.

"Let's turn the corner," he said.

She sensed something wrong and merely followed. They sat on a bench, as if waiting for the tram.

Two guards held the woman, one with her documents in his hand. She continued protesting, but now more loudly. A black Trabant sped down *Friedrichstrasse,* travelling faster than surrounding traffic. The car screeched to a halt in front of the guards. A man got out, dressed in a black suit, studying the area around him, glancing furtively up and down the intersecting boulevards.

"Hofer!" Kirstin exclaimed.

"Who's Hofer?" Marino asked.

"He's looking over here!" She grabbed him around the neck, pulled him close, and kissed him, tentatively at first, but then a bit more forcefully. The kiss lasted several seconds, started as a diversion, but ended far differently. It was Kirstin who broke away.

"I'm sorry," she said, eyeing the border warily. "He's a Stasi officer, highly placed. I couldn't let him see me."

Marino didn't reply. He pulled her close and kissed her again. She didn't resist. They clung to each other, tentatively and then more passionately, until Kirstin reluctantly pulled away. She gazed at him vacantly, as if feeling emotions that had long been dormant.

"That was nice," she whispered.

He smiled and noticed the S-bahn approaching. "Come on," he said quietly, not wanting the moment to end. "We have to get out of here."

They boarded the tram and, as it pulled away, watched an

aggravated Karl Hofer, animated and frustrated, handing the blond woman her passport and letting her cross the border.

"That was a trap," Tony said softly, nuzzling his face in Kirstin's hair, drinking the scent of her perfume. "They were looking for you."

53

I t was just after 7:30 when Kirstin walked through the front door of her townhouse. Steiner was sitting in the parlor, listening to the radio – the news program he seemed to favor. He looked toward the door as it opened, and then rose from his chair and approached her.

"What happened?" he asked. "I was worried about you."

"I left your dinner on a plate in the refrigerator," she said. "Didn't you heat it up?"

"Yes, I did, but that was almost two hours ago. Where have you been?"

"I told you I might wait in line," she said. "And I saw a friend from the publishing company so we stopped for a glass of wine and something to eat."

"You had dinner?" he asked, seeming to relax.

"Yes, I did," she replied. She then fished through her pocketbook, retrieving cosmetics that had been there for weeks. But she knew Steiner wouldn't know the difference. "And I got this – rouge, lipstick, and some eye shadow."

"That's what you waited in line for?"

"Yes, with dozens of others," she replied. "But it was worth it."

"Where did you see your friend?"

"She was just ahead of me in line."

"Where did you eat?"

She felt beads of perspiration forming on the back of her neck. He was suspicious, and she was being questioned, just as the Stasi would question any suspect. She had to be careful. She didn't know what he already knew. She could have been observed, other Stasi agents could have been watching her.

"Kirstin?" he probed, waiting for a reply.

"I'm sorry," she said. "The radio program had my attention for a moment. We ate at the Berlin Café."

"On *Friedrichstrasse*?"

"Yes, by the department store." She intentionally didn't mention the checkpoint, the most common landmark on the boulevard.

"Seems a bit far for some cosmetics."

"Far? Really, Steiner? Why don't you buy my lipstick the next time?"

"I thought there was a shortage of wine?" he asked abruptly.

She hesitated. It seemed a question someone asked when they already knew the answer. "It wasn't really wine," she said trying to recover, "although that's what they called it. It didn't have alcohol in it. It was probably some sort of juice."

He studied her for a moment, as if digesting her statement. Then he turned away, walking back to his chair. "Karl Hofer asked about you," he said.

Her heart started to race. She felt like a mouse running on a wheel, moving faster but not going anywhere. Or a fly about to be caught in a spider's web. "Hofer?" she asked. "What did he want?"

"He's concerned about you," he said. "But I assured him there's nothing to worry about."

"Why would he be concerned?"

"He's focused on how you helped Dieter Katz the day the border was closed," he told her. "He didn't actually say it, but it's my impression he thinks you're trying to escape. I told him you're not that foolish."

"That's ridiculous," she said as she sat on the chair across from him. "I only helped Dieter because the guards attacked him."

"I don't think Hofer likes Dieter."

"I thought he was rehabilitated?"

"He goes to the right school and will learn a good trade," he said. "There are no guarantees, but hopefully he'll become a border guard or a Stasi agent."

She suppressed her anger. "Hofer should be suspicious," she said testily. "Dieter was a brilliant student. If he remained at the Technical University in the West, he probably would have been a doctor or a scientist. But maybe we should be grateful that we'll have another border guard. The profession seems to be in such high demand."

His eyes widened and his face paled. "Kirstin, how could you say that?"

"How could Hofer say he rehabilitated Dieter?" she asked. "He didn't rehabilitate him. He destroyed him."

"Dieter was provided an opportunity that few in his situation warrant," Steiner said. "He should be grateful."

"I'm sure he is," Kirstin muttered sarcastically.

"Hofer is worried about Dieter's western girlfriend. Eileen, I think her name is."

She felt her cheeks flush, both from anger and because she knew she had already said more than she should have. "He should worry about something else," she said, "Like ending the shortages."

Steiner didn't reply. "I'm concerned about you, Kirstin," he said gravely. "Very concerned."

54

The following day at noon, Tony Marino approached Frieda's Café, tucked in a row of quaint buildings on *Anklame Strasse*. The weather was pleasant, the few outdoor tables scattered along the pavement mostly occupied. He saw Kirstin sitting in a corner, two men at a table beside her, one older and the second young, perhaps a college student. She was chatting as if she knew them when he walked up and pretended to search for a seat. After a moment passed, he motioned to an empty chair beside Kirstin.

"Please, sit down," she said, knowing the charade was for anyone watching. It was a weak excuse, but all she could manage.

She turned to the adjacent table. "Dieter Katz and Dr. Werner, this is Tony Marino."

The men nodded discreetly. Marino studied those around them, the waiter who served them, the cashier just inside the door, and the pedestrians walking by. All seemed innocent, although some were probably not. "This is the last time we all meet," he said.

"Yes, of course," Katz said, looking nervous, as if he was

about to be caught doing something he shouldn't. "Thank you for helping us at the cemetery."

"You're welcome," Marino replied. "I wish the ending was better."

"Kirstin told us it didn't go well last night," Werner informed him.

"No, it didn't" Marino said. "It was a trap. The Stasi were waiting at the checkpoint."

"I suppose the passports won't work," Katz said.

"It's too soon to tell," Marino replied. "But I have another plan, something more reliable, and a method that allows many people to escape at once."

"You have our attention," Katz said, smiling slyly.

"Yes, what is it?" Kirstin asked.

"A tunnel," Marino said softly, eyeing those nearby.

"How are we going to manage that?" Werner asked.

"You're not," Marino said. "I am. Everything will be done from the West. When the tunnel is ready, I'll provide the time and location – or a courier will. But I'll let you know when we're close. I hate to be so secretive, but I think the less everyone knows, the better. For now, I'll assume seven people, but it'll be much more by the end."

"Who will dig this tunnel?" Katz asked.

"I have someone who can arrange it," Marino said.

"How about supplies and equipment," Werner wondered aloud. "Where will you get the money?"

Marino knew the next topic might be controversial. "I'm a writer," he told them, "and my publisher is going to finance tunnel construction."

"And you'll write a book about it?" Katz guessed.

"Yes," Marino admitted. "I'll be documenting our efforts to get you out."

"You can't use our names," Kirstin said, as if a bit disappointed. "The Stasi are everywhere. They'll retaliate against family and friends."

"I realize that," Marino said. "And I promise no real names will be used. And no photos that show faces."

"Photos?" Katz asked. "Isn't that dangerous?"

"It can be," Marino said, "if I let it. But I won't."

"How will we know what's happening?" Werner asked.

"We can't meet in public," Marino said, looking at his watch. "And this meeting will be ending in a minute."

"Then how will we know?" Katz asked.

"I'll communicate through Kirstin," Marino said.

"And I'll relay information at church and through an occasional office visit to you, Doctor Werner," Kirstin added, implying that she and Marino would remain in close contact.

"And with that, we need to leave," Marino stated. "We can't be this careless anymore."

"Just one question, Mr. Marino," Dieter Katz said.

"Yes, what is it?" Marino asked, as he stood to leave.

"You write a book and make lots of money," Katz said. "What's in this for us?"

"Freedom," he said tersely. "Right now, that's all I can promise."

He walked away, Kirstin following a few feet behind him.

55

Marino watched a man approach, walking from the S-bahn down *Bernauer Strasse*, the avenue shaded by linden trees. The man was cautious, glancing around the urban landscape, but it didn't seem he expected to find anything. As he came closer, Marino saw it was Josef Kramer, a few minutes early for their scheduled appointment.

"You're punctual," Marino said, glancing at his watch.

"I try to be," Kramer said with a smile. "But I'm not always successful."

"It's a good quality to have," Marino said. He turned, pointing to the building behind him. "This is it."

Kramer looked at the three-story brick building that occupied most of the block. "An old factory?"

"Yes, I think ball bearings were made here during the war. The center section was bombed, but never rebuilt. The far end is a metal fabricator and the end closest to us is vacant."

Kramer studied the building, scanning the façade. It was built in another era, and he seemed to appreciate the detailed construction, corbelled bricks in different designs with an Art

Deco influence. It was as if the engineer in him valued the craftsmanship. He then gazed at the modern four-story apartment building next to it, more functional than decorative, sleek straight lines of concrete and glass. It was an interesting contrast. Lastly, he looked at the twelve-foot wall that hid his view of East Berlin, and the slice of cemetery on the western side of it.

"It's interesting how the wall intersects the edge of the graveyard," he remarked. "Not even the dead can escape the conflict."

"It doesn't say much for civilization," Marino commented. Then he pointed to the destroyed portion of the factory. "Sixteen years after the war and the city still has bombed buildings."

"There are more in the East than West," Kramer said dryly. "And most will be there for another sixteen years."

Marino studied the factory, the entrance accessible from the street and hidden from an East German watchtower. "I tracked down the owner," he said. "He's planning to demolish the building someday."

"Probably for another apartment building," Kramer said. "I'd like to talk to him. Maybe I can persuade him to turn this beautiful building into apartments instead of creating another modern monstrosity."

Marino grinned. "I'd be happy to give you his contact info."

"I may take you up on that," Kramer said. "Is he willing to let us use part of it?"

"He's willing to rent it."

"That's nice of him," Kramer commented, "considering most of it is rubble."

"The portion nearest the apartment building is sound," Marino said. "The walls are sturdy, the roof intact. The floor is relatively free of debris."

"Did you tell the owner what we're using it for?"

"He never asked," Marino related. "But the building is next to the wall. I'm sure he suspects something."

"Isn't that risky, depending on a stranger like that?"

"I had no choice," Marino explained. "But the rent helped him understand it was in both our interests. This part of the building has been vacant for years."

"Have you been inside?"

"Yes, the owner took me through."

"Is there space to store the dirt we excavate?" Kramer asked.

"More than enough," Marino replied. "Come on, I'll show you."

Marino unlocked a door near the corner of the building and they entered. The first floor appeared to have once been an office, desks and chairs still occupying the space, cobwebs strung between them. Large industrial windows were spaced around the walls, dirt and grime making them opaque, some cracked, others broken. The room was about fifty feet square; a brick wall that was bulging but still standing separated it from the destroyed center section. A door to the factory hung from its upper hinge, crooked, the jamb splinted. The scene beyond was one of broken brick and timber, covered in dust and laying in piles where they fell, like a time capsule. The back wall of the factory was intact, as was the section beyond it – now the metal fabricator.

"We can put the excavated material in this destroyed section," Kramer said as he eyed the building's interior. "And we can separate this office space, put in a partition with some couches and tables and maybe a coffee pot. But we'll need electricity."

"I was hoping one of your helpers might be an electrician," Marino said. "Maybe we can run a line from the apartment building."

Kramer walked to the front door and peered out. "That might work," he said. "Or even a temporary service from the street."

"You can take care of that?" Marino asked.

Kramer nodded. "Yes, it's the least of our problems," he said. "We'll also have to cover these windows. We don't want the border guards to see lights on and guess what we're doing."

"I hadn't thought of that," Marino admitted.

"It's just a precaution," Kramer said. "I'm sure they know this part of the building has been vacant for a long time. We don't want to arouse their suspicions. How far from the border are we?"

"I'll show you," Marino said, guiding him toward the back wall.

Marino used his sleeve to wipe clean a window pane centered in the brick, and they looked directly at the wall, maybe fifteen feet from the factory, twelve feet high with a circular tube on top that made it difficult to climb.

"We aren't far at all, are we?" Kramer asked as he peered out. "Is there a stairway to the second floor? We'd have a better view of what's on the other side."

"Yes, just on the other side of the dividing wall."

Marino led him through the door with the broken hinges into the remnants of the factory, climbing over piles of brick to reach a stairway, partially buried in rumble, some of the treads missing.

"We'll have to repair this," Kramer said as they carefully started to climb. "We don't want anyone hurt. The tunnel will be dangerous enough."

They reached the second floor, the original factory mostly destroyed, the level above partially collapsed upon it. Patches of open sky were visible through the damaged roof, cottony clouds drifting by.

"Be careful where you step," Marino cautioned as he led him to the window on the back wall.

"We'll have to clear a walkway through here," Kramer said, "so we can check periodically."

They stood at the back window and looked at the other side of the border. Guards patrolled the cemetery, up to the wrought iron fence that defined it, while others walked the vacant area behind the clothing company. Some had dogs with them.

"What is that building?" Kramer asked.

"It's a clothing manufacturer," Marino replied. "I think it's closed on weekends, but there's quite a bit of activity there through the week."

Kramer was quiet, perhaps mentally marking the distance from the factory to the clothing manufacturer. He looked back and forth, towards the cemetery and then in the opposite direction, toward *Strelitzer Strasse*.

"What do you think?" Marino asked.

"One of the mausoleums would be better," Kramer said. "But the guards are too close to them and we don't know for sure how much vacant space is inside them."

"Does the clothing company work?"

Kramer hesitated, still studying the landscape. "It's close, maybe a hundred and fifty feet," he observed. "Has anyone been inside the building?"

"No," Marino replied. "Not yet."

"That can be a problem," Kramer said. "We won't know what we're walking into, and it could be harder to get the escapees into the building."

"I saw someone exit the side of the building, right near the cemetery fence," Marino said. "They stepped outside for a cigarette. We might be able to bring people in through there."

Kramer nodded. "That would work," he said. "The shrubs along the cemetery fence hide the area. And there's not much light there at night. At least there's no streetlight in front of it."

"Do you have any other ideas?" Marino asked.

Kramer continued surveying the landscape, looking at the cemetery, the church, different mausoleums spread throughout the graveyard, and the row of townhouses adjacent to the church. "We may have to use another route, but we have time to figure that out."

"What do you need for materials?"

"Assuming we use the clothing manufacturer, or at least define the distance of the tunnel, I would guess twenty thousand marks, thirty at most."

Marino considered the estimate, having already discussed the funding with Ned Simpson. It was a lot of money – the equivalent of eighteen months salary for the average American. But he didn't want to cut costs on the tunnel and have someone die because of it. "Let's do this," he suggested. "Form your team and choose the route. I'll pay for the supplies. Any additional money my publisher offers can be split between you and the diggers. As long as you think the project is doable."

Kramer smiled. "It's doable, all right," he said. "We'll dig the best damned tunnel you ever saw. There's just one condition."

"Which is?"

"I told you before," Kramer reminded him. "My cousin gets out. That's not negotiable."

Marino wanted to ask the obvious question, especially after having two escape attempts thwarted, possibly by an informant. "I assume your cousin brings no additional risks."

"He's not an informant, if that's what you mean," Kramer replied, seeming a bit offended. "But every refugee brings risks, especially him. But that's why they're escaping."

Marino thought about Kirstin and her husband, the Stasi informant, and her motivation, an elderly grandmother and a daughter she had never seen. She would do anything to escape, which might make her careless. He realized Kramer was right.

"Fine, "he agreed. "But I should meet him before we get too far."

"When are you going East again?"

"Tuesday," Marino said.

"That works," Kramer said. "You'll meet him then. He'll know you, but you won't know him."

56

Karl Hofer sat behind his office desk, wondering what went wrong at the checkpoint. He left explicit instructions for the guards, warning that a blonde woman would attempt to cross the border with a fake Swiss passport. But apparently, they apprehended the wrong blonde woman. Or he had bad information.

A map of the Mitte section of Berlin lay sprawled upon his desk. It was very detailed, complete with the infrastructure needed for a city the size of Berlin. The drawings showed sewer lines, U-bahn and S-bahn stops and stations, utility lines – gas piping and power lines – shared by the sectored city, and any streets that intersected West Berlin, including the exact location the wall crossed the boulevard. Watchtowers, so critical for surveillance of the newly constructed border wall, were currently being built, and the location of those already in place were clearly identified.

He studied the area adjacent to the wall, especially where border defenses were insufficient: parks and cemeteries that still had barbed wire, waterways, closed S-bahn or U-bahn stations, buildings near the border. He imagined what weakness he would exploit if trying to escape and what method he would use to do it. With a pencil, he marked several locations worthy of investigation that he planned to check in upcoming days.

The cemetery escape had been clever, leveraging a section of barbed wire only accessible from one side, the wrought iron fence splitting the guards' patrol and rendering response to a threat less than adequate. It was hidden in shadows, sheltered by trees and shrubs. Tombstones and mausoleums offered sanctuary for refugees moving furtively across the landscape, places to hide when a guard approached. It was a good plan. Someone had researched the guards and their routines, choosing exactly the right location, and finding the most opportune moment. It would have been easy to escape through the breached barbed wire – had he not known in advance.

The fake passport proved more difficult. Although use of forged documents had been successful just after the border was closed, police were now more observant. Newly enforced regulations, such as imposing restrictions on travel, documenting when the passport holder entered East Berlin, forcing foreigners to leave the city by midnight on the day of their arrival, all made escape more difficult. You couldn't leave East Berlin, no matter how good your passport was, if you couldn't prove you entered.

Hofer suspected no further fake passports attempts would be made from those his informants were watching. The planning was too difficult. The refugee had to use a counterfeit passport or someone's documents who resembled them. Either approach left too much margin for error. The refugee also had to speak the language of the country from which they supposedly came and answer questions about their life – details border guards could often verify. The trap he set at the border, even though it hadn't snared the culprit, had certainly been witnessed by the perpetrator, and the results would have spread throughout the refugee population. Fear was an extremely effective motivator.

He was convinced the next attempt would be different, more detailed, better planned, something requiring more effort. The most viable option, involving more people, was a tunnel. But it would be difficult for those involved to keep the secret. Someone always talked, making it easy for the Stasi to thwart the escape. If any attempt was underway, he knew he would find out before it was completed. But as he scoured the map, he realized there were dozens of places where a tunnel was practical, where buildings were close to the border on both sides of the wall. It would prove difficult to find the exact location, unless the information his spies obtained was detailed and accurate.

The knock on his door was light, almost timid, even though it was expected. He folded his map. He didn't want his informant to see it. It was better that the information came directly from them. Why influence their judgment, maybe cause them to invent or modify an escape based on incomplete sentences of an eavesdropped conversation. He would rather not.

"Come in," he called, as he put the maps and folders into a drawer.

The door opened, closed a few seconds later, and the sound of footsteps echoed across the wooden floor of his office.

"Sit down," Hofer said, motioning to the chair in front of his desk, "and tell me what you have learned."

57

The border guard studied Marino's passport closely, as if not convinced it was authentic. "Pennsylvania, U.S.A," he said. "What is special about Pennsylvania?"

It was the fifth senseless question the guard had asked. Marino's patience was waning. "The Philadelphia Phillies."

"What is Philadelphia Phillies?"

"A baseball team."

The guard eyed him warily. "You're a funny man, aren't you?"

Marino shrugged and didn't reply.

The guard picked up the phone. Holding the receiver close, he spoke quietly for a moment and then hung up. He looked at Marino. "Someone is coming to talk to you."

Marino sat on a wooden bench by the front door. About ten minutes later the door opened and a handsome man in a black suit walked in.

"There he is, Mr. Hofer," the guard said, pointing to Marino

The new arrival walked behind the counter, joining the guard. He eyed Marino curiously for a moment, as if determining whether or not he posed a threat. "I'm Karl Hofer of the Ministry for State Security."

"Tony Marino, American writer."

Hofer stared at Marino with a hint of amusement. "May I see your passport?" he asked.

Marino walked to the counter and handed his passport to Hofer.

Hofer took the document, fingered it gently, as if gauging the authenticity of the binding, but his eyes remained on Marino. It was an awkward impasse, neither man speaking.

Marino stood quietly, not expecting trouble but knowing it could arrive at any moment. Hofer was obviously someone important, a person who made decisions that altered people's lives. Marino maintained eye contact, wondering why this man thought he was so interesting, so deserving of such a vital state official's time.

"You come to the East frequently, Mr. Marino," Hofer said, still not looking at the document. "Why is that?"

"I'm a writer," Marino explained. "I come for research."

"And what are you writing?" Hofer asked. He lifted the passport toward his face, as if smelling the ink, his eyes still trained on Marino.

"A history of Germany," Marino replied.

"Why write a history of Germany?"

"I've written histories of France and Belgium," Marino said. "My editor wanted Germany done next. I don't pick the countries, Mr. Hofer. I only write the books."

"What is so fascinating about East Berlin?" Hofer asked, now gently rubbing the texture of the passport cover.

"The library is good," Marino said. "And I visit historical buildings."

"Really?" Hofer asked. "You come to sightsee. Maybe you enjoy seeing bombed buildings. Is that it, Mr. Marino?"

Marino was starting to feel uncomfortable. His interrogation no longer felt like a formality, designed to intimidate visitors of East Berlin. It felt planned, as if Hofer had an agenda. Marino just couldn't figure out what it was.

"I asked you a question, Mr. Marino," Hofer said sternly.

"I come to absorb the history," Marino said. "And to do my research."

"Why don't I believe you?"

"There's no reason not to."

"Maybe you really come to spy for America," Hofer said, putting the passport on the table and eyeing him coldly.

"I'm not a spy."

"But you speak German very well."

"I used to be an interpreter," Marino said. "I speak Italian and French, too."

"Amazing linguistic abilities," Hofer said. "Perfect qualifications for espionage."

"I'm not spy," Marino insisted.

Hofer picked up the passport and examined the photograph before leafing through it, slowly turning the pages, pausing to study a documentation stamp or two. He then put it back on the counter. "What is it that you're looking for, Mr. Marino?"

"Nothing," Marino replied. "I'm doing research for my book."

"Maybe you only pretend to do research for your book. Maybe you have a far different reason for coming to East Berlin."

"Why don't you follow me?" Marino said, daring to be brave, hoping Hofer wouldn't call his bluff.

"Maybe I already have," Hofer smirked. "Do you really think much goes on in East Berlin without me knowing?"

Marino hadn't considered that Hofer already knew the answers to the questions he asked. Why wouldn't he? That's what the Stasi did. They spied on people, they knew everything about them, likes and dislikes, where they went, what they thought. Why should he be different, just because he was American? If the Stasi was interested in him, they probably already had all the information they needed.

"You find that alarming, don't you, Mr. Marino," Hofer said. "You hadn't considered that I may know more about you than you know yourself."

Marino studied the man before him. He suspected he had no fears, no conscience, little or no compassion. He wasn't the person to pick a fight with. "No, Mr. Hofer," he said, "I hadn't considered that."

Hofer chuckled. "You don't believe me, do you?"

Marino shrugged, smiling tritely.

Hofer leaned forward, bridging the gap between them. "What if I told you that Johnny Callison of the Philadelphia Phillies was your favorite baseball player?"

Marino's eyes widened with surprise, his heart beating rapidly. How could Hofer ever know that? Where did he get his information? How long had he been watched?

Hofer laughed lightly. "Mr. Marino, you seem shocked. If you are a spy, I don't think you're a very good one."

Marino chose a different tactic. "I suspect you do know everything that goes on in East Berlin. And given that, you already know that I'm not a spy."

"Why should I believe you?"

"Why shouldn't you?"

Hofer studied him a moment more, apparently convinced. He pushed the passport across the counter. "Enjoy your stay in East Berlin, Mr. Marino."

"Thank you," Marino replied. He grabbed his passport and started for the door.

"Mr. Marino," Hofer called as Marino prepared to exit.

"Yes?"

"I'll be seeing you again. You can be certain of that."

58

Marino left the guardhouse, finding his confrontation with Hofer perplexing. He knew East German authorities often intimidated visitors, but it was unnerving that Hofer knew so much about him. It made no sense, but then, after giving it some thought, he wondered if maybe it did.

He continued to the library, continually looking over his shoulder to see if he was being followed. He paused at shop windows, pretending to gaze at merchandise while watching the reflection of passersby in the glass. He saw no one suspicious and, after a while, he realized he probably wouldn't. Even if he was being spied on, he had no idea who it might be. Stasi agents came in all forms – friends, family, lovers, grandmothers and children. If someone was watching him, he would have no idea who it was.

He wondered if he should meet Kirstin at a different location, especially after Steiner may have seen her at the library, but he realized that might look even more suspicious. He told Hofer he frequently came to the East to do research at the library. If he still came to the East, but didn't go to the library, the Stasi might know something wasn't right. And even if

Steiner had seen Kirstin, and was suspicious of her intentions, he probably wouldn't expect her to go there again; he would assume she went somewhere else.

His next dilemma was whether or not to tell Kirstin what happened with Hofer when he crossed the border. He finally decided not to. She was anxious enough about the escape. It wouldn't be wise to add more suspense to the emotional roller coaster she was already riding – a Stasi husband, a dependent grandmother with no one to depend on, a daughter lost to adoption sixteen years before that she was now ready to meet. The less Kirstin knew about the escape or anything related to it, the better.

He arrived early, did some research needed for his book, and then went to the third floor to meet Kirstin in the remote corner where they normally met. There was a wooden bench against a wall and he sat there and waited, a book opened before him, a notepad on the bench beside him. Thirty minutes later, Kirstin arrived.

"Hello," she said warmly. She took a book from the shelf and sat beside him.

"It's nice to see you," he whispered, smiling. He liked her, even though he knew that wasn't meant to be part of the equation. Now somehow it was. He wondered if she had feelings for him. The kiss they shared at the border proved that she did. It seemed much more than a diversion. There was more behind it, passion and emotion.

She glanced around the library and, after ensuring they were alone, asked, "What have you determined?"

"I assume the passport frightens you," he said.

"It does," she replied. "There's too much risk."

"Because of the document?"

"And because I'm not much of an actress," she told him. "I don't think I could do it. If pressed by the Stasi, I would collapse."

He nodded, pensive, trying to imagine crossing a border you had no right to cross. "What would you prefer?"

"Something like the failed escape," she replied. "I would rather slip across the border, hidden by darkness, than confront the Stasi."

"Do you think you can do the tunnel?"

"Yes, if it's well constructed."

"It will be."

She turned, seeming surprised. "Have you started?"

"No, net yet. But we're about to. We're getting material now."

"Who is helping you?"

"The less you know the better," he said. "At least at this point. But it's some college students. As I told you before, it'll mean more refugees than in our original attempt, as many as thirty."

"Where will the tunnel lead to?"

He hesitated. "We're not sure yet," he said. "Somewhere near the church." He suspected someone in their group was Stasi, or at least an informant for Stasi. When they tried to cross the border, guards were waiting with searchlights. When they tried to cross with a fake passport, a blonde woman was detained by the Stasi just ahead of them. Even if both were coincidences, they still had to be cautious.

"When will it be ready?"

"In three or four weeks."

"That may not be soon enough for Dr. Werner," she said.

"What do you mean?"

"The Stasi are pressing him harder, still falsely accusing him of financial misconduct."

"Why?"

"They want information from him," she explained. "If he doesn't provide it, they'll make it very bad for him."

Marino knew what socialism was. People were ruled by lies

and fear – lies retold so many times people swore they were true. "I can't even imagine," he said.

"It isn't enough to imprison you," she explained softly. "They also destroy you and your family."

He felt a sickening feeling in his stomach, as if Nazism hadn't died. Maybe it now lived in socialism. "What did they do?" he asked hoarsely.

"They're claiming Dr. Werner committed sex crimes, the most perverted acts imaginable."

"But surely no one will believe that," Marino said in disbelief. "Doesn't the man have an impeccable reputation?"

"It doesn't matter," she said with a hint of disgust. "People believe what they're told to believe."

"That's horrible," he said, the Stasi tactics almost unthinkable.

"And after they've destroyed him, they'll start on his family," she continued. "They'll claim his daughters are prostitutes, or maybe even his wife. Or that they stole money from orphanages or killed someone."

"But I don't understand how they can do that," he said. "Even if the government does control the people. Especially with no evidence."

"They create the evidence," she said somberly. "Just as they create the crime."

59

Sunday service ended and the parishioners slowly filtered outside. Each stopped to speak to the minister, who stood at the door of the church as people passed by. He greeted the Becks, Kirstin and Steiner, three other couples, and then Dr. Werner and his wife.

"An interesting sermon," Steiner said as he and Kirstin stood on the pavement in front of the church. The morning was brisk; autumn had arrived.

"Yes, it was," Kirstin said, eyeing Dr. Werner as he left the church, his wife stopping to talk to another woman. She paused, letting them reach her.

"Kirstin, how is your ankle?' the doctor asked as they approached.

"It's doing well," she said.

"Hello, Doctor," Steiner said. "How are you today?"

"Not looking forward to winter," Werner replied. "But then, who is?"

"Professor Beck," called a parishioner, an attractive middle-aged woman. "Do you have a minute? I wanted your opinion on the sermon."

"Of course," Steiner replied, smiling and nodding politely. Then he turned to Werner. "Excuse me."

Kirstin eyed the woman, not sure who she was, and waited until Steiner was out of earshot. Then she cast him a look of disdain. "I thought he would never leave," she whispered to Werner.

Werner looked at her anxiously. "Have we made any progress?"

"Yes," she replied. "I talked to Tony the other day."

"The tunnel has started?"

"It's about to," she said guardedly.

"How long will it take?"

"Three weeks, four at most."

"I may not have four weeks," he hissed.

Dieter Katz exited the church and furtively walked toward them. "Are they digging?" he asked quietly.

"Almost," Kirstin replied. "They're gathering material."

"Where is the tunnel coming from?" Werner asked.

"I don't know," Kirstin replied. "Actually, I didn't even ask."

"More importantly," Katz interjected, "where is it going to?"

"I don't know that either," Kirstin said. "But many plan to use it."

"How many?" an anxious Werner asked.

"Probably near thirty."

Katz gasped. "How will thirty people keep a secret?" he asked. "Especially when we may have been betrayed already."

"I think any information provided will be limited," Kirstin informed them. "At least that's what Tony told me."

"We'll still need some advanced notice," Werner said "And at some point, we'll need to know where to access the tunnel."

"Tony said they'll use couriers to notify everyone, probably Eileen for us," Kirstin replied, referring to Katz's girlfriend. "Maybe a few others."

"She did tell me that they needed her help," Katz said.

"She's not one of the diggers, is she?" Werner asked.

"No," Katz replied. "She'll be relaying messages, running errands and getting supplies for the others."

Werner looked at them anxiously. "Is there any way they can speed the process?"

Kirstin shrugged. "I'm not sure," she admitted. "But I did tell Tony you needed to get out as soon as possible."

"Does he understand how serious my situation is?" Werner asked.

"Yes, he does," Kirstin said. "He was shocked when I told him."

"Will he try to go faster?" Katz asked. "I need to get out too. The Stasi watch me constantly. It's only a matter of time before I make a mistake."

"He understands the urgency," Kirstin assured them. "I promise he'll do the best he can."

"I'm desperate," Werner said. "Tony needs to understand that. I don't have four weeks."

"Maybe they can't do it any faster," Katz reasoned.

"I may have to escape without you," Werner said gravely. "I'll be dead if I don't."

60

Tony Marino walked into the factory and saw stacks of plywood cut into three-foot squares beside a pile of posts about three feet in length. A roll of electrical wire lay on the cement floor next to several lengths of flexible hoses, three or four inches in diameter. Two small fans were next to the hoses and, leaning against a wall, there were straight wooden ladders of various heights. Dark sheets had been strung across the windows; a few floor lamps were placed about the room.

"I see you obtained supplies," Marino said as he studied the pile of lumber. "Is this everything you need?"

"Not even close," Josef Kramer replied. "But we have enough to get started."

"Did you solve the electrical problem?"

"Yes, we did," Kramer replied with a sly grin. "It was easier than we thought."

"The apartment building?" Marino asked.

"No, we actually tapped into the factory next door. I doubt they'll even notice."

Marino smiled and pretended to cover his ears, as if he hadn't heard. He was impressed with Kramer. The college student was personable, well-organized and determined. All traits that lead to success. "Let's hope they don't," he said. "It's only for a few weeks."

"At most, I would think."

"The sooner, the better," Marino said. "There's a man in the East that's in trouble with the Stasi. He's hoping we can get him out quickly."

"We'll see how the digging goes," Kramer said. "A lot will depend on the soil consistency."

"Do you have your team lined up?"

"Yes, everything is set," Kramer informed him. "Eileen will help with supplies. And we have three four-man teams. They'll dig eight hours a day until we break through."

"Can they be trusted?"

"Yes," Kramer replied. "They all have loved ones in the East they want to rescue."

"Did you tell them about the money?"

"Not entirely," Kramer replied. "I gave them each some money as an incentive and told them there would be more when all the refugees are standing safely in this room."

"That should give them something to work towards," Marino said.

"I think they would have volunteered anyway," Kramer said. "They want to help those on the other side."

Marino could understand that. He was doing the same thing, only contributing in a different way. He had come so far in such a short amount of time. It felt good. "What's the plan going forward?"

"We were fortunate enough to find a lumber yard that will cut all the wood to size," Kramer informed him. "I decided to make the tunnel a little larger than planned, with some additional recesses every fifty feet or so."

"I don't understand," Marino admitted.

"We can stage one of our diggers at each of these recesses

during the escape," Kramer explained. "They can help those having difficulty. We don't want anyone too frightened."

"Is that a lot of extra work?"

He shrugged. "Yes, a bit," he said. "But we'll get through it."

"What are the other supplies for?"

"We'll run the wire the entire length of the tunnel and install lights."

"I'm impressed," Marino said.

"I told you it would be the best tunnel you ever saw."

Marino laughed. "Since I've never seen a tunnel before, that shouldn't be too hard."

"You'll marvel at our engineering and construction skills," Kramer said jokingly. "I only wish our professors could grade us on it."

Marino thought for a moment and considered the photographer. "Maybe they can," he suggested. "We'll have the photographs."

"Probably not a good idea," Kramer said. "The Stasi are everywhere."

"Even college professors in the West?"

"Yes, believe it or not," Kramer told him. "It's better not to take the chance."

"Are you absolutely certain we can trust everyone involved?"

"Yes, I think so," Kramer replied. "They all have a vested interest in our success."

Marino studied Kramer a moment, but was satisfied by his response. He glanced at the pile of supplies. "Are the fans and flexible duct for ventilation?"

"Yes, one blows air in, the other exhausts air. That should provide good circulation."

"I still want the exit kept a secret, just between those involved," Marino said. "We'll tell the refugees where to go on the day of the escape."

"Agreed."

"When do we start?"

Kramer looked at his watch. "The first crew should be here in about an hour."

Marino walked to the edge of the building where a square had been drawn in the concrete slab a few feet away from the brick wall. "Is this the entry?"

"Yes," Kramer replied. "We'll dig about fifteen feet down, maybe less if the soil is stable, and then it's a straight shot east."

61

Karl Hofer parked his Trabant across the street from the Church of Reconciliation and got out of the vehicle. The Beck residence, the end townhouse, sat to his left, a row of similar nineteenth-century brick buildings continuing to the corner. The fourth was damaged by a bomb during the war, the roof laying in a crumbled heap in what once was the second floor. Behind the row of townhouses sat a portion of the cemetery, tombs and mausoleums, trees and shrubs that dotted the landscape. And at the edge of the cemetery stood the concrete wall, what the Socialist government called the Anti-Fascist Protection Barrier – border guards patrolling it.

He walked past the church, where the cemetery reached the street, and continued along the pavement for a couple hundred feet to the wrought iron fence that defined the edge of the graveyard. He turned and moved along the fence, the clothing company to his right, and studied the concrete wall that sliced through the cemetery, leaving parts in the West, the rest in the East. A brick factory stood on the other side of the wall, next to a four-story modern apartment building that consumed the rest of the block, only a few feet from the wall. When the wall was still barbed wire, this corner had been the site of the foiled escape, and he suspected the next attempt would come somewhere nearby

As he approached the wall, he met a border guard and showed his Stasi credentials. "Good afternoon, sergeant," he said. "Have you noticed any unusual activity in this area?"

"No, sir," the sergeant replied. "It's been quiet."

"Stay vigilant," Hofer said.

"Is there something I should be aware of, sir?"

"No, just some preliminary information," Hofer replied. "I haven't been able to validate it."

"Are you expecting trouble?"

"We should always expect trouble," Hofer informed him. "Then we're prepared should it ever arrive."

"I'll be sure to tell the others," the guard said. "Do you suspect activity in the cemetery?"

"Perhaps," Hofer answered. "If not, then nearby."

"Do you know how an escape might be attempted?"

"Not yet," Hofer replied. "But I will soon."

He left the sergeant at his post and walked away from the wall, farther into the cemetery. A large mausoleum attracted his attention. He studied it for a moment, its proximity to the wall, the ease with which he suspected the vault could be accessed, and he then stared at the brick factory on the other side of the concrete barrier.

"Is something wrong?" a voice behind him asked.

Hofer turned to find Steiner Beck. "Professor Beck, what brings you to the graveyard?"

"I saw you arrive," Beck said. "When you started walking through the cemetery, I wondered why and thought I would ask what's going on."

"I don't know that anything's going on," Hofer told him. "But I think something soon will be."

"May I assist in any way?"

"Yes, I think you can," Hofer replied. "Much like we discussed previously, I suspect some of the churchgoers may be causing trouble. I need you to observe them."

"I will," Beck replied. "I've been very cooperative, as you're aware. And I always have been."

Hofer didn't reply, but continued examining the tomb. Beck's devotion was well-documented and he had no need to question it. But he could always do more. After several moments had awkwardly passed, Hofer stepped away. "You're not doing enough," he said.

"I'm watching those in the church," Beck told him, "even the minister. And I've gathered information on all that remain. Many lived in the French sector and, now that the wall has been built, they no longer come to service."

"You see no evidence of capitalist tendencies?"

"No, I don't," Beck replied. "Even Dieter Katz appears to be acclimating."

"I find it unusual that no one is worthy of being watched."

"I have already provided information on several subversives," Beck reminded him. "And as soon I notice anything unusual, or I have any information from my informants, you'll be the first to know. As you always have been."

"I appreciate your devotion," Hofer said. "It's a loyal trait."

"Thank you," Beck said humbly. "I only seek to serve."

"But you haven't provided information on the most important member of the congregation," Hofer said. "The one I suspect as the ringleader of the operation."

"Who is that?" Beck asked curiously.

"Your wife."

62

"All the material arrived last week," Tony said as he sat with Kirstin in the rear of a secluded café near the art museum.

"Have they started digging?"

"Yes, and they've made a lot of progress."

"How are they doing this?" she asked. "Especially without being seen."

"They're working from inside a warehouse," he explained. "As long as they're careful entering and exiting, even the guards in watchtowers won't notice them."

"Are you helping them dig?"

"No, not really," he said. "But it's fascinating to watch. They started by cutting a square in the concrete floor. Then they dug vertically twelve feet or so and inserted a wooden ladder."

"I wish I could see it," she said. "I'm so appreciative. All those people working for me and a handful of others to escape."

"They're also doing it for family and friends," he said. He sipped a glass of wine, which was once again available in most restaurants and cafés, glanced at some of the other patrons, and leaned forward. "And I think they enjoy it."

"Are you sure it's going to be safe?" she asked. "It would be horrible if it caved in."

"They're taking every precaution imaginable," he assured her.

"But the tunnel is underneath the border guards," she said. "What if they hear something? Or what if they drive a vehicle over it and it collapses?"

"I'm not worried," he replied. "Those working on it are accomplished students, and the tunnel is a marvel of engineering. They're being very cautious."

She was quiet for a moment, as if digesting the information. "How far did they get?"

"They made a small room at the base of the vertical shaft, maybe eight feet square, and fortified it with posts and planks. Then they installed lights and ventilation, and a small hoist to remove pails of soil. Once they completed that staging area, they started the horizontal dig."

"Have they crossed the border yet?"

He shrugged. "It's hard to say, but I think they're close. About twenty feet from their starting point."

"Is the tunnel large enough to fit through comfortably?" she asked. "Some of those escaping might be children. They could get frightened."

"I think the diggers have done a good job balancing tunnel size, and the ability to fortify it, against the time required to dig it."

"How big is it?"

"About three feet square," he said. "They have a cart that they wheel in and out with the dirt. When it's time for the escape, they can even wheel people through the tunnel, if needed."

She still seemed worried. "It sounds dangerous," she said.

"But I suppose it's no worse than trying to get through the barbed wire. How much longer do you think it'll take?"

"I'm not sure," he admitted. "They've made great progress so far. Two more weeks, maybe three."

She was quiet for a moment before speaking. "Why won't you tell me where it exits?" she asked quietly.

"To protect you," he replied with no hesitation. "It may not be a coincidence that border guards were waiting for us on our first escape attempt. And it probably wasn't an accident the Stasi were at the border, looking for blondes with a fake passport, at the exact time you were supposed to cross."

She sipped her wine and, for a moment, seemed lost in her thoughts. "I told you my husband is Stasi," she said softly.

"But he would have no way of finding out."

"He may have seen us at the library," she pointed out.

"But it's more likely he didn't," he countered. "If he did, he would have asked why you were there."

"Or he might have someone following me."

"Yes, he could," Marino replied. "But even if he did, he still wouldn't know about the escapes. He would only know where you were."

She hesitated, as if digesting his comments. "I hate to think one of the others is an informant."

"They may not be," he said. "It could be someone they know. An informant would need a motive."

"Dieter Katz was kept in solitary confinement," she told him. "And then he was interrogated, berated, and humiliated while the Stasi reinforced the evils of capitalism. He may not be the man he once was."

"Maybe he's the informant," Marino suggested.

"I hope not," she said. "He seems like such a nice young man."

"How about the others?" he asked.

"I don't know Dieter's friend, or the doctor's wife or friends.

But I already told you the Stasi are threatening the doctor. He may try to escape on his own if the tunnel isn't finished soon."

"Are they still making false accusations?"

"Yes, and each day gets worse," she said. "He's trapped, caught in the web they weaved around him."

Marino was quiet for a moment, assessing the doctor's predicament. "He could regain his reputation by turning us in. Maybe that's what the Stasi wants."

"I suppose it's possible," she said, "but it doesn't seem like something he would do."

"Then it could be someone in the West, Eileen Fischer, or someone she confided in."

"Again, it seems unlikely. She's so devoted to Dieter."

"It could be one of her friends, or the friend of anyone else in the group that tried to escape."

Kirstin sighed, slowly shaking her head. "I suppose that's why it's best we don't know where the tunnel is," she said. "If no one knows any details, no one can betray us.

"It protects everyone," Marino affirmed. "You'll know by courier on the day of the escape. I realize it's the last possible moment, and doesn't allow much time to prepare, but it's just another precaution."

"What happens next?"

"We keep digging," he replied.

"Anything else?"

"I think it's time for me to visit the Haynors," he said. "I want to meet your daughter."

63

After eight days of digging, the tunnel extended beyond the factory wall, crossed underneath a fifteen-foot expanse of lawn and then the border wall, before continuing into East Berlin for almost twenty feet.

Sometime around noon, a digger named Klaus climbed the ladder from the tunnel and hauled a bucket of soil up with the wench. "You had better come look at this," he said.

Kramer was sitting at a table near the work site, compiling a list of refugees and what couriers would be used to contact them. He looked at Klaus strangely, rose from the chair, and walked to the excavation site. "What's wrong," he asked.

"Look how moist this soil is," Klaus said.

Kramer put his hand in the bucket, finding the excavated material more like mud than dirt. "Is this the first bucket like that?" he asked.

"No, I already removed a bucket just as moist."

"Is it groundwater?"

The digger shook his head. "No, I don't think so."

"Did you hit a pipe?"

"No, we didn't hit anything," Klaus said. "The water isn't coming from where we're digging."

"Then where's it coming from?"

"Farther back in the tunnel, closer to the building."

"Is the leakage constant?"

"It's too soon to tell," Klaus said. "But it seems to be."

Kramer paused and considered his options. "See if you can locate the source," he said. "I'll find Marino."

———

An hour later, Tony Marino stood beside the tunnel entrance with Josef Kramer. Klaus came up the vertical wooden ladder. His clothes were soiled, much more than usual. His partner, an architecture student named Edsel, was a few rungs behind him. His clothing was worse, damp and dirty, smeared with mud.

"How does it look?" Kramer asked anxiously, eyeing their clothes.

"It started to drip just after you left," Klaus said. "Every seven or eight seconds. But now it's a pencil-thin stream."

"Can you tell where it's coming from?" Kramer asked.

"The top of the tunnel," Edsel replied.

"We won't last long with water leaking like that," Kramer said. "The tunnel will cave in."

"How difficult is it to find the leak?" Marino asked.

The three college students eyed each other anxiously. "It all depends," Edsel said.

"We have no choice," Kramer said. "We have to find it and fix it, or abandon the tunnel and fill it back in"

Marino stepped to the edge of the hole and peered below. "Can you determine the source?" he asked.

"At first, I thought it was ground water," Kramer said. "But when the leak worsened, I realized it couldn't be."

"What do you think it is?" Marino asked.

"I think we damaged a water line," Kramer said.

"But we didn't puncture any piping," Klaus informed them.

"We didn't have to," Kramer said.

"I don't understand," Marino replied.

"It took me a while to figure it," Kramer said, "but I think I know what happened."

"Do you mind telling me?" Marino asked. "Because I have no idea."

Kramer was pensive for a moment, as if searching for the easiest explanation. "Many pipes in the city's water system are made of a clay material. They remain intact from the pressure placed upon them by the soil. When we excavated underneath the piping, and alleviated the pressure, it started to leak."

Marino sighed, knowing the problem could have disastrous consequences – especially if it was on the wrong side of the wall. "Do we know exactly where it's located?" he asked.

"I'm certain it's on the western side of the wall," Edsel said. "Between the edge of the building and the border."

"How do we fix it?" Marino asked. "Do we dig down from the surface and repair it?"

"That was my first thought," Kramer said. "But then I realized we don't know anything about repairing clay pipes that are decades old."

Marino rubbed his chin, searching for solutions. When the most obvious came to him, he looked at Kramer and then chuckled when he saw the college student's grin. "It seems we came to the same conclusion."

"Yes, we did," Kramer said.

"Please enlighten us," Edsel requested.

Kramer looked at him and Klaus and smiled. "We call the water department."

64

I t was the following day, just after nine a.m., when the water
department employee arrived. Kramer and Marino were
waiting in front of the building when the truck rounded the
corner. They motioned the driver forward, making sure his
truck was parked in front of the factory, hidden from the East
German border guards perched in a watchtower at the far side
of the cemetery.

"You reported a leak?" the man asked. He had on a gray pair
of overalls, a name tag affixed to the right breast pocket.

"Albert?" Marino asked, looking at the tag.

"Yes."

"I'm Tony and this is Josef."

Albert nodded but looked at them strangely, as if
wondering why introductions were more important than fixing
the leak.

"The leak is on the other side of the building," Marino said.

"Can I get my truck back there?" Albert asked.

"No," Kramer said quickly. "The ground is too soft. And
there's not much room."

Albert studied the two men for a minute, and then asked, "Can you show me where it is?"

"Yes, come on," Kramer said. "It's right this way." He led them around the corner of the factory, wary of the guard tower.

"Is there any surface water?" Albert asked.

"No, not really," Kramer replied, eying Marino warily.

Albert stopped just as they rounded the building. "Then how do you know there's a leak?" he asked.

Neither Marino nor Kramer replied. They stood at the edge of the factory, the cemetery wall in front of them, the concrete border wall behind it. Just a bit farther north, the cemetery ended at a wrought iron fence. They both studied the man as he eyed them curiously.

Several awkward seconds elapsed as the man observed each of their expressions and then averted his gaze, studying the landscape. He looked at the wall, separating the city, twelve feet high, and then back to the factory, partially destroyed. Then he studied the narrow strip of land in between. It took several seconds, but a knowing look crossed his face. He again gazed at each of them, then to the wall, and back to the building.

"Do you understand?" Marino asked. He risked trusting the man, even though he was a West Berlin city employee. He could be Stasi, or he could report them to authorities, but it was doubtful.

Albert looked at him, apparently deciphering the clues. "Yes, I think so," he said, suddenly looking uncomfortable.

"Will you help us?" Kramer asked.

Albert paused, as if evaluating risk and reward. "Show me the leak," he said, offering no commitment.

Kramer led them past the edge of the cemetery to the green strip of grass between the building and the border. He walked twenty feet farther and stopped.

Albert folded his arms across his chest, a smug expression

on his face. Without even looking at the ground, he said, "I don't see any water."

Marino eyed Kramer. It seemed the city worker was going to be difficult. He had hoped for someone who would support their cause, maybe even ask to participate, helping people escape. But it didn't look like that was going to happen.

"I assume there are old clay pipes in the city's water system," Kramer said. "As I understand it, the piping maintains its integrity due to the pressure of the soil upon it."

"Yes, that's correct," Albert said, now looking down at the grass.

Marino decided to blatantly state their case and put themselves at Albert's mercy. "If the soil is disturbed – either above or below the piping – one of the joints could potentially leak. Is that correct?"

Albert seemed to relax. "Yes, that's correct." He bent down and put his hand on the grass, feeling around for indications of moistness. "It seems that's what happened here."

"Will you help us?" Kramer asked.

Albert stood and stared intently at Marino and Kramer for a moment. Then he nodded. "Yes, I will help," he said. "But on one condition."

Marino eyed Kramer warily. "What is that?" he asked.

"I have a sister in the East, with a child and a husband," he said, pointing to the border. "Three blocks on the other side of that wall."

Marino studied the man's expression, judging his sincerity. "What are you trying to say?"

"I'll fix the water leak if my sister and her family can escape through the tunnel."

65

"Hello, mom," Marino said when his telephone call was answered.

"Tony?"

"Yes, it's me. How are you?"

"It's Wednesday."

"I know."

"What are you calling me on Wednesday for?" she asked. "Is something wrong?"

Marino rolled his eyes. "No, everything is fine," he assured her. "Why would you think something's wrong?"

"Because you call on Sunday."

"I called on Thursday a few weeks ago."

"And something was wrong," she insisted. "That's when you told me about your girlfriend."

He laughed lightly, missing her more than he'd admit. "Everything is fine."

"Are you coming home for Thanksgiving?"

"I'm not sure yet," he said. "But I'm trying to."

"Why wouldn't you come?" she asked. "I promised your

aunt you would be here. And you're a famous author now. The whole neighborhood is waiting to see you."

"Ma, I'm not a famous author," he said. "I write history books."

"You're famous to everyone coming for Thanksgiving. None of them ever wrote a book. They'll be disappointed if you don't come."

He paused, trying not to get irritated. "Please, mom," he said. "No guilt, all right?"

"What do you mean no guilt?" she asked. "I'm talking about having a holiday dinner with your mother and your aunt and uncle. What's wrong with that?"

Without even realizing it, a smile turned the corner of his lips. "I'm sorry," he said. "You're right. It's just about holiday dinner."

"Yes, holiday dinner," she replied. "Is your lady friend coming?"

He chuckled. "I'm not sure I would call her a lady friend, but I would like to bring her. I just have a few complications to work through first."

"Complications?" his mother asked. "What kind of complications?"

"Problems to solve."

"She's pregnant," Mrs. Marino stated firmly. "Dear Lord, what are we going to tell Aunt Marie. How could you do this Tony? You were always a good boy. You couldn't get married first? What will the priests say? I can't believe -"

"Ma, will you stop," Marino interrupted. "She isn't pregnant, all right? We're just friends."

"Don't tell me that, Tony," his mother scolded. "She's more than a friend, I can tell."

"All right, she's more than a friend," he admitted. "But not much more. At least not yet."

"If she isn't pregnant, then what's the matter?" she asked.

"It's hard to explain."

"She's not Catholic, is that what your worried about?" she asked. "I'll talk to Monsignor Galanti. She can convert."

"I don't know if she wants to convert," he said. "I never asked her."

"It's easy," she told him. "She just has to take some classes. Joey Milano, the kid that lives on Porter Street – the one you used to play stickball with – just married a Jewish girl. The Monsignor made her a Catholic. It only took a few weeks. I'll talk to him tomorrow. We'll get this straightened out."

"Mom, it's her papers," Tony said, partly telling the truth. "It has nothing to do with religion. There's some issues with her visa, her documentation. I need to get that straightened out."

"Oh," Mrs. Marino said. "That doesn't sound too hard."

"It can be, believe me."

"Well you get that straightened out so we can all meet her on Thanksgiving."

"You mean you and Aunt Marie and Uncle Luigi can meet her on Thanksgiving," he said, correcting her.

"No," Mrs. Marino said. "There's more than that. The priests from St. Mary's are coming, and so is the butcher and his wife from down the street. And when I told the neighbors that my Tony had a girlfriend, they all wanted to meet her, too."

"Isn't that a bit much?"

"Wait, there's more," she said. "Once I made a list of everyone coming, it was too many to fit in the house, so the Monsignor said we should have Thanksgiving dinner in the church basement. Everyone's bringing something to eat, so it'll be a feast, all types of food and bread and wine. And when I told the mailman he said he wanted to come too, so I -"

"Mom! Enough already," Marino said. "You're going to scare her away. And me too."

"Everybody wants to see you, Tony," Mrs. Marino said. "They all love you."

"The mailman?" he asked. "You even told the mailman?"

"He's the nicest man, Tony," she told him. "He's an older Italian gentleman, so sweet. It isn't the same man who delivered the mail the last time you were home. We have someone different now."

Marino paused, wondering why his mother was so complimentary of the mailman. She rarely gave anyone compliments. For a moment, he wondered what was going on. But then he dismissed it.

"Maybe someday you'll come home and not go away anymore," Mrs. Marino continued.

"Maybe someday, I will, mom," he said, suddenly realizing what a special person his mother really was. "That would be nice."

66

Dr. Jacob Werner was treating a young girl with a bruised ankle when the Stasi came. Two men dressed in black suits, conspicuous in a physician's office, told the receptionist they had to see the doctor immediately. They shoved past her and went back to the examining room, barging in before she could stop them.

"Come with us, Doctor," directed one of the men. "We have some questions for you."

"I'm sorry, Doctor," his flustered receptionist said. "I couldn't stop them."

Werner was annoyed, a bit frightened, but not surprised. For a moment, he ignored them and spoke to his patient, a young girl with pigtails who looked at the intruders curiously. "Now Anna, I don't want you to play outside," he said, probing her ankle delicately. "You need to rest."

"I'll tell her mother," the receptionist said, a sickening look crossing her face.

"She's to rest for three or four days," Werner clarified. "She should read or listen to the radio. No physical activity."

"Of course, Doctor," the receptionist said softly, as if she knew it might be the last words she spoke to him.

Werner turned to the Stasi. "Let's get this unpleasantness over with."

The Stasi led him through the waiting room, filled with patients, only a single chair vacant. Most stared, shocked and afraid but not surprised. They had often seen Stasi take friends and neighbors away. Some returned and some didn't. And an appointment that couldn't be kept was just another inconvenience – like empty stores shelves.

"You should all go," one of the Stasi agents said loudly. "The doctor is being arrested."

A few in the waiting room gasped, but most minded their own business. They knew not to make eye contact, it was best to stare at the floor, pretend you didn't see anything, pretend you didn't hear.

The Stasi led Werner out of the office to a black Trabant parked at the curb. Passing pedestrians stopped to stare, but then continued, not wanting to get involved. Werner sat in the back seat, a Stasi agent sliding in beside him.

"Where are we going?" Werner asked.

"To *Rusche Strasse*," the driver replied. "You'll be interrogated at Stasi headquarters."

Werner knew interrogation meant torture and imprisonment, possibly forever. His life would never be the same. He wondered what they would do to his family, what accusations they would make against his wife or daughters. He had spent his whole life trying to do right, to be a good person. And he had chosen medicine as a profession to help people, to make their lives better, to ease their suffering. But in the end, he wondered if any of it really mattered.

As they raced down the block, the car weaving in and out of traffic, he watched the city of Berlin speed by, as if he would never see it again. Smoke from the city's factories filtered through the autumn sky, blotting clouds in a hazy mist, painting a smeared picture of what was actually there. Just like the Stasi had painted a portrait of him – one that didn't describe what really was.

The drive lasted fifteen minutes and then the car halted in front of Stasi headquarters. The driver got out and opened the rear door. The agent in the back seat pushed Werner from the vehicle and climbed out behind him. The driver grabbed Werner's arm and roughly guided him up the steps toward the front door.

"Will I be charged with a crime?" Werner asked, trying to sound brave. "I have a right to know."

"You have no rights," one of the Stasi agents said coldly. "You never did."

They led Werner into the building, down a narrow hallway to a flight of steps. The driver pushed him toward the stairs and Werner stumbled, almost fell, but at the last moment grabbed the handrail and caught his balance.

"Hurry," the Stasi agent commanded.

Werner didn't reply. He quickly moved down the steps. When they reached the bottom, he saw rows of doors with a small window centered in each on both sides of the hallway. He tried to peer in the rooms as he passed but saw nothing but darkness beyond.

They took him to the last room on the right. The agent opened the door and pushed him inside. It was a cell, vacant except for a cot with wooden legs and frayed fabric. There were no windows. The door was slammed shut, the room dark, only the light from the hallway filtering in, until a cover was placed over the window and the room was consumed by darkness.

Werner stumbled forward, blinded. He held out his hand until he touched the cot. Fumbling, he sat upon it, blinking his eyes, trying to see in the darkness. He sat still, listening, wondering if anyone was in adjacent cells. He glanced at his wrist watch but couldn't see it. He couldn't see anything, only blackness.

He waited, his heart racing. He knew he would be tortured. But how much pain could he endure? Would he tell the Stasi whatever they wanted to know? Or was he braver, more courageous than he realized? He wasn't sure. But he did know that, as each minute passed, the anxiety heightened, the fear increased, and his heart began to pound as his mind filled with vivid images of what was about to happen.

He had no concept of time. It was difficult; his senses were numbed. He couldn't see and there was nothing to hear. He counted to estimate passing seconds, but because he was frightened he counted too quickly and then overcompensated, counting too slowly, until he was too frightened and confused to even count at all.

When he was certain an hour had passed, he wondered why no one had come to get him. Did the delay mean anything? Did they want his fear to mount, fueled by his imagination? Did they know his heart was racing, his stomach nauseous, his hands trembling? His feet nervously tapped the floor, his eyes staring at a room he couldn't see, his ears listening for sounds he couldn't hear.

He laid down on the cot and forced his mind to wander, to think of anything except what was about to happen. He thought about his life, starting with his earliest memories: his mother and father, a brother and sister, his friends from school. There were sports that he played, and girls he had loved – or only thought he had loved. And then there was the university and medical school, marriage and his two daughters. But that was all before the war – the hellish tragedy that almost ended civilization.

He rose from the cot and stretched his arm out in front of him. He counted the steps until his hand touched a wall. He turned around and crossed the room, touching the other wall.

He did this over and over, trying to release the restless energy that kept his body shaking. He tried to guess when another hour had passed and then stopped, returning to the cot.

His thoughts drifted to mistakes he had made, bad decisions, poor choices, and he wondered how he could have been a better person. If he was ever released, he wanted the chance to correct everything, but he knew that would never happen. He knew he was about to die in a damp prison basement.

He laid back on the cot, guessing he had been there for three or four hours. He closed his eyes, trying to find peace, knowing he had lived his life the best that he could. His breathing slowed and he slept, exhausted from the stress of not knowing his fate.

Sometime later – either minutes or hours – he jerked upright. He didn't know how long he had slept or how long he had been in the cell. He didn't even know if it was the same day. And then he got up and paced the floor, again reflecting, before returning to the cot and sleeping again.

When he woke he grazed his hand across his face, trying to judge time by the growth of the whiskers on his face. There was stubble, he needed a shave, so perhaps it was the next day, or at least late in the evening. He stared straight ahead, seeing nothing, and counted – for no reason at all.

It was some time later when he heard heels clicking along the corridor, two sets of footsteps. He sat up, listening, his entire body quivering. Someone was at the door, fumbling with a lock. A second later the door opened and light streamed in, blinding him. He covered his eyes, squinting, trying to get accustomed, but was grabbed by the arms, pulled from the cell and jerked into the hallway, where a man stood, watching him, a smirk on his face.

"Just imagine what I could do if I wanted to, Doctor Werner," Karl Hofer said. He then turned to the guard. "Take him home."

67

"The tunnel is more than halfway finished," Marino told Ned Simpson. "Another ten days and we'll be done."

"Has the photographer been there?"

"Yes, he's been taking photos from the beginning."

"Are you sure you can trust him?" Simpson asked.

"Yes, I made a deal with him."

"What kind of deal?"

"His mother and father will be among the refugees," Marino said.

"Can you arrange that?"

"Yes, I think so," Marino replied. He paused for a moment, reflective, and then said, "This has been an overwhelming experience for me."

"What do you mean?"

"So many friends and families are separated," Marino told him. "A few months ago, they lived blocks apart. Now they might never see each other again."

"I want that personal angle in the book," Simpson said.

"It's taught me a lot," Marino continued, ignoring him.

"Especially about life and love. Even commitment and responsibility."

"Am I hearing you right?" Simpson chuckled. "I thought you hated responsibility."

"I'm serious, Ned," Marino replied. "You have to live through this to know what I'm talking about. People will risk their lives to reunite family. That's an extremely powerful dynamic, not to mention the whole political angle."

"Which is?"

"Freedom," Marino told him. "We take it for granted. People in East Berlin will risk their lives for it. It's fascinating. We could all learn from the people here."

"That's moving, Tony," Simpson said. "It really is. Get it on paper and make your readers feel it like you do. Tear at their hearts. And we'll have a best seller."

Marino didn't reply. He wasn't sure Ned understood, or if he was even capable of understanding. Maybe you had to be in East Berlin to grasp it, to feel what they felt, to know what they lost.

"How many do you think will get out?" Simpson asked.

"We're compiling a list now," Marino replied. "I think there's more than thirty."

"Do they know where the escape originates?"

"No, only Kramer, the diggers, and I know that the clothing company is the real location. The others think it's a mausoleum in the cemetery."

"If someone is an informant, and the Stasi are at the mausoleum, can they see the refuges entering the clothing company?"

"No, there's a wrought iron fence at the edge of the property, bordered by shrubs and evergreen trees. We haven't been inside the clothing company, but there's a side door near the fence. We're trying to have the tunnel exit near that door. The refugees will walk along the fence for thirty or forty feet. Then they enter the building and go right into the tunnel."

"Have you been in the tunnel yet?"

"Yes, I inspect in every day."

"Is it safe?" Simpson asked. "The last thing we need is some sort of cave-in, a catastrophe that's all over television."

"No, it's very safe," Marino assured him. "We lost some time with the water leak, but once it was fixed and everything dried out, the diggers shored it up and kept moving."

"What's it like?"

Marino thought for a moment, visualizing the escape path. "It's like an earthen box, about three feet square."

"This'll be a great success for Green Mansion," Simpson said. "I want an article ready for the day it happens, maybe two thousand words. We'll give rights to the *New York Times* and use it as a prequel to the book. Can you send me something, so I have it ready?"

"Sure," Marino replied, "I'll write it now. But don't print it until I confirm the escape."

"Agreed," Simpson promised. "I'll wait until I hear from you." He paused for a moment, as if jotting down notes. "What else is left?"

"I contacted Lisette's adoptive parents," he said, looking at his watch. "I'm meeting the father at a local café in an hour."

"I want the kid standing at the tunnel exit when Kirstin comes through," Simpson said. "And make sure the photographer is ready. I want plenty of pictures."

Marino felt uncomfortable, as if he was betraying Kirstin. It would be a nice surprise – having her daughter there when she escaped – but it was private.

"Did you hear me?" Simpson asked.

"Yes, Ned, I heard you," Marino replied and looked at his watch again. "I have to go. I'll check in later."

Marino hung up the phone and headed for the door. He left

the apartment building and walked down the street, catching the S-bahn to the British sector, near the *Kurfürstendamm*, one of the most famous boulevards in Berlin. When he got to the café, he ordered a coffee, so readily available when across the border it wasn't – like so many other products and services.

A few minutes later a man approached, late forties, a receding hairline, glasses, but a kind expression. "Mr. Marino?" he asked, in halting English.

Tony stood and shook the man's hand. "Thank you so much for coming, Mr. Haynor. I'm so grateful."

"It was the right thing to do," Haynor said as he sat down. "If Lisette has the opportunity to meet her natural mother, I want her to have it."

"That's so kind of you," Marino said, thankful for his consideration.

Haynor nodded and motioned for a waiter. He ordered a coffee and watched the pedestrians stroll down the boulevard for a moment. Then he spoke. "My wife and I weren't trying to adopt a child," he said. "We have two sons, grown now, several years older than Lisette. We were a happy family."

"What prompted you to adopt Lisette?" Marino asked as the waiter put a cup of coffee in front of Haynor.

"A friend of their family told us what happened," he said. "The story was so moving that we wanted to help. So we did."

"How did you do it if you lived in West Berlin?"

"We lived in East Berlin then," he explained, "but moved to the West when we had the chance. I'm a chemical engineer. There was so much more opportunity for me in the West. It was easy to do back then."

"It's a lot harder now."

"I know," Haynor said. "We were very fortunate. And we never regretted adopting Lisette. She's greatly enriched our lives."

"You're very compassionate," Marino said, impressed by the man who sat before him.

Haynor sighed, stirring the cream in his coffee. "It was a time so evil that, in retrospect, it doesn't seem it could ever happen. But we must all accept that it did. My wife and I felt that, if there was any way we could bring happiness to what was otherwise a horrific situation, we would."

"It's a tribute to you and your family, that you're willing to take this next step."

"We love Lisette and we only want the best for her. She knows what happened to her mother and why the State put her up for adoption. She understands. And I do, too."

Marino took a sip of his coffee and studied the man sitting before him. Mr. Haynor seemed like such a wonderful human being. Tony knew he could learn a lot from him, especially about the man he hoped he could become.

68

Kirstin Beck stood at her second-floor window and scanned the graveyard that sprawled behind her house, spreading several blocks to the north where it ended at an ornate wrought iron fence that was at least a hundred years old. The cemetery was sprinkled with trees and shrubs, most over-grown, and cobblestone lanes where mourners could walk among the mausoleums. The farthest lane, some thirty feet from the short stone wall that marked the edge of the cemetery, was now the site of a twelve-foot wall, splitting the cemetery just as it divided the city.

She watched her husband walk through the lanes and she wondered what he was doing. He had left the house, walked along the street, and then crossed into the cemetery, moving slowly up one lane and down the next. He didn't seem to be looking for any particular grave, but paused to examine the larger mausoleums, studying them closely, circling the perimeters. It seemed as if he was searching for something, but he didn't know what it was.

She couldn't remember when she first realized he spied for

the Stasi, providing information on family and friends, parishioners from church, students in his classroom. She had caught him in clandestine meetings with Stasi agents, or at least those whose dress or demeanor gave every indication they were Stasi. And she had often seen him sequestered in his college office, or in some café in a remote part of Mitte, and even on streets near their house, engaged in whispered discussions with faceless strangers – informants or agents, she wasn't sure. And as time passed, and the meetings increased, he had become more distant until she finally didn't know him at all.

Tony Marino was different. He had no hidden objective, offered no discussions designed to detect differing views, made no requests or demands. Initially, he was only a stranger, someone she asked for help without fear of Stasi reprisal. He wanted nothing in return and, even if his publisher did finance their escape for rights to their stories, Tony seemed a distant part of it, as if he only did what was asked without considering the repercussions of what that request might be. He was just a normal man from the streets of Philadelphia, and it didn't seem as if he wanted to be anything more. And although it had never been her intention to fall in love with him, somehow, without really trying, she had.

Steiner was far more complicated. When he was a professor, and she was a naïve student, she was overwhelmed by his intellect, attracted to his dashing good looks, jealous of the other women who fought for his affections, hoping they might be next to attract his attention or even share his bed. Ultimately, she was triumphant, and now she wondered why she fought so hard. Maybe he was a worthy prize at the time, but as years passed they both changed, travelling in different directions. Now he was cultured, refined, aloof, so very different from the charming man she had wanted so desperately to share her life. She couldn't see his soul; he was too guarded. She couldn't guess his thoughts; they were hidden, locked away, used as weapons to twist and contort the truth, creating an idealized concept from a thread of reality. And they couldn't have a conversation, because every word spoken, every thought revealed, was dissected and analyzed, and compared to the doctrines of the Socialist Party. When had he changed? Or maybe he hadn't. Maybe she changed while he stayed the same. She wasn't sure. But she knew it no longer mattered.

She realized the stark contrast between Steiner and Tony was symbolic of the difference between East and West Berlin. Steiner, the East, was older, rigid in his socialistic dogma, and one-dimensional, gray, unimaginative, like the newly constructed buildings. Whereas Tony represented West Berlin, alive and vibrant, willing to take risks to reap rewards. He seemed so much more than a man. He symbolized freedom of thought, speech, and movement, offering her the ability to go where she chose, express any thought she wanted – traits that didn't live in Steiner, who violently and vehemently opposed any view that differed from his own, refusing to either listen or entertain. Two men so different, just like the East and West.

She watched Steiner walk to the rear of the cemetery, close to where their first escape attempt had been made. He called to a guard and they talked for a few minutes, each enjoying a cigarette. She wondered what they discussed. Was it a casual conversation, or was it more sinister? A few minutes later Steiner walked away and continued his examination of the larger mausoleums, but in more detail. He approached one tomb near the corner of the cemetery and crouched beside it, his hands close to the ground.

She got her binoculars so she could see more clearly. She watched as he pushed pieces of marble, testing the construction, ran his finger along mortar joints, studied cracks or crevasses as if searching for something that didn't seem to exist. When unable to find what he was looking for, he left that mausoleum and walked to the next, conducting the same detailed examination, searching for anything loose or disturbed, any hint that access to the tomb could somehow be gained.

It was only then that she realized what he was doing. He knew about the tunnel. And he was looking for the exit.

69

D ieter Katz sat in a classroom as his professor discussed the dogmas of socialism, the genius of Lenin and Marx, the leadership of Stalin and the prosperous future the Soviet Union offered Communist countries around the world. It was a riveting lecture, the professor an accomplished speaker and, for a moment, Katz stared at the motto sprawled across the top of the chalkboard: *The past is the present. The future is the past.*

"Democracy fails because it's an election of perception," the professor told his students. "Who does the voter deem most qualified to preserve and protect his own self-interests? Which politician stages the best show, or has the prettiest face? Who sounds the best, seems the most compassionate and sympathetic, whether they truly are or not? The politician makes promises to secure a citizen's vote – whether he intends to keep them or not. And therefore, this extremely flawed system of self above the collective is doomed to fail."

The professor eyed his students intensely and then lowered his voice, as if sharing a secret. "Socialism is the greatest form of government ever created," he informed them. "Our leaders, the best and brightest mankind has produced, make decisions rooted in the interest of the greater good, whether it concerns food, shelter, healthcare, wages, or even entertainment. All is done for the collective, neutering the need for individuality. Our citizens need not be concerned with problems or process. The State is, and always will be, parent to the people."

"Since we're governed by the most gifted," the professor continued, "the State needs a method to identify those with the greatest potential. The Industrial School, and our very class-room, is a fertile ground for tomorrow's leaders, those capable of fulfilling the needs of the State. It's here that young men like our own Dieter Katz are chosen, developed, indoctrinated – recognized for their intellect and compassion, as well as their ability to preserve Socialism and all it stands for."

Dieter was surprised he was chosen as the best in his class. He wasn't sure he deserved the recognition. He had always thought socialism was one party with one creed, where opposi-tion was brutally repressed, where no one could challenge the supremacy of the State, and where there was no tolerance for opposing views, innovative concepts, contradictory thoughts or dialogue. He assumed the Party was all that there was and would ever be; all that ever could be. But maybe he had been wrong. Especially if his abilities were acknowledged by the very leaders he thought he despised.

He looked at those in the class and wondered how many were like him – living in a cage, pretending to accept the unac-ceptable, but not really sure, wondering if they might be wrong. Most tried to prove they were changing, showing the Stasi they had become good Socialists, denying their subversive roots. More likely, the constant lectures eroded their resolve, brain-washing them into cult-like acceptance of all that was said and done, knowing it was for the good of the Party. The lectures were often so intense, so undeniably true, that even those exposed to western ways recognized the evils of capitalism when contrasted to the glories of socialism.

He was confused, wondering if he was any different from those that sat beside him. He thought he wanted freedom, but he wasn't really sure. He once wanted to come and go as he pleased, live and work where he wanted, think for himself, earn a living – or fail at earning a living. And he often thought he would do anything to attain those goals, no matter what the cost. But he knew thoughts and dreams like his were incompatible with the Socialist system, and they always would be. Now he tried to understand why. If his professor identified him as a future Party leader, maybe he should play the role that destiny provided.

When his class was over, he left school and went to Checkpoint Charlie, on *Friedrichstrasse*, to wait for Eileen Fischer. She appeared a few moments later, exiting the S-bahn on the western side and entering the small hut manned by the United States Army. She emerged a moment later, crossed the border into the East, and went into a guard shanty to have her documents examined. Ten minutes later she exited and walked towards him, a broad smile on her face.

"I missed you," she said, as she hugged and kissed him.

"How long can you stay?" he asked, not wanting to let go.

"All day," she replied. "I just have to be back by midnight."

"Wonderful," he said, planting a kiss on her lips. "I was hoping we'd have some time together."

"Let's go to the café on *Ackerstrasse* for lunch," she suggested. "And then we can go to your apartment."

"That would be nice," he said, taking her hand.

They walked down the street, as two lovers would anywhere in the world, and tried to forget that their lives were separate, divided by both a wall, with capitalism on one side and socialism on the other, and the restrictions those two worlds imposed. She managed a few visits a week to the East, where he was trapped, although he could never use that description.

Residents of the East were expected to accept what was, not to dream of what could be.

"How are your classes?" he asked.

"They're going well," she replied. "I enjoy my political lectures the most. The professor is fabulous. I take as many of his classes as I can."

"Why is he better than the others?" Dieter asked. "I thought all the professors were very good."

"Professor Keitel was originally from East Berlin," she told him, "so he has a different perspective. He taught at Humboldt University but fled to the West."

"What is so fascinating about his lectures?"

"He has perspectives on all forms of government and traces their roots to Ancient History. He loves the Greek philosophers."

"I do miss those stimulating discussions," he muttered. "It seems like centuries since I've been to the West."

"It changes daily," she said. "Roads rebuilt, buildings constructed, new stores and restaurants. And no shortages."

"I miss it," he said as they entered the café. "And I miss the Technical University."

"How's the Industrial School?"

He shrugged. "It's different," he told her. "Mostly lectures. But I find it very interesting. I have an excellent professor, also. He makes me see what I never saw before."

They sat down and scanned a menu. Coffee and soda weren't available so they ordered two glasses of white wine and beef goulash with spaetzle.

After they were settled, and Dieter had the chance to study those sitting near them, he leaned close to Eileen. "How's the tunnel?" he asked.

She glanced around before replying. "It's going well. We need another week, but no more."

"Is the exit still through a mausoleum?"

"Yes, I think so."

"Do you know how many are escaping?"

"At least thirty," she whispered. "The diggers have friends and family who want to get out."

"Is the tunnel safe?"

"Yes, it's very well built," she informed him. "It has wooden posts for support, and it's equipped with lights and ventilation. You would be impressed."

"I thought you said there was a water leak."

"The water department fixed it," she said, and then leaned closer. "Although now we have to get the city worker's sister and her family out. That was the price for him not reporting it."

"How will everyone know when and where to go?"

"We have several people with access to the East," she explained. "They'll each have a list of people to notify. Those people, in turn, will inform others."

"Will you be my contact?"

"I'm not sure," she said. "I might be waiting in the West, at the tunnel exit, helping those who escape."

"Then who will it be?" he asked anxiously.

"It'll be someone you know," she assured him, "but I don't know who."

He thought of Dr. Werner, or Kirstin, or maybe the American, Tony Marino. It might be one of them.

"One week from today?" he asked.

"Yes, one week from today," she affirmed. "Or even sooner."

70

Tony walked to the third floor of the library, back towards the Medieval section and found Kirstin sitting on the bench waiting for him. She rose as he approached.

"Hello," she said smiling. She looked down the aisle to ensure no one was coming and then hugged him, holding him tightly for several seconds before giving him a quick kiss on the lips.

"That was nice," he said.

"Then we should do it again," she said coyly.

He kissed her, his mouth lingering on hers for a moment, and then broke away. "We shouldn't draw attention to ourselves," he hissed, glancing around the library. "It's risky to even come here."

As she sat on the bench, he walked to adjacent aisles to ensure no one was nearby. Although his encounter with Hofer had made him more cautious, he never felt like he was being watched or followed. He returned to the bench and sat beside her.

"When's the escape?" she asked.

"Saturday night at seven."

"In two days?" she asked. "Dieter told me a week."

"That's what we wanted everyone to think."

"Why would you do that?" she asked.

"Because we may have an informant among us," he said. "It's better if no one knows any details."

"We know Steiner is an informant," she said. "But we're not sure about anyone else."

"But we should assume we can't trust anyone and act accordingly. Especially after two failed escape attempts. And I doubt Steiner knew about either of them."

"I'm not sure what he knows," she told him. "But I do know he's dangerous."

"Just be careful," Marino warned. "Don't underestimate him. You only have two more days and then it's over."

"What should I do on Saturday?" she asked. "Just go to the cemetery and look for an open mausoleum?"

"Someone will come and get you," he said. "Someone you know. They'll take you to the right place."

"What about Steiner?"

"Don't worry," he told her. "I'll take care of him."

"How can you possibly do that?"

"The less you know the better," he said.

"All right, if you say so."

"Just trust me."

"I do," she said, and then squeezed his hand.

"I have some good news for you."

"What is it?"

"I met with Mr. Haynor."

She froze, acting excited but prepared for disappointment. A few awkward seconds passed before she responded. "What did he say?"

"He wants you to be part of Lisette's life."

"Oh, Tony, that's fabulous," she said, hugging him. "That's the best gift anyone ever gave me."

"I'm meeting with the family tomorrow night."

"I can't wait to see her," she said, wiping tears of joy from her eyes.

"It won't be much longer."

"I don't know how to thank you," she said. "So many good things are happening. I'll have my daughter, I'll have my freedom." She paused and smiled impishly. "And I'll have you."

He leaned forward and kissed her, wrapping his arms around her, not caring who saw or heard. He then moved his lips about her face, kissing her cheeks, her nose, her eyes, and then returning to her lips. When he heard footsteps, he pulled away and they both giggled like teenagers.

"This is going to be complicated," he said, making sure she understood what her new life would entail.

"I like complicated," she said, and then stole another quick kiss. "Can we live in West Berlin, so I can be near Lisette, at least until she's grown. Then maybe she'll go to school in America and we can all be together. The Haynors can come too."

Tony smiled. He had never made anyone that happy in his entire life – except his mother. Maybe commitment and responsibility weren't so bad after all. "There's one condition," he added.

She paused, not knowing what to expect. "What's that?" she asked.

"You have to agree to learn something."

She seemed confused. "I suppose I can do that," she replied. "What would you like me to learn?"

"First of all," he told her, "the number nine is very important."

"What's the number nine?"

"There are nine innings in a game and there are nine players on the field," he explained. "The objective of the game ..."

71

"We had another leak," Josef Kramer announced as Marino entered the factory.

"Is it fixed?" Marino asked, alarmed.

"Yes, the workmen left a few hours ago."

"We're so close," Marino sighed. "I hate to see anything go wrong."

"It was worse than the last one, not an easy repair."

"Where was it?" Marino asked.

"A few feet from the wall," Kramer told him. "I called Albert, our friend at the water department, and he came right away."

Marino was relieved. So many people were depending on him, their dreams so close to coming true, that a tunnel failure would be devastating. "How did they fix it?"

"They shut the water off with a valve in the street," Kramer explained. "Then three workers arrived, excavated the piping, and replaced it."

Marino cringed, visualizing all the activity. "Did the guards in the watchtower see anything?"

"I don't think so," Kramer replied. "We were very careful."

"Did they use any machinery?"

"No, they dug by hand."

Marino was pensive, weighing the risks. "No leaks since?"

"None," Kramer said. "And we shored up that entire tunnel section with plywood and posts. Just to be sure."

"Can we trust the other workers?" Marino asked, worried about an informant.

"Yes, but we made the same deal."

"What do you mean?" Marino asked.

"We have the same agreement with them that we have with Albert," Kramer explained. "We have to rescue family members – cousins, friends – whoever they request."

"How are we going to manage that?" Marino asked. "Can we even notify all these people in time?"

"Yes, I think so," Kramer replied. "We assigned groups to each courier based on geographical location. And each person the couriers notify will, in turn, inform their friends and family"

"Will we be ready by Saturday?"

"We'll be ready before then, maybe Friday night."

"I checked the clothing company and verified the business is closed on weekends."

"Then we should break through the floor on Saturday morning, ensure everything is alright, and send couriers to deliver instructions."

"Are you sure no one knows the tunnel destination?" Marino asked.

"Yes," Kramer assured him. "Only the diggers. Anyone else who supports the project, delivering food or supplies, thinks we're using a mausoleum in the cemetery."

"I checked with some of the refugees," Marino said. "They all think it's a mausoleum, too."

"We'll provide the real destination on Saturday."

"We have to be cautious," Marino advised. "We may have an

informant in our midst – either among us or one of the refugees."

"Do you expect the Stasi to act?"

"Yes, I do," Marino replied. "Assuming there is an informant. I think the cemetery will be crawling with guards by seven p.m. on Saturday."

"While our refugees slip into the tunnel a hundred feet away."

"Exactly," Marino said.

"Won't the Stasi notice all the activity?" Kramer asked.

"The trees along the wrought iron fence will screen the escape route," Marino said. "And people will crowd the street to see what the Stasi are doing."

"Then the refugees can filter through the people and sneak into the side door of the clothing manufacturer," Kramer said.

"Will your cousin participate as planned?" Marino asked.

"Yes, and he'll do everything he can to make sure we're successful."

"How many have we listed as refugees?"

"Forty-eight," Kramer replied. "Some may not make it, for whatever reason, and there may be a few stragglers."

"Forty-eight?" Marino asked, surprised. "I didn't realize the number had grown so much."

Kramer shrugged. "We did all that work on the tunnel," he offered. "The more people that use it, the better."

"Yes, I suppose you're right," Marino agreed.

"If we can get the first wave out, we should consider further notifications."

"Agreed," Marino replied.

"Is there anything else?"

"I'll have the photographer in the factory taking pictures of the escape. He'll have an assistant, someone to record names and ask if anyone needs anything."

"Most have relatives in the West they can stay with," Kramer noted.

"And I have a contact at the refugee center," Marino said. "After the escape, I'll notify him and we can get everyone new documents – passports and any visas they might need."

"Don't say anything in advance," Kramer warned. "The Stasi may have agents at the refugee center."

"I'm sure they do," Marino said, thinking of those who gave him advice. He wondered of any notified the Stasi. Maybe he was being followed. But not in East Berlin, as he suspected, but West Berlin. "Maybe they're watching me."

"They could be," Kramer said. "The Stasi are everywhere, even in West Berlin."

Marino took a deep breath, feeling the stress. "Forty-eight people whose lives will change forever. I hope we can pull this off."

Kramer nodded, pensive, as if rolling the events of Saturday evening through his mind. He then looked up, his eyes on Marino. "This is a good thing you're doing," he said. "You're reuniting families, giving people their lives back."

Marino smiled and wrapped an arm around Kramer. "You mean it's a good thing we're all doing. Not just me."

72

Tony Marino sat in the parlor of Gertrude Manstein, Kirstin's grandmother. It was a cozy room, dated striped wallpaper accented by white crown molding. An area rug covered a portion of the hardwood floors, hiding blemishes from a hundred years of wear. On a coffee table in front of the couch sat a tray of pastries and two coffee mugs, half-empty.

"I'm so nervous," Gertrude said anxiously. "After all these years, I finally get to meet my great-granddaughter."

"It's so good of the Haynors to do this," Marino said.

"What if she doesn't like me?" Gertrude asked, a worried expression on her face.

"How could anyone not like you?" Marino asked, smiling. "I don't think you have to worry about that at all."

"I just want everything to go perfectly."

"I'm sure it will."

"The Haynors must be very brave," Gertrude said. "And secure in their relationship with Lisette."

"Mr. Haynor seems like a very understanding man."

"It would be so wonderful to have Kirstin and Lisette with

me," she said, daring to wish the future would be as bright as she imagined. "Who could ask for more than their family?"

Marino was quiet for a moment, listening and learning. "Yes," he said, "I suppose family is what life is really all about, isn't it?"

"Yes, it is."

He watched the elderly woman he had become so fond of, sipping her coffee with a trembling hand. She was such a good person, as were all the people he had met in Berlin, from Kirstin to those digging the tunnel, to the lumber yard personnel providing the supplies, to the men from the water department that fixed the leak. And now so many families and friends were about to be reunited. He was proud of what he had done, the risks he had taken, and the rewards to be reaped.

Promptly at 2 p.m. there was a knock on the door. Gertrude looked at Tony apprehensively. "They're here," she said with the anxious look of someone who wants to be accepted but is afraid they might not be.

"I'll get it," he said, moving toward the door.

He paused with his hand on the doorknob and took a deep breath. Kirstin had found her daughter after years of searching, and now a family would be reunited. Many people's lives were about to change, and he was partially responsible for it. He only hoped they changed for the better.

He opened the door to find Mr. Haynor standing there, a smile on his face, a woman and a teenage girl with him. "Please come in," he said.

They stepped across the threshold and Marino closed the door behind them. "Come, make yourself comfortable," he offered, motioning toward the parlor.

Gertrude stood by the chair in which she had been sitting, looking frail and frightened as the group approached.

Marino provided introductions. "I'm Tony Marino," he said,

"friend of the family. And this is Gertrude Manstein, great-grandmother to Lisette."

Mr. Haynor removed his hat and held it in his hand. "I'm Gustav Haynor," he said. "Mr. Marino and I have met."

"I'm Maria Haynor," said his wife, a woman of average height, her complexion dark, her hair black. She seemed frightened, as if she was about to lose something she couldn't bear to part with.

As if sensing her mother's apprehension, the teenage girl moved closer, wrapping her arm in her mother's. She was tall, a willowy blond with blue eyes, a younger version of Kirstin. "I'm Lisette," she said simply, although no introduction was needed.

"Please, come in and sit down," Tony said, trying to ease the awkwardness. "Have some pastries. Would anyone like coffee?"

"Please," Mr. Haynor nodded, "for my wife and me."

"Lisette?"

She shrugged. "It doesn't matter."

"Coca Cola?" he asked.

"That would be fine," she said, smiling shyly.

As Tony left the room for the kitchen, he could hear the conversation, pleasantries about the weather, the upcoming winter, different events planned for the city of West Berlin. He returned a moment later and served everyone, sitting in a distant chair, allowing the family to dominate the conversation.

Eventually, Mr. Haynor came to the point. "Lisette has always known she's adopted," he explained. "My wife and I also have two sons, several years older than Lisette."

"My daughter and I would never do anything to interfere with your family," Gertrude then said, her voice trembling. "The debt we owe you for raising Lisette can never be repaid."

Mrs. Haynor nodded, as if in gratitude. "Thank you, Mrs. Manstein," she said. "Lisette is part of us, as I'm sure you understand."

"I do," Gertrude acknowledged. "And even though the State

took Lisette away from us, at the time it seemed best for everyone." She hesitated, as if not sure how to continue, but then added softly, "Given Kirstin's age and condition at the time, and the circumstances surrounding the birth. But hardly a day goes by that Kirstin and I don't regret it."

It was Mrs. Haynor who now spoke, having also lived the horrors of the final days of the war. "No one would ever judge you," she said.

"Thank you," Gertrude said quietly.

"Even if you fought the State's decision, it's unlikely you would have been successful," Mr. Haynor said. "We know what happened to Kirstin. And the impact it had on her mentally and physically."

Gertrude nodded, her eyes misting. "We had only hoped, Kirstin and I, to be a part of Lisette's life, even if in a simple way. If you could be so kind as to share such a treasure."

Lisette rose from her chair and went over to Gertrude. She sat beside her and hugged her, holding on tightly for a moment before releasing her. "I would like nothing more than that," she said warmly.

73

"I think this is the most likely mausoleum," Steiner Beck said as he stood in the corner of the graveyard, close to the wall.

Karl Hofer examined the tomb carefully. "I don't see any sign of disturbance, as if it was opened."

"I would guess they're breaching the tomb tomorrow evening as planned."

"Or at least as your informant claims," Hofer said, correcting him.

"The informant has been correct on two other occasions."

"Actually, they were almost correct," Hofer said. "We never apprehended any escapees or enemies of the State."

"No, we didn't," Beck agreed, "but that could change quickly."

Hofer looked beyond the concrete wall that ran down the last lane of the cemetery, and then to the brick factory building beyond. A long building that dominated the city block, the ends were intact, apparently housing active businesses. The center had been bombed during the war and still lay in a crumpled heap of bricks, boards, and shingles.

Beck looked at the building also. "Do you think they're watching us?"

"Probably," Hofer replied. "We had best not stay here if we think this is the tomb. Let's walk a bit."

They continued along the wall, nodding to the guards on patrol. There were several large mausoleums nearby, any one of which could be the target of the tunnel's exit. And there were also others, farther away from the wall.

"They could choose a tomb in the center of the cemetery," Hofer said, glancing back at the brick factory. "Then they'll be farther from the wall."

"And the border guards may not see them," Beck said. "But since we're supplementing our guard force, it may not matter where they exit."

"If they're observing the graveyard from the upper elevations of the factory, they might be scared off if they see more guards."

"Agreed," Beck replied. "We'll have to be careful."

"Maybe we can hide soldiers near the church," Hofer said. "Or even in the street."

"The far end of the cemetery would work, too," Beck suggested. He then turned and looked behind them. "Near the watchtower."

Hofer glanced in both directions. "I'm sure those that organized the escape will have someone near the cemetery, watching. If they see us, they may change their plans."

"And we won't catch anyone."

"We just have to be smarter than they are," Hofer said.

"What are you going to do?"

"I think I'll stage a dozen men throughout the cemetery," Hofer replied, "but back towards the wall. They can hide behind the larger tombs. And then I'll place others at the far end, behind the townhouses."

"What will happen once the tomb is opened?"

"First, we need to know which tomb it is," Hofer said. "But it should be easy to find once the refugees migrate towards it. Then we'll arrest whoever we find in the graveyard."

"What if we don't see anything?" Beck asked. "What if they're suspicious and wait until later in the evening or another day?"

"Then the escape will be foiled, like the last two, and we'll be prepared to thwart the next one. But I want to apprehend as many people as possible."

"It would also be good to publicize their capture," Beck suggested. "As a deterrent for anyone else with similar ambitions."

"They seem to be watching us," Hofer mused aloud. "I just wonder how." He scanned the graveyard, the church that anchored it, the clothing manufacturer, and the row of townhouses adjacent to the church. His gaze shifted upward, to the second-floor window of one of the townhouses.

Steiner Beck also looked upward. He then glanced at Hofer who was watching him watch Kirstin, standing in the second-floor window.

74

"We're ready to break through the floor of the clothing company," Josef Kramer said. "Do you want to be there when we do?"

"Absolutely," Marino said. He glanced at his watch. It was almost noon. The refugees would arrive in seven hours.

"Then let's get into the tunnel," Kramer said. "Just don't interfere with the operation."

In the hole cut into the factory floor, a wooden ladder had been placed against the side. Across from it was a truss with a pully hanging from it, and a man standing ready to take five-gallon pails of dirt and carry them to the bombed section of the factory for deposit. He then returned with the empty pail and sent it down to a man at the bottom of the pit.

Marino followed Kramer down the ladder, pausing where a man knelt by the tunnel entrance. "How's it going?" he asked.

"We're almost through," the digger, a man named Ernst, replied. "We're hitting coal slag now."

"Coal slag?" Marino asked, confused.

Kramer noted his perplexed look. "Many buildings have

coal slag under the foundation," he explained. "It's used for insulation."

Wooden planks lined the tunnel floor, and a flat cart with large wheels and a heavy rope attached to it was used to transport soil. Ernst put the empty bucket on the cart and tugged at the rope. At the far end of the tunnel, the digger pulled the cart toward him. Two ventilation ducts were attached to the tunnel's upper corners, small fans in front of them. One blew fresh air in; the second exhausted stale air out.

"Are you ready?" Kramer asked.

"Yes," Marino replied. "Let's go."

They got on all fours and started through the tunnel. Wooden posts were periodically placed against the sides, holding horizontal struts and plywood on the ceiling to reinforce the excavation. Every fifty feet or so, a small recess was cut into the side, large enough for someone to wait, eventually to assist the refugees as they crawled down the corridor. Strung down the center of the ceiling were lights, a dim bulb hanging every forty feet, casting eerie shadows on earthen walls.

Although the tunnel was only two hundred feet long, Marino felt like he was crawling for hours. It was close, dimly lit, the air stank, but it was a path to freedom for as many people as they could get through. He marveled at the work the diggers had done, mostly college students in different engineering disciplines. They employed the skills they had, the material they were provided, and donated hours of hard work to help other people – all for no personal gain. Marino took a minute to marvel at the human spirit. We can disagree, we may not even like each other, but when someone needs help, we respond.

Throughout the journey they heard hammering, material crumbling, and more hammering. When they reached the end, there was another staging area, maybe six feet square, with the cart and bucket, which was now full. As Marino and Kramer moved out of the way, the digger tugged at the rope and the cart disappeared down the tunnel.

"We're almost there," Marino said to the man by the cart, a student named Klaus.

"Yes, he's breaking through now," Klaus said, pointing upward where a man stood on a ladder, hitting concrete with a hammer.

Pieces of stone fell to the floor, followed by larger chunks, and then a tiny stream of light pierced the concrete. The man at the top of the ladder took a few more swings, the concrete falling to the ground in larger chunks until a hole was visible, roughly two feet square.

"We had best take a look," the man on the ladder said.

"Come on," Kramer said. "Let's go."

He scrambled up the ladder with Marino behind him, and they squirmed through the hole. The digger stood waiting, a West German policeman named Franz whose wife and three children were in the East.

"How did we do, Franz?" Kramer asked.

"I'm not sure where we came through," Franz replied, sweating and covered with dust. "It looks like an office."

Kramer and Marino emerged from the hole. They stood in a small room about eight feet square, a desk against the exterior wall. There was a narrow window above the desk, higher on the wall, where sunlight shone through. They were between the desk and a wall with a closed door.

"I'll move the desk and make the access hole a little larger," Franz said, "assuming we're in the right place."

"Let's have a look around first," Marino suggested. "Just to make sure it's safe."

They opened the office door and paused, listening closely. After hearing no sounds, they stepped out into a hallway. Ten feet to their right was a door. They walked toward it and saw it was bolted from the inside. They opened it a few inches, and then a bit more until they were staring outside, the wrought iron fence of the cemetery barely eight feet away. The street was forty feet to their left.

"This is the entrance we wanted to be near," he told Franz and Kramer. "The refugees can come in through here."

Kramer and Franz glanced out the door and then came in. "What's in this room?" Kramer asked, opening a door between the office they had tunneled into and the exterior wall.

"It looks like a storage area," Marino said. The room was lined with shelves, although there wasn't much on them. Some reams of paper and cleaning supplies, not much else.

"This is where we were trying to come through," Kramer said. "In the corner of the building by the side door."

"It's better where we are, in the office," Marino told them. "We have more space. You did such a fabulous job. The length was perfect."

Kramer lightly slapped Franz on the back. "We have a good team."

"And we all worked together," Franz echoed.

"Let's check the rest of the building and make sure there are no surprises."

There was another office next to the one they had entered, much larger, the furniture nicer. It had a window on the exterior wall and another facing the interior of the building.

"This must be the manager's office," Marino noted.

"And we tunneled into his clerk's office," Kramer said.

They walked to the end of the corridor and opened the door, exposing the factory beyond. There were rows of tables with sewing machines spaced every five or six feet. Large tables at the end of each row contained piles of cloth, while other areas had buttons and zippers.

"At least no one is here," Marino said. "Just as we expected."

"I wonder how many people work here," Franz asked as they walked the factory floor.

"It looks like quite a few," Kramer replied.

"We have until Monday morning to get as many people as we can through the tunnel," Marino said.

"I'll enlarge the opening, clean things up a bit, and we'll be ready to go," Franz said.

"And I'll dispatch the couriers," Kramer added.

75

At 6 p.m. Tony Marino walked through the factory, filled with those who helped construct the tunnel, and ensured everything was prepared. He approached the photographer, an older man named Helmut, who had documented the tunnel's construction with pictures.

"Are you ready?" Marino asked.

"Yes, I am," Helmut assured him. "I have plenty of film, the lights are properly set, and I'm anxiously looking forward to the escape."

Eileen Fischer stood beside Helmut, a notepad in her hand. "I'll provide any assistance the refugees need," she said. "Food, clothing, a place to stay, sympathetic contacts in West Berlin."

Marino glanced at his watch. "It won't be long now," he told them.

Standing just off to the side, fifteen feet from the tunnel entrance, were the Haynors, Gustav, Maria, and Lisette – who was anxiously waiting to meet her natural mother.

Marino studied them for a moment, their lives about to drastically change, and admired both their kindness and courage. Maria and Gustav were Lisette's mother and father in every way parenthood is defined, save one, yet they willingly offered to share their precious daughter, knowing it could create more questions than answers, more hurt than happiness. Marino noticed their expressions, anxious and afraid, and he wanted to reassure them, to tell them their family would not grow smaller, but larger, and they would never regret the compassionate decision that they had so bravely made.

Eileen Fischer motioned toward them. "They're a lovely family," she said softly.

"They are," Marino replied. "And such good people."

"The natural mother must be so excited," she said, knowing the story but not the identity. "I hope she's among the first to escape."

"I do, too," Marino said, hiding a smile.

"We're all ready and waiting," Eileen said. "It almost seemed like this day would never arrive."

"But I'm so glad it did," Marino said. "I just hope it goes as planned."

"I'm sure it will," Eileen said. "And a lot of people will soon be free."

"Do you know how many the couriers are contacting?"

"Forty-eight that we know of," she replied, "although I don't have any names. But we expect friends of friends to be notified at the last minute, increasing the number."

"No one knows the names," Marino told her. "It just seemed safer. We don't want to expose everyone if a single person is apprehended."

"A wise decision," Eileen commented. She paused a moment and glanced down the hole. "It's ingenious routing the tunnel into the cemetery. The refugees can hide behind tomb-stones and trees, crawl through the shrubs if they need to. And the border guards will never suspect a mausoleum is the tunnel entrance."

"I hope not," Marino replied, pleased no one knew the true

destination. "We've done everything we could to help people escape."

Josef Kramer crossed the room and came to Marino's side. "It's time," he said.

Marino turned to the Haynors. "We're ready," he told them.

"And what happens now?" Mr. Haynor asked.

"Josef and I will lead the refugees to the tunnel entrance in East Berlin," Marino said. "Kirstin should be among the first to escape."

"How will we know who she is?" Lisette asked.

"You can't miss her," Marino replied, smiling. "You look just like her."

Fifteen minutes later, Marino, Franz and Kramer climbed the wooden ladder and emerged from the tunnel in the clothing company office. They searched the building to confirm it was empty, and then Marino unlocked the side door, cracking it open to peek out. He would guide the refugees in, while Franz and Kramer helped them into the tunnel. Klaus, one of the diggers, would wait in the staging area, urging them through to West Berlin. Other helpers were positioned along the route, ensuring the flow of refugees continued unabated.

Even the minutest detail had been meticulously planned. As many as fifty people would soon be reunited with family and friends, enjoying the freedom they had so callously been denied.

As long as everything went according to plan.

76

K irstin Beck looked anxiously out her second-floor window. Border guards briskly walked along the wall, one with a German Shepherd, others with machine guns. Soldiers searched the cemetery, closer to the street, hiding behind shrubs and tombs and sneaking through the graveyard as if afraid to wake the dead.

Troop trucks emptied and more soldiers arrived, crawling like ants across the landscape. A handful hid behind the church, a few more near the watch tower. As she scanned the cemetery, she saw her husband coming from the street with Karl Hofer. The Stasi seemed to know their plans, just as they had during prior attempts, but she didn't know how they found out.

She glanced at her watch. Marino said someone she knew would come to get her. It was almost seven p.m. They would arrive any minute. She looked back at the graveyard and saw Steiner talking to one of the guards. It was as if he wanted to be part of whatever was happening, whether he deserved to be or not.

She went downstairs and waited by the door, her stomach

churning. She dreamed of seeing her daughter and beloved grandmother, and she thought of Tony and whatever their future held. It all seemed too good to be true. But she realized much had to go right before she escaped and the view from her window proved it might not.

The knock came a moment later, loud and distinct, promptly at seven. She rushed to the door, the leather satchel with her money and documents slung over her shoulder. She took one last look towards the kitchen to ensure Steiner hadn't returned and then opened the door.

"Good evening, Mrs. Beck," Karl Hofer said, standing on the steps. "Were you about to go out?"

Kirstin's heart sank. As victory arrived, defeat took its place. "I was going to run some errands," she said, conscious of the bag over her shoulder.

"Why do you need a satchel?" he asked. "You already have your pocketbook."

"I use it for smaller items, like cosmetics," she explained. "Whenever they're available."

"You're shopping will have to wait," Hofer said smugly. "You're coming with me."

"Why?" she asked, her heart racing. "I have things to do."

"Not now you don't."

She knew she had to get rid of him. "I should tell my husband," she said. "He's over by the church."

"I'll make sure he's notified."

"No, he'll worry. I should tell him."

"Come with me," Hofer ordered. "Now."

Kirstin felt a tear trickle down her cheek, but she quickly wiped it away. She left the house and closed the door. She wondered what had gone wrong. Who had betrayed her?

Hofer grabbed her elbow and forced her down the steps. He stared straight ahead, his face taut, not speaking, not looking at her.

She glanced across the street, wondering if the courier watched, waiting to see what happened.

"My car is past the church," Hofer said, yanking her roughly by the arm.

He led her past a few pedestrians. Two empty troop trucks were parked in front of the church. There were some people on the street, not many, although more were gathering. They were curious – neighbors and passersby – wondering why so many soldiers were behind the church and if another escape through the cemetery had been attempted.

"Are you sure this can't wait?" Kirstin asked, her voice trembling. "I really do have errands to run."

"No, it can't," Hofer said.

"Can you tell me what's going on?"

"Did you see all the activity in the graveyard?"

She feigned ignorance. "No, I didn't."

He nodded toward the trucks. "Soldiers are searching the cemetery. We think one of the mausoleums leads to a tunnel."

"What does that have to do with me?" she asked, trying to be brave.

"I want to ensure you're not part of it."

They continued down the pavement. He held her arm firmly, pushing her forward. As they walked past the church he paused, looked at the troop trucks as if to ensure no lingering guards remained, and shoved her.

"Come on," he said coldly. "Just a bit farther."

A soldier appeared from the side of the church. "Do you need help, Mr. Hofer?"

"No, I don't," he said. "Return to your duties. I'm taking this woman to Stasi headquarters."

"Is she part of the escape?"

"She's probably one of the instigators," he said, looking sternly at Kirstin.

"I know nothing about an escape," she insisted, although no one cared.

"Call me if you need anything," the soldier said as he returned to the cemetery.

Kirstin looked up and down the street. More civilians gathered, curious, but fearful, wondering what was happening. Most migrated toward the church, knowing it provided sanctuary in uncertain times. Others peeked from drawn curtains in their living rooms. She noticed no soldiers on the street, just civilians, and no obvious Stasi, only Hofer. When he pushed her past some pedestrians, just at the edge of the church, he momentarily relaxed his grip and she yanked her arm from his grasp and started to run.

"Stop!" he ordered, chasing after her.

77

Kirstin darted down the pavement, Hofer just behind her. She turned and saw his arm outstretched, reaching for her. She swerved to avoid him.

"Stop!" he demanded, rapidly closing the distance between them. "You won't get away."

She veered to the right and leaped across the curb, almost tripping. She bumped into an obese woman she had never seen before, stumbled and almost fell before she caught her balance.

"What's wrong?" the woman asked, shielding her from Hofer.

"Out of the way," Hofer commanded, withdrawing a pistol from a holster on his belt.

The woman gasped, her eyes wide, and moved aside. Half a dozen others scattered, afraid Hofer would shoot.

Kirstin ran down the street, bumping into those she couldn't avoid, the crowd starting to thin. She turned, saw Hofer gaining, and hurried behind a parked car, not knowing how to escape, searching frantically for the courier who was supposed to help her.

Hofer stopped in the street, on the opposite side of the car.

"Don't be stupid, Mrs. Beck," he reasoned. "If you come with me now, it'll be much easier."

She edged down the side of the car, toward the rear. He followed, just across from her, and then rushed around the vehicle, trying to grab her. She changed direction and raced around the front bumper, across the street, feigned running back toward her townhouse but turned and sprinted in the opposite direction.

Hofer matched each step she took, scrambling after her, only a few steps behind.

As she approached the end of the cemetery, she felt her hair being tugged. Her head snapped back and she slowed, crying out in pain.

Hofer pulled her toward him. "I said to stop," he said coldly. He lifted his right hand and put the pistol against her temple. Speaking loudly for the benefit of those nearby, he added, "I'll shoot if I have to."

Kirstin lowered her head, gasping, tears dripping down her cheeks. She had been so close. But somehow everything had gone wrong. She fought to regain her composure, knowing she didn't have the strength to fight him. She had to outsmart him.

"You're coming with me," Hofer said softly, lowering the pistol and returning it to the holster. He grabbed her by the arm and pulled her forward. "This way."

"What do you want with me?" she asked defiantly. "I've done nothing wrong."

"I'll be the judge of that."

She saw observers dispersing, frightened by Hofer's pistol. They didn't want to be witnesses, having seen something they wished they hadn't. Most were neighbors. They knew Kirstin. But they still didn't want to be involved.

Hofer led her to the edge of the cemetery and, just as they reached the iron fence, he pushed her down the alley between the graveyard and the clothing company.

"Where are you taking me?" she asked, fearing for her safety.

"Hurry," he hissed, looking over his shoulder.

They had walked another thirty feet when a side door to the building opened and Tony Marino stepped out. "This way," he directed.

"Tony?" Kirstin asked, confused. She looked back at Hofer, who was nervously watching the street.

"Come on," Tony urged. "We have to hurry."

"I'll get the others," Hofer said.

"Make sure you have time to get out, too," Marino said.

Tony took Kirstin's hand and led her into the building.

78

"What's going on?" a bewildered Kirstin asked.

"We're escaping," Marino replied. "This is Franz, one of the diggers, and Joey Kramer, the tunnel's architect. He's also Karl Hofer's cousin."

"Hofer is Stasi!" Kirstin hissed.

"Yes, he is," Marino said. "But he's also one of us. He'll be coming through the tunnel later."

"But he foiled two other escape attempts," a shocked Kirstin reminded him.

"No, he didn't," Marino explained. "It only seemed like he did. An informant betrayed us. Hofer arrived to ensure you didn't get caught."

"How long have you known all of this?" she asked.

"Only for a few days," he replied.

"There's a group of six approaching now," Franz said as he peeked out the door. "You had better get going."

"Come on," Tony said as he took Kirstin's hand. "It's time to go."

"Be careful," Josef Kramer called as they started down the ladder.

"See you on the other side," Marino said to Kramer.

They climbed down the ladder, finding Klaus at the bottom. "How many have come through?" Marino asked.

"Eight so far," Klaus replied. "She makes nine."

"There's six more coming," Marino informed him. He turned to Kirstin. "You go first. I'm right behind you."

They started through the tunnel, crawling on their hands and knees. "I can't believe it," Kirstin said. "When I saw Hofer, I thought I was doomed."

"He wasn't supposed to come for you," Marino explained. "He was distracting Steiner. But we only had a few minutes to get you to the tunnel. We couldn't wait for the courier."

"Is Steiner Stasi?"

"Yes," Marino replied. "And he's much more than an informant."

They kept crawling, moving down the dimly lit tunnel. Kirstin started to sob, unable to believe freedom waited minutes away.

"It won't be long now," Marino assured her. "We're almost there."

They reached a recess in the tunnel, where one of the diggers was prepared to assist if needed.

"There's a group of six behind us," Marino told him as they passed.

They kept crawling, the short journey seeming like it would never end. Soon they reached the site of the water leak, plywood bracing the ceiling and walls.

"We're in West Berlin," Marino said. "Just a little bit farther."

Minutes later they reached the staging area. Tony guided a trembling Kirstin up the ladder, remaining a few rungs behind her. They climbed to the top and the cameraman flashed photographs as they emerged from the tunnel.

Kirstin stepped on to the factory floor, a bit dazed and

disheveled, as if unable to accept she was free. "We made it," she said in disbelief.

Marino was right behind her. He kissed her and pulled her close, not wanting to let go. But after a few seconds, he did. "There's someone waiting for you," he said, gently spinning her around.

Standing a few feet away, with her parents beside her, was Lisette Haynor. Kirstin could only stare, open-mouthed.

"Hello, *Mutti*," Lisette said softly.

"Oh, Lisette," Kirstin said. She hugged her daughter, tears of joy running down her cheeks. "I thought this day would never come."

"But it did," Lisette said. "And that's all that matters."

79

The refugees continued to emerge from the tunnel, each with a look of disbelief, overcome with joy as they stepped onto the factory floor. Marino greeted each arrival, while the Haynors and Kirsten sat off to the side on a couch and some chairs the diggers had used when resting. Marino watched them, crying with joy, sometimes laughing, as sixteen years were discussed and described, and the expanded family got acquainted.

The next group to pass through the tunnel was Franz's family, the digger and West Berlin policeman, his wife and two teenage sons. Marino greeted them once they all had exited safely.

"Your father made all of this possible," Marino said to Franz's wife and sons. "He's truly a hero." He motioned to the refugees clustered nearby, shedding tears and hugging loved ones. "He saved all of these people."

The family embraced, crying with joy, and stepped aside as more refugees climbed up the ladder. Seconds later, Albert's family arrived, the city worker who had fixed the water leaks, his sister and brother-in-law and a small boy, aged five. The boy was a bit shaken, flight through the tunnel intimidating for an adult, but even worse for a child.

Marino walked up to them. "Your uncle made all of this possible," he said, motioning to the refugees. "He's a hero. The tunnel would have never been built without him."

Thirty minutes later, Dr. Jacob Werner emerged with his wife, his sister-in-law and her husband, as well as other friends, a group of eight people. They were all a bit shaken, soiled, but elated.

"I don't know how to thank you," Werner said, shaking Marino's hand and then giving him a quick hug.

"It was a team of people," Marino said, immensely proud that he was able to change so many lives. "The college students designed and dug the tunnel, with help from Franz and a few others, and the city workers ensured any leaks were repaired."

Werner's eyes suddenly widened, and fear flickered across his face. "Hofer!" he exclaimed.

Marino turned as Karl Hofer climbed from the tunnel entrance, an attractive woman and two small girls, apparently his wife and daughters, just ahead of him. As Hofer ensured his family was safe, Marino approached.

"Thank you so much," Hofer said, grasping Marino's hand and shaking it firmly. "This is my wife Anna and my daughters Ingrid and Beatrice."

"Thank you for helping us," Anna Hofer said to Marino. "You changed our lives."

"I'm so glad I could help," Marino replied. "But we couldn't have done it without your husband. He's truly a hero, ensuring all of these people were able to escape."

Anna Hofer kissed her husband on the cheek as his two daughters gazed at him lovingly. "He's a good man," she said.

"He is," Marino agreed. "And we had a whole team of good people, all dedicated to freeing as many as possible."

Hofer removed a framed portrait from a satchel and showed

it to Marino. It said: *The past is the present. The future is the past.* After Marino read it, Hofer smiled grimly. "Lest I ever forget."

Hofer then stepped away from his family and approached Dr. Werner. "You may never realize it, but I saved your life."

"You're right," Werner said angrily. "I'll never realize it. And if I could, I would kill you."

"Without me, you never would have left solitary confinement," Hofer continued. "I made you disappear, at least your case file, to give you enough time to escape."

"Why did you do it?" Werner asked. "Why destroy me?"

"I did it to prevent others from doing worse," Hofer replied. "And I hope someday you'll understand."

Dieter Katz emerged from the tunnel with four college friends. He also gasped when he saw Hofer, and angrily approached.

"Hofer has been helping us," Marino said, intervening. "His cousin was one of the diggers."

"Why?" Katz asked, looking at Hofer, trying to understand. "Why did you do that to me?"

"As I told the Doctor," Hofer said, "I did what I did so others wouldn't do worse. I walked a tightrope. I had to please my superiors while protecting you. The Stasi watched me just as they watched you. I hope someday you'll understand."

"I won't," Katz said.

"And neither will I," Werner echoed.

"What are you even doing here?" Katz asked.

Hofer looked at them, his eyes pleading for understanding. "We all live for our children, hoping they grow in our image. When I looked in the mirror, I didn't like what I saw. When I looked out the window, I saw a stark, depressing city I didn't want to live in. And I realized a long time ago, that I didn't want to be part of it, I didn't want to be like them."

"Then why did you prevent two other escapes?" Werner asked, still angry.

"I had to," Hofer explained, "because it was the only way to save you."

"We were almost through the wire," Katz said. "But you stopped us."

"The border guards had orders to shoot," he told them. "You never would have crawled across that border alive."

"What about Kirstin's fake passport?" Werner asked.

"If a citizen of East Berlin is caught with a fake passport, they're imprisoned for life," Hofer said. "Hardly worth the risk."

Katz and Werner stood with friends and family, still glaring at Hofer, but their stares began to soften. Now they were free. And maybe that was most important.

The line of refugees continued until almost ten p.m. when Josef Kramer returned with the diggers that had been staged throughout the tunnel. In all, fifty-seven East Germans had successfully escaped.

At some point during the evening, as evidence of the successful escape became apparent, Eileen Fischer had slowly slipped away, fading into darkness.

EPILOGUE

The tunnel remained undiscovered until Monday morning when workers at the clothing company reported for work and found the hole cut in the office floor. Several more escapes occurred on Sunday, as couriers frantically combed East Berlin, encouraging other relatives and friends to flee. In the end, sixty-nine people successfully escaped to West Berlin.

Eileen Fischer was the Stasi informant, recruited by her college professor who worked with Steiner Beck. Although Marino had often suspected her, there was never any solid evidence and most of what she knew was also known by Dieter Katz and others. She vanished from West Berlin that evening and was last seen in Vienna, Austria. It's believed she's still employed by the Stasi and may have married her college professor.

Steiner Beck remains an invaluable Stasi agent, molding the minds of the most impressionable, students who trust those that teach them. Originally on the fringe of intelligence operations, he eventually developed an entire stable of informants –

from his professor friend in West Berlin to Eileen Fischer to dozens of students, professors, parishioners, and those convinced, as he was, that Socialism was destined to dominate the world.

The refugees assimilated into West Berlin society, some emigrating to West Germany or other countries. Karl Hofer became a member of the West German Intelligence Office, serving until he retired from service. His cousin, Josef Kramer, graduated from college and went on to build bridges, earning a reputation as a daring and innovative designer. Dieter Katz, at first devastated by what Eileen Fischer was and all she had done, soon fell in love with a college student from West Berlin and married her a few years later. After earning his advanced physics degree from the Technical University, he worked for the West German government on projects that remain secret and highly classified, even to this day.

Green Mansion Publishing released Tony Marino's book, *Freedom At Any Price*, two months after the escape, along with countless magazine articles beforehand designed to promote it. The book was on the *New York Times* best seller list for over thirty weeks and was eventually made into a movie that earned many millions of dollars. A portion of the profits was awarded to those involved in the escape, including the refugees.

Tony Marino visited his mother that Thanksgiving and, with help from Otto at the refugee center and some assistance from the West Berlin government, Kirstin Beck joined him in Philadelphia for the festivities. A few months later, Marino's mother married her postman in one of the largest weddings the neighborhood could remember, courtesy of Tony Marino. They live just off Shunk in South Philly, a block past Broad, in the house Tony was raised in,

Kirstin Beck eventually married Tony Marino and they settled in West Berlin with her grandmother, just off the

Kurfürstendamm within walking distance to Lisette's home with the Haynors. They spend summers in Philadelphia, Tony, his mother and her new husband, Kirstin, and Lisette. All are devoted fans of the Philadelphia Phillies.

THE END

Dear reader,

We hope you enjoyed reading *For Those Who Dare*. Please take a moment to leave a review, even if it's a short one. Your opinion is important to us.

Discover more books by John Anthony Miller at https://www.nextchapter.pub/authors/john-anthony-miller

Want to know when one of our books is free or discounted for Kindle? Join the newsletter at http://eepurl.com/bqqB3H

Best regards,

John Anthony Miller and the Next Chapter Team

You might also like:
God's Hammer by Eric Schumacher

To read the first chapter for free, head to:
https://www.nextchapter.pub/books/gods-hammer-historical-viking-adventure

ABOUT THE AUTHOR

John Anthony Miller was born in Philadelphia, Pennsylvania to a father of English ancestry and a second-generation Italian mother. Motivated by a life-long love of travel and history, he normally sets his novels in exotic locations during eras of global conflict. Characters must cope and combat, overcoming their own weaknesses as well as external influences spawned by tumultuous times. He's the author of the historical thrillers, To Parts Unknown, In Satan's Shadow, When Darkness Comes, and All the King's Soldiers, as well as the historical mystery, Honour the Dead. He lives in southern New Jersey with his family.

A note from the author ...

When WWII came to a close, the Allied victors – the United States, the United Kingdom, France, and Russia – carved spheres of interest from the European continent. The former Allies soon became enemies, the U.S., U.K. and France pitted against Russia and the Cold War began, a global conflict drawn on ideological principles – capitalism versus communism.

The German nation, initiator of the global cataclysm, was divided among the victors. West Germany was administered by the U.S., U.K. and France, East Germany was overseen by the Soviet Union – Russia and her satellites. Germany's former capital, the city of Berlin, was also split into East and West with the same administrators. West Berlin, located one hundred miles within East Germany, became a capitalist island in a socialist sea, a remote outpost of freedom often used as a pawn in a global game of chess.

Initially, East and West Berlin had no controlled borders. Residents worked and worshiped in either sector, had friends and family on both sides, and were free to pass from East to West, or West to East, with no repercussions. But socialism soon became a symbol for suppression and stagnation, a society that trampled invention and innovation, stemmed the free flow of ideas, and offered no reward for those who took risks – the entrepreneurs who ultimately transform civilizations. The professionals in the East, those with desirable skills like doctors and developers, architects and engineers, scientists and psychologists, fled to West Berlin to better their lives. Between 1945 and 1961, two and a half million East Germans escaped to West Berlin, some fifteen percent of the entire population. The Socialist government in East Germany eventually took drastic measures to stop the unwanted exodus. In August of 1961, they built the Berlin Wall, wrapping West Berlin in concrete and barbed wire to prevent any more in the East from escaping.

I decided to write this book because I was intrigued by those who risked everything for dreams of a better life, determined to escape East Berlin regardless of the method – tunnels, sewers, fake passports – and regardless of the personal cost. Many were successful. Many more were not. Although *For Those Who Dare* is purely fiction, it's based on fact, inspired by a political system that has failed repeatedly throughout the course of human history, but is continually reinvented with different faces and footprints, as if the muddled masses won't recognize it and somehow embrace it for all eternity. The stark reminder to which I always return, is that in East Berlin in

August of 1961, people risked and often lost their lives to obtain the freedom that most in the world are now so fortunate to enjoy.

Made in the USA
Monee, IL
23 July 2022

10176654R00215